HIGHER

LOVE

JOY ECKERT

Published by Doorbell Books.

Typeset in Berthold Bodoni. First printed in 2019.

A CIP catalogue record for this book is available
from the British Library.

ISBN: 978-1-5272-4817-5

ABOUT THE AUTHOR

Joy Eckert was born in Newcastle-upon-Tyne. She moved to Germany for one year after meeting her future husband Tim in Spain.

She went on to live and work in America, Tim's homeland, for fifteen years.

Returning to the UK in 2001 with Tim and their daughter Sara, she worked in the hospitality business in Northumberland.

After several years they went to live in Great Malvern in Worcestershire, then Stratford-upon-Avon in Warwickshire before returning home to the North-East in 2018.

Joy now lives and works in Northumberland at the seaside with Tim and their dog Rose.

I will never leave.

I will always be around.

Prologue

I'm sitting here alone, chewing on my finger nails in this small room, waiting. I've never liked waiting for anyone or anything, so I'm getting more restless by the minute. My breathing is becoming harder to cope with as I'm now prone to having panic attacks.

I try to take my mind off my situation, so I look over at the colourful prints on the walls (this is part of my therapy while I've been in here) and concentrate on the colours. I see pinks and yellows and greens and then I take in the picture more carefully and see a meadow of wild flowers. I continue to concentrate but I'm scared. I feel as if any minute I will keel over and be lying on the floor unable to move. My imagination is running riot. I must stop fearing the worst. I must concentrate until my breathing slows down and the sweating has stopped. I know I must move to stop my adrenalin taking over, but I feel weak. How can I accomplish my goal without keeling over anyway?

I pull my sweaty and shaking body carefully off the chair. Putting my hands flat onto the table in front of me, I move my legs back and forwards as if I were running. I hurt but I need to do this. I look up at the colourful painting once again. Concentrating with all my being, I feel now as if I'm running through that beautiful meadow. I continue with this playful imaginary thought until my body is eventually calm and under control.

I sit my painful body back down on the hard office chair, with a feeling of depression. I wonder why this is happening to me. I don't like this deep, harsh, dull sensation of a dark cloud over my head.

With my hands covering my eyes, I cry, until (I think) that there are no tears left.

With a feeling of so much frustration that I have never encountered before, I stand with more force in my body than usual angrily grabbing the large box of tissues off the table in front of me, causing the box to tear and the contents to fly all over the small room. Whilst cursing and trying to pick up the majority of the mess from the brown lightly stained carpet, I use a couple of them to wipe the snot poring from my nose and the tears once again flowing from my swollen eyes. I sit again and ponder why I am here.

I'm here to get help and they told me they could help me get my life back. I have quite a sizeable tube inserted in the top of my arm which they tell me is an experimental treatment to help me to stop the shaking and the depression I've encountered.

Earlier I overheard a doctor saying that I've had a memory block due to traumatic events. What could I have encountered to have a memory block? After hearing that shocking news, I try hard, day and night, to dig deep into my mind to pull out any memory that I do have of my past. This struggling to remember *anything*, has the power to deny me of sleep at times, causing my daytime 'mind digging' to be weak. Either way, I'm getting nowhere fast.

I think my name is Ailish O'Neill because lying on a table in front of me is a file with that name written on the top of it. Some woman, who I've never seen before, was with me a minute ago. She mentioned that her name was Rachel. My ears pricked up at that name, but I don't know why. Then she suddenly rushed out of the room. I start to get hot and sweaty again. I wish I wasn't alone as I need a glass of water. Why can't they open the window?

My hair feels greasy and I told them I must wash it today, but they have ignored me. My body is shaking again and I don't want to wait any longer. I decide to stand up. With my legs feeling like jelly I walk towards the door to look for someone to help me get that cold drink. I'm scared shitless once again, I don't want another panic attack.

Just as I'm about to open the door to leave the room, it is opened by the woman who left me. She must have known what I wanted as she is carrying a jug of water and two glasses on a tray. When I get back to my chair I take the glass from her with my shaking hand. I find it very difficult to put it to my lips. I eventually manage but not before dribbling some of it onto my legs. I watch her looking at me, which makes me feel more nervous. I stare back to study *her* face which is long and narrow with a large nose, big round blue eyes and long black hair. It's *so* shiny it looks like a wig. She has on a blue sweater with a Christmas tree brooch pinned on her right side. So, it's Christmas time! One thing I *do* remember is a huge, beautiful Christmas tree sparkling with gold baubles and pink bows and crackers tied on the branches. I know I saw it somewhere nice but where? I haven't a clue.

I carefully put my glass down on the table and tell her what I have just remembered. She listens intently to what I tell her and then goes on to calmly ask if I remember any more. I tell her that I know I was in Germany to see my sister Carly but I'm not sure whether she's still over there or not.

Sometimes I see Carly as a blur standing in front of me, but when my mam comes to visit, my sister is not with her, only Riona, my aunt. She doesn't comment on what I've just said. I find this very weird, so I carry on.

I do remember some things from when I was in Berlin, such as shopping and the friends I had there. I also know that I went to London for some reason, but did I go alone or with a friend? When I close my eyes I get flashbacks, seeing things as if I've just dreamt them. I sit back in this chair I have been put in, and want to remember, but I am too scared, I think I must have been through something bad or what would be the point of me being in here? I begin to tell her about my past, when I was younger and all the things I *do* remember. There is one thing she does ask me to talk about: my sister Carly. So, I tell her from the beginning. October 30th, 1996.

I was five years old when I first met my sister.

Mam looked at me and Dad with sheer happiness as she held her baby in her arms in that hospital bed.

She beckoned me over to look at my baby sister. So, I wandered over to check her out. I glared and thought my sister looked a bit ugly. I didn't touch her yet.

I was a smart arse when I was a kid. I knew this as I

used to hear Mam talk to friends and family when I was in earshot. I would hear her say quite arrogantly as I had a book in hand, "Our Ailish with her reading, she's a little smart arse isn't she?"

I had learnt to read by the time I was three years old. So, when I started school, I was the only kid in class who impressed Miss O'Reilly by reading a story out loud. Gave her a break I'm sure.

So, I read the chart at the bottom of my mams bed and read out loud the name she and Dad had chosen for this *ugly child*. "Carly Rose, seven pounds and eleven ounces". Then thinking about how I felt about the name by twisting my mouth back and forth I decided that it was cool.

So, I blurted out quite proudly with a huge smile on my face "I think that name is fuckin' lovely".

Sadly my smile disappeared rather quickly.

My mam turned as white as the sheet she was laying on and said "WHAT! Do you know what that word means Ailish. And where'd you hear it?"

I answered Mam by telling her that I'd heard the word from Dad. I'd noticed that Dads eyes were getting bigger by the second at this point.

"He was on the phone..." I said quite loudly. Mams mouth opened wide as she listened to my explanation "and I heard him tell someone that the roses were fuckin' lovely, and..." I said whilst pointing at my baby sister "her middle name is Rose so..." I was immediately stopped in my tracks by Mam almost leaping out of her bed.

Finding out much later, Dad had been talking to his newly acquired assistant telling him that he'd done a great 'fuckin' lovely' job engraving the said flower on the edge of a desk that he'd recently made.

Mam grabbed my arm and, looking me right in the eye, said very angrily "I don't want to hear that word coming out of yer mouth ever again. Understood?"

I just nodded my head feeling very confused.

I've never seen Dad move so fast. "Toilet, I need the toilet" he stuttered. Then he was out of that room in a flash as if he'd been sitting on a mass of hot coals.

Mam shouted out at him to stick a bar of soap in his mouth while he was at it.

I was on a mission to find out what the F word meant.

Unfortunately, I didn't find out until six years later when I was eleven years old.

I will put this in brief terms: School hide out, me, friend, smoking, boy and *hard on*. Then Treasa the friend shouting "I'll fuckin' kill yer, yer horny bastard" to the boy.

My friend taught me many more words that day. (Including *hard on*.)

At first, I was jealous of Carly. Once I threatened to run away from home, but I was just ignored. My Dad said he would pack my bag for me. I was so mad at him for saying that, I walked out of the house with a bag I had packed myself, then heard him shout "See yer then". I only got to the end of the street, had a cry and turned around.

As we got older, Carly looked up to me, so I was never jealous again.

I told Rachel I was getting tired, so she stopped our session. I was taken back to my bed, where sleep took over instantly.

PART ONE

CHAPTER 1

Ailish and Carly O'Neill live in big old house that in the last few years has become a shrine to their Dad. Kathleen O'Neill, their Mother, hasn't changed anything since her beloved husband Michael passed away, even though she should as he was fixing it up a bit before that dreadful day. The wallpaper on the living room walls has seen better days. The whole house could do with a good lick of paint in a lot of places, but Mam likes it just the way it is.

One thing Dad had done, acting on an order from his younger daughter, my bossy younger sister Carly, was to build her a big wooden shed to play in. It was filled with lots of shelves to put toys and books on, then painted in bright pink with yellow stripes, as that's what *his* Carly had asked for. Mam saw it and told him it looked like a stick of rock and to paint it a different colour. It became more of a burgundy shade (just what he had handy) which Mam *still* thought looked like shite. So, it ended up being painted yellow. It's now faded to the colour of a lemon sherbet sweet, but he painted the inside pink and yellow stripes instead, just to stop the sulking and keep the peace.

One morning, not long after he had finished that most important piece of work, he suddenly became weak and decided to stay in bed, which wasn't like him. Before he could even think about seeing a doctor he passed away peacefully in his sleep that very evening. The post mortem stated he had had a massive heart attack. Nobody knew why it happened. He had his own business as a carpenter, always took regular days off and never got stressed. Just one of those unexpected, distressing things in life.

Ever since Dad died, things around our house have changed. He was always the one who kept the family together because he didn't put up with any nonsense. Not only that, he was kind and funny, we miss him dreadfully.

We both try to help our Mam around the house doing our delegated chores. But I catch Carly in her bedroom, drawing plans of the house she wants to live in, when she should be sorting her laundry out or drying the dishes. My sister has always said she wants to be an architect when she gets out of school. I'm not as ambitious as her. I take life as it comes so whatever will be will be, which was also my Dads philosophy on life.

That was eight years ago, when we had to put our life in order and change our routine. Our Mam didn't have to worry about going to work to keep us, as she was left a huge life insurance policy that Dad had taken out. Plus, she receives her widows' pension, so we aren't hard up.

I work at a travel agency. I started as an apprentice and loved it, so I stayed and worked my way up to become part of a fully-fledged top sales team. Carly is sixteen and can't wait to leave school to go to college to do her architect training. She has kept her dream going; I'm not surprised as she always was a go-getter.

Unfortunately, she hangs around with a girl called Sandra Delaney.

I know I shouldn't judge but the reputation this girl has is a bit rough. Carly as a loyal friend, accompanies her from school most days.

Sandy, always the show off with her short skirt and too much eye make-up, swinging her large silver hooped earrings as she talks, will stand in front of our house as the two of them chat.

Mam will watch with arms folded at the window of the front room as she curiously peeps through her pristine white sheer curtains. staring mostly towards Sandra and swearing under her breath at the same time at the way that girl is dressed. Embarrassing is the word she would use out loud when I am in ear shot. But I know better when I'm not. The air no doubt will be blue.

As I pass the living room via the staircase toward the kitchen, I hear Mam shout out. "Apparently, her parents have allowed her to have a tattoo. At the age of sixteen. What's that all about Ailish?" I don't respond, thinking better of it.

I leave her to her ritual of trying to put a spell on this girl, wishing she would just piss off and leave her beloved younger daughter alone to find a more decent friend.

Although Mam has a strong religious background, she normally wouldn't say nasty comments about another human being, so her reaction to Sandra is, well, not normal. The thing is I secretly agree with her!

But I know she wants better for Carly, so do I, but I leave her to it.

Christ though, thinking what Mam said, I would hate to think where and what this artistic skin engraving is. The name of a boy maybe or even the face of something evil? She'll regret it in the future I'm sure. Or she may not. Might go on to have several more and enjoy them.

Me, Ailish O'Neill, the perfectionist and always the prude. My downfall at times. Sometimes I think I should just say to hell with it all and get a tattoo myself. Most likely though I would end up running out of the tattoo parlour and into the nearest book shop looking for a self-help book that can stop my out of hand behaviour.!

Going back to Carly's friend, the lovely *Sandy*. Mam tries not to bring her name up in the house, especially during meal times. All I would hear would be "Don't mention her, I'd like to enjoy my food thank you very much." So, my mouth stays shut.

Sitting at the table debating the usual, thinking what to have for our next meal, we hear the front door open.

We wait for her usual response but Carly doesn't say a word as she enters the house. We hear her run up the stairs two at a time, then the bang of her bedroom door. This a bit strange, walking into the kitchen with the same question, "What's for tea?" is the usual.

I look at my Ma and she's giving me the look of, *something's up.*

Oh God, I know for a fact that it will be little old me

that will be knocking on Carly's bedroom door asking what the hell is going on. Sometimes I wish Dad was still around, he would know what to do and say.

Mam gets up off her chair and wanders out of the kitchen.

I ask her where she's going. "To look for something" answering in a couldn't care less manner.

She loves to wander off in her own world. I sometimes hear her singing, but not as much since Dad passed.

I lay my head on my hands on the hard wood of our old and lovely worn table and think of him and mumble to myself 'Oh Daddy, why aren't yer here when I really need you?'

I just have a gut feeling that things are going to be difficult.

I hear Mam and the sound of her floppy purple slippers coming back into the kitchen.

"Ailish, I heard you talking to someone." I look up at her and nod. "It was yer Dad wasn't it?" she asks sitting back down.

She waits for me to answer but I don't.

Then says "I can feel him around sometimes, you know. I smell his after shave..."

A quick pause then, "That expensive one I bought him the last Christmas he was here. He never really liked it, you know. He wore it just for me."

She smiles and continues with her story, "I watched him pouring some of it down the sink one day. He never knew that I caught him in the act."

I couldn't speak as I had just filled my mouth with tea,

so my answer came out as a spurt of liquid (far better than choking). I'm now covered in tea from my mouth, slipping down the chin to the bosom area.

While I clean myself up with the nearest cloth after that fit of laughter, Mam finishes telling the story of how she saw him refill the bottle with water. She almost got caught herself, as he kept looking behind in case *he* was caught.

She was so shocked almost wetting her pants in the process, trying not to laugh as she continued peeping around that door. Mam has always kept her sense of humour no matter what.

We continue the laughter until our stomachs ache just thinking about it.

When we've calmed down, Mam pulls herself up from the kitchen chair, stretching her arms out in front of herself, trying to speak whilst yawning loudly at the same time.

"Can't be bothered to cook tonight love, take-out be okay?"

Without hesitation I reply "Yep, I think that would be a good idea Mam".

I'm not really that hungry as I'm feeling anxious. But it might get Carly to come down and make an appearance if she knows that we are having a Chinese or fish and chips, don't know which yet.

It doesn't take long to decide as when I dig in our junk drawer the first menu that appears was for Chinese. We decided on our usual chow mein with duck egg rolls.

I shout up the stairs "Carly we're havin' Chinese what d'yer want?"

I wait, hoping that I won't get ignored.

Then "Eh, not really that hungry Ailish" she throws back at me.

But I know as soon as the smell hits her nose, she will want some, plus I'm certainly not sharing. So, when I make the call to order, I include her usual too.

We only wait fifteen minutes before we're ripping into the paper bags and taking out the hot containers, then sitting down and stuffing our mouths full of that (can't get enough of) crispy duck.

As I'd predicted, Carly eventually and very quietly enters the kitchen while we still have our heads in our food. I notice her taking a peek in the foil containers while Mam and I keep quiet. Then Mam speaks.

"There's plenty there, so take what yer want."

Still being as quiet as a mouse, my sister plates the food and off she goes heading back up to her room without saying one word.

"There's something up with her" Mam says.

"That's obvious" I reply.

Then I get *the look* again. "Yes, I'll go up and find out…not until I've had seconds though"

So much for not being very hungry.

My anxiety on a scale from one to ten is a definite eight. I must relax. I feel like my shoulders are touching my ears.

I tap on her door as I hear music playing; it's not to my taste at all. It sounds like a load of crap, obviously she doesn't think so.

She doesn't answer so I knock a bit louder this time. I hear her moving around; I swallow hard then take a long drink of the water I'd brought up with me. Eventually her door slowly opens.

Carly peeps around the door. "What do you want?" She looks at me in a way that I would say repulsive, yes that's it Ailish you look repulsive!

"Yes, I'm fine" I lie and shout as the music is *so* loud.

Shouting even louder I say "Just wanted to see if I can help you, if you had any problems, that's all". I swallow nervously.

"Mams worried...you never spoke to her when you came home from school" I still can't hear myself speak.

Then she says "*You* seem to be the one with a problem Ailish; you're looking a bit pale".

"Can you turn your music down a bit? I just want to come in and have a chat with you. Please?" I answer.

So, she lets me in, turning down that shite and locks the door after I walk in her room. Feeling trapped (and nauseous), I have thoughts of escaping out of the window, as I notice it's open. This is most likely to get rid of the smell of the food she had brought up with her. I take in a deep breath. Then I begin...

"How's your day been at school, do you still enjoy it?" (I say half heartedly as this is not what I want to find out, not really.)

"Okay, I suppose."

"And?" I question, feeling slightly calmer.

"I've just been feeling a bit tired and run-down that's all" she tells me while flicking her hair back with her hand. I feel I have to get down to finding out the truth, to ask the *real* question.

"Why do you hang around with Sandy Delaney? She doesn't seem to be your type of friend." She looks at me with horror.

"Why are you asking me this?"

"I'm worried about you and so is Mam" I reply. "And I'm sure you know the reputation she has around here."

Then answering me with a bit of anger in her voice. "Sandy loves the boys, I know that, but she is a good friend. She's not teaching me any sex tricks if that's what you mean."

I thought, God damn hope not!

Then I tell her, "I was thinking about taking a holiday." Wasn't planning on it, but what the hell, I need one.

"I'm owed some weeks from work, so I was thinking of taking Mam to Valentia Island for a few days. She's got happy memories from when she and Dad went there years ago, bought that special shell from there. You know that pink one? I caught her looking at it just the other day. She needs to have a break Carly."

She doesn't say a word as she is still picking at her Chinese take-out, so I continue.

"You said you were feeling a bit tired. It might do yer some good. What do yer think?"

She thought for a bit. "Maybe."

I'm waiting for the next question.

But…"Yes, maybe, but…could I bring Sandy?"

I just had the feeling she would ask. My face *must* have paled up again as I can feel the blood draining from it.

Then, "Are you alright Aili?" she asks.

I sit on the edge of her bed (thinking shite; I don't

want that girl coming with us and showing off her red lips and tattoos). Carly comes over and puts her arm around my shoulders.

"Yes, I'm okay." Then I said, "I thought it would just be a family get together Carly. Would you not like that?" I was really hoping she would agree.

"Why do you want to bring Sandra anyway, aren't your Mam and me enough for you?"

God, as I make that remark I could eat my words, it sounds so pathetic.

Looking a bit upset, she obviously wants her friend with her. She lays her head down on her pillow and sighs.

"Do you really want to know?"

I can see her eyes are tearing up. Now I am starting to worry. With my heart pounding faster now, I look down at her angelic face, and hope it's not what I am thinking.

She returns the look, and then I say, "Carly you're upset; you need to tell me what's going on with yerself".

Her tears stream down her face now, but no cries come from her mouth.

Looking at me again, she hesitates. Then it came to me like a karate chop to the throat, "I'm pregnant Ailish!"

Oh my God! How am I going to tell our Mammy? The thought goes around my brain, amongst a hell of a lot more thoughts like, shall I scream now or later. After what seems like hours, the sensible part of my brain comes to the rescue and ignores those terrible things. I decide not to tell, (anyone) *yet*.

I continue nervously. "How far gone are you?"

"Two months" she replies, now crying.

I hold her in my arms and gently kiss her face. I have to ask who the father is but the thought of asking her makes my heart rate increase again. I feel quite sick. But I eventually do ask and then I wait. Tears are coming to *my* eyes now. I don't want to cry, it would make things worse so I wipe them quickly away. More thoughts are racing around my brain.

I ask "Has this anything to do with Sandra and the bad influence she obviously has on you? Were you at a party with her and alcohol was flowing?" She looks really annoyed now and wipes her eyes and face on the sheet on her bed.

"No nothing like that happened. If you must know Sandy is helping me"

I am now very confused.

"Helping you with what?" I asked, trying not to shout.

She puts her head in her hands and mumbles, "I want to have an abortion."

"WHAT." I'm shouting now. "What did you say?"

"An abortion" she replies much quieter. But I hear very clearly.

"That's what I thought you said" I mumble back to her with my fist practically in my mouth.

She continues. "Sandra has had one and said she would help me get through it without anyone else knowing."

She starts crying again. I once again hug her, thinking what the hell am I going to do. I feel so much love for my sister, I need to help her.

"Carly I will always help you. You cannot just go and

have an abortion without a lot of thought. The Father may want to know too. Have you never thought about that?"

Silence in the room now. I rock her in my arms for what seems like ages. Carly pulls herself together and says "I really don't think I want the baby. I want to have the career I have always dreamt of. I want to go to college and to do my training to become an Architect. You know I've wanted to do that since I was a little girl." She collapses on the bed crying so hard, will she never stop. I wait until she has calmed down and then a huge sigh comes from my mouth.

"You *still* have not told me who the Father is. You need to tell me. I think it's a very important part of the equation here."

She lays back down again and tries to calmly tell me her story of the day she met "*this man.*"

Carly tells me that she had gone into her regular newsagents in Dublin where she bought her monthly architect magazine. Walking to the counter to pay she noticed this attractive looking man standing behind her who was tapping her on the shoulder and commenting on what she had just bought, whilst showing her that he had bought the very same magazine.

Very forward of him I think.

Noticing he was maybe somewhere in his late twenties, very good looking and spoke with an English accent, she said she liked his eyes; they were dreamy deep blue, (her very words). Also lovely black wavy hair that just fell over his collar.

They'd went on talking about their one thing in

common, architect stuff (her words again). As they were walking out of the shop he asked if she would like to go for coffee with him at the cafe just down the street. Becoming a bit nervous, as she fancied him and he noticed this. He told her not to worry, that he just wanted to keep chatting about "architect stuff" with her, as that was what he did for a living.

I am secretly thinking that she is *so* innocent and naive.

As they entered the café he was greeted by the portly man behind the counter.

He called the man she was with Ross; they found a table at the rear of the cafe where he ordered their drinks and then comfortably starting chatting. He told her his name was Ross Carmichael and that he was an Architect. He had offices based in London and Berlin. He said he was opening a new office in Dublin, his reason for being in the city. He also told her that he was looking for a female apprentice for his new place. Telling me that she got really excited at the prospect of maybe taking up his offer. Then told him that she had to talk to her Mam first as she had planned to go to college. He understood. Then he had asked how old she was.

When Carly tells me this, my first thought is...right, the first step to seducing my sister. I keep quiet and she continues.

He wanted to meet with her again, so they exchanged mobile numbers.

He was staying at The Westbury in the city. God almighty, very posh he's obviously made of money.

They arranged to meet again at the same café where

they first met. She says she likes him a lot as they seem to have a lot in common. I think, something in common alright, he liked sex and she was willing? I keep my thoughts to myself.

One week later they met again. She says he made her laugh and felt grown up in his company. He told her he had a lot of books about Architecture in his hotel room. Carly decided to go with him to *"Look at his books."*

Jaysus! I cannot believe it!

Then going on to tell me that she willingly had the most wonderful out of this world sex she could ever imagine. I feel I am going to have a full-blown panic attack at this point.

This went on every week for two months and she never saw him again after that. He returned to London. "He doesn't know does he?" I ask her, my whole body shaking with the shock of it all.

"No, he doesn't. I don't want him to know anyway" she replies quietly. "I don't know where he is either, Aili. He never told me where in London his office is. I love him a lot and I miss him".

Noticing her tears, I put my arms around her again, feeling so sorry for her. I desperately need to help her. She had been looking forward to going to college. God knows what was to become of that now.

I'm wondering how our Mam is going to react when finding out. I tell Carly to calm down; I will sort everything out to help her with her baby.

I leave her to it and go into the bathroom to splash cold water on my face and down my throat as I am so thirsty after all that salty Chinese food, before going back downstairs.

I pop my head around Carly's door and tell her to wash her face and just come and say hi to her Mammy. She just nods.

Ten minutes later, the three of us are sitting at the old wooden kitchen table enjoying a cup of tea out of the worn out old brown tea pot as if everything is normal. I look at Mam and smile. She returns the smile and I can tell what she is thinking, that I will chat with her later, to let her know what the outcome was of my encounter with her younger daughter.

I have decided not to tell her anything yet, as Carly said wait just a while. Unfortunately, Mam does ask me, so I tell her that her boyfriend has dumped her and that Slutty Sandra was helping her out. I feel terrible lying to her, but I've made a promise to my sister.

Well, nine days later, life has changed, *again*. Stress had set in with Carly and she had a miscarriage. She had been getting ready for school. I was in my bedroom and heard her crying in the bathroom. I knocked on the door, she told me to wait one minute. When she *did* open it, I noticed a lot of blood in the toilet.

"Oh no Carly, you will need to go to the hospital, NOW"! I was scared I must admit.

"Come here I will help yer, oh but hang on a bit" I took off out of there with sweat pouring from my armpits.

I ran into her bedroom to grab a clean pair of knickers, trying to bypass the small black lacy things while searching for something more comfortable.

"Clean yourself up a bit. Don't worry about Mammy; I will make something up."

I did. "Very bad nose bleed Ma."

WHAT!! Well, what could I say? I had minutes to think. She wanted to come with us.

I immediately put a stop to that. I grabbed my bag and my sister then ran to the car.

The hospital took great care of Carly. She was in there most of the day; just as well I'd told work that I needed the whole day off.

I hung around for a long time in that place. When it was time for her to go home, we knew we had to keep this to ourselves.

Crying is not good when I'm driving but I just couldn't help it. Glad that there was a box of tissues at hand. Normally used for my sweaty armpits, thanks to my nervous disposition that I was probably inflicted with when I was dragged out of my mother's womb. Difficult birth she told me.

I glanced over at Carly in the passenger seat; she was out for the count, mouth wide open and saliva running from the corner. I wiped my tears away with the back of my hand this time and thought, it could have been worse I guess?

When we arrived home, Mam was at the door with a worried look on her face. I parked the car in the drive adjacent to the house and she ran over as we were getting out.

"Is she alright now Aili? You were at the hospital a long

time. Why was that"? She asked looking concerned. Think, Ailish, think.

"It was very busy. A lot of emergencies in today" I answered too quickly really.

Phew! I think I got away with that. She replied with a look that made me think differently. She knew. I just know it. She's not daft.

"Hmm. As long as she's alright, that's the main thing."

Then as she was walking back inside, I heard her say, "I'll make us some tea."

Whilst in the kitchen, I could hear her sniffling. I think she *does* know, but will never mention it. I know what she's like. I'm sure Dad in the afterlife listens to what goes on in this house and tells her all about it. Who knows?

I walk up to my bedroom as I need to lie down for five minutes. I think about what just happened today and cry. I also think I do need a holiday, *desperately.*

CHAPTER 2

Two years have now passed. How'd that happen?

I still work for the travel agent and I still live with my Mam. Well, I love my Ma plus I have nowhere else to go!

Carly is now eighteen and it's her last day at school before going to college in September, to becoming a fully-fledged Architect at last. I am so proud of her.

It's my day off and it's mostly been a nice relaxing day at that. Usually I catch up with things I've put off until the last minute but I've been a bit lazy, but who cares, not me.

I'm sitting in the kitchen with Mam, having a casual chat about the price of food. It's the usual exciting conversation between mother and daughter with tea as the chosen beverage, when Carly runs in the house looking very rosy cheeked and cheerful.

"I *love* this day. I just can't wait for the next few months to pass by" she announces. shouting out loud and slamming her bag on the table with a big smile on her face. The talking continues.

"I've wanted to let you know something." She hesitates whilst turning towards the cupboard to get a mug for her tea. She says, "I'm travelling to Europe with a good friend next week". She is looking at me and her Mother so I ask her when had this been decided on.

"Oh, not that long ago" she replies. I rub my hand over my forehead as if I have a headache (one on the way I am sure). I ask why she had not booked it with me, knowing I could have got a reduced fare.

"I booked it with your company Ailish, last month, Molly helped me out."

Molly is my work mate. Why hadn't she told me Carly had been in though? I just thought of something quite important, where did she get the money from to book a holiday to Europe? She isn't getting her inheritance until she is twenty-one.

I look at Mam shrugging her shoulders. Behind her back, I signal to Carly, jerking my head toward the sitting room so we would be alone. She lazily drags her feet toward the room.

I calmly ask her. "How are you paying for this holiday?" She looks rather nervous before answering my question.

"My friend is treating me." I notice that she swallows hard. Hmm, I wonder what is going on, so I ask her.

"So which friend are you going with, who is treating you to this lovely holiday?"

Then I add "Where exactly are you going in Europe?" I try to hide my suspicion.

"Ah, well, Germany. Not sure where else until we get there", still looking like she is a bit nervous. Well, I think, I am going to ask the obvious.

"Is your friend a male by any chance?" Now she is

looking terribly anxious, as if she is holding her breath before answering. I damn well feel like I am, waiting for *her* to answer!

"Yes, he is, my friend that is, a male" she says still sounding nervous.

"So, who is it Carly, this boyfriend of yours?" Suddenly, she runs out of the room and out of the house into the garden. How I knew, I don't know. I just had that gut feeling again. Or is it just obvious? I slowly go after her. Don't want to panic by running hysterically down the garden path shouting and screaming after her. That would only make her run even farther out of the back gate. Then I would have to run after her. Don't even want to think of that scenario.

Mam is in the kitchen in a world of her own, pottering about studying her recipes. Thank the Lord I don't have to explain anything to her.

I find my sister hiding in our old wooden shed that Dad had made for her years ago. She has her head in her hands. I sit next to her, putting my arm around her.

"You've met up with Ross again, haven't you?" She takes her hands away from her face and looks at me. "I love him. I told you, two years ago. I love to be with him and make love with him. He excites me and he has ever since the day we met." She stops for a minute to take a breath.

"We met about a month ago at the same place. It was meant to be, I just know it. I was buying my usual magazine and there he was. We arranged to meet. We had wild sex again, *unbelievable sex*!" She stops again and I daren't imagine what is going through her head as I watch her reminisce.

"He asked if I wanted to come to Berlin with him to look at his office and make a holiday of it at the same time. I said yes, of course."

I interrupt her. "You haven't told me how old he is."

She looks extremely annoyed.

"What difference does it make? I *am* old enough to choose who I want to be with." Not that it is really important. Maybe I am being a bit of a prick, but she is my sister and I am worried about her. But she decides to tell me anyway.

"If you really want to know, he is twenty-eight. That's what he told me anyway. It doesn't matter to me really. He could be *thirty*-eight and I would still want to be with him." She glows when she talked of him. "He is very kind to me. Treats me like a princess and buys me princess things too. Look, he bought me this", showing me a very sparkly expensive looking piece of jewellery hanging from her wrist.

"WOW! Are those *real* diamonds?" I ask her.

"He definitely has good taste hasn't he", telling me, looking very pleased with herself. I am happy for her but there is one thing I need to say to her.

"Make sure you are on the pill Carly. I hope you are. I don't want you to go through having an unwanted pregnancy again. Please?"

I am wondering why she doesn't want me to meet him. When I think about it, I've never asked. I'm sure she will in her own time. If the relationship lasts she might. Who knows if it will?

A week later I arrive home from work and my sister has already left for the airport to join her boyfriend. I ask Mam if he had come to pick her up. She told me Carly had gone in a taxi this morning and was meeting Ross at the airport. I am pretty annoyed about that. I had wanted to tell her I love her and to stay safe. And the important thing I wanted to say to her again was to stay on the pill. I mention this to Mam. She says that she had told her the exact same thing. We exchange smiles, while I'm thinking, great minds think alike.

We decide to change the subject to discuss Dad, as we miss him a lot. I do feel though, that he would have wanted to know more about her boyfriends before she wandered off around the world. This starts me thinking. I used to hear Dad talking to Mam "Kathleen, you are too soft with that girl. I know she's the baby in the family but she needs to know right from wrong. She gets away with murder sometimes." Dad was soft with her too but in different ways. I just want to keep her out of trouble. I worry about her more now as she's only eighteen after all, but she needs to be frickin' streetwise! I need to find out more about this boyfriend of hers. When I eventually *do* meet him, I just hope he doesn't merit the bad gut feeling that I have about him. Cannot wait until she's home.

CHAPTER 3

There are times when I want to have some quiet time, when I need to be alone. There are also times when I like the company of someone to talk to. Molly, my friend from work, suggested meeting for a quiet drink tonight. I just didn't fancy that idea at all. For one it's only Tuesday, and two I have too much on my mind. The thing is I just don't want to discuss how I'm feeling with Molly. I just want my Mother's company tonight. I have thoughts about taking a holiday as I had mentioned to Carly. But now that she has buggered off to Germany, it's made me think more seriously about actually making it happen.

I decide to tell Oonagh, my boss, that I don't feel too good. So, I leave at three instead of five thirty. I feel a bit guilty though, I could have got through the rest of the day as I only have a bit of a headache. But that holiday is on my mind and I want to discuss it with Mam. I tell all at work that I will be in tomorrow as usual. Something strange goes through my mind as I walk out of the door.

I have a weird feeling that I won't be working at this place for too long. It is *very* weird, as I like my job. Why would I want to leave?

As I drive home I can't shake off the feeling that things may be going to change quite soon. I stop at a red light and notice a girl that reminds me of Carly. She is walking toward the car and wearing the same type of clothes, the hot pants and the tight T-shirt. Now my thoughts turn to my sister. I do worry about her. I just hope she's safe with this Mr Ross Carmichael and he's taking care of her. I would really injure him severely if he hurt her and I *would* try to do it too. I think that's only normal, isn't it? Mm, maybe I would sleep on it, just for her sake.

I'm nearly home now. I'm looking forward to kicking off my killing me on the toes shoes.

I open the front door and she is nowhere to be seen or heard. Usually when I get home, I hear the radio playing in the kitchen and her singing along to her favourite music, which is very loud at times. She denies being a bit deaf but I know better so I shout out.

"Mam, I'm home."

No reply.

"Ma, where are you? I'm home early." I eventually kick off those heels and wander into the kitchen. No sign of her. I pop my head around the door of the sitting room, not there either. I need to go for a pee. Running up the stairs I now hear her singing. Ignoring my desire to use the toilet, I follow the sound of her lovely voice. As I look around the door to her bedroom, I see her sitting on her bed with some photos in her hands. She notices me.

"Oh, Ailish, you're home early. Everything alright love?"

I answer. "Yes, fine. Just a bit of a headache, thought

I'd leave early for a change. What you got there?" while looking down at her loved ones.

"This one is of Daddy. Look, it's when we went to Valentia Island. We had such a good time there. It's very beautiful there you know. You smile just like him, the way that you both tilt your head to one side." She shows me the other.

"And look at this one of Carly. It's on her tenth birthday. She's so cute with that pretty pink dress on." Mam looks so happy, and then appears to look sad. I move to where she is sitting on the bed. I put my arm around her and say, "Mam, I love you. Let's take the box of photos downstairs. We can look at them in the kitchen while you're making me a lovely cup o' tea." We both laugh.

"Come on then Ailish." We pick each other off her bed, still giggling as Mam is struggling to get her arse off the comfort of her mattress. I go into my own room to change into my stretch pants and T-shirt so I'll feel more comfy, then head toward the stairs. I sit at our old familiar kitchen table while she makes that much needed tea.

I pick up one of the pictures of Mam and Dad when they were in Valentia Island.

"Look at this one Mammy. You look so young then and you're both smiling at each other like two love birds, Ah, very *tweet*." I nudge her and we both laugh.

"Ah, it was lovely there, we had so much fun. It's a very spiritual and calming place to be, I'll tell yer. We also got the ferry back over to Cahersiveen just for one afternoon. It was nice there too, with the few shops an' all."

Pouring the tea from the old brown teapot that we've

had in our family for an absolute age, she chooses a chair next to me and as the legs make a screeching sound as she pulls it across the floor, I cover my ears. "Ooh sorry Ailish" trying to cover her ears at the same time.

"Dad always said he would do something about the legs on this chair. I don't want to touch it now." I laugh and tell her I am used to it now anyhow. We pull out more pictures and see another of Carly.

"I'm still worrying about Carly being over there in Germany on her own" telling me with a look of gloom on her face.

I tell her. "She's not on her own. I understand how you're feeling but you're not getting yourself anywhere by worrying are you?" Sighing, she gets up from the table to refill her tea. I look over, stretching out my arm with mug in hand, hinting for more tea. I'm enjoying chatting with her. I realise how much I *do* enjoy her company, then I make a decision.

"Mam, I think we should have a holiday together. You enjoyed Valentia Island with Dad. What if I book a holiday there for us both? I would love to see it." She turns around from her tea pouring and looks quite excited and happy.

I add "That took you by surprise didn't it? Well?" I can see her thinking. A few minutes of silence follow as we sip our hot tea. She eventually answers my question.

"You know Ailish" hesitating for a few seconds, then..."I'd love to go with you. We could do with some excitement. We haven't been anywhere since you're Daddy passed. Carly's on *her* holiday so, we should have one too." She claps her hands together and her face lights up with excitement like she was a child again. I get up from the table and kiss her cheek.

I tell her "I'll get that booked as soon as I get back to work tomorrow. We'll go next week before Carly gets back from hers."

I'm excited at the thought, I really am. I feel in my heart though that this holiday will be the calm before the storm. I don't know why I feel like this, I just have that old gut feeling coming back.

Mam puts a small bag of goodies in front of my face as I'm trying to drive. Then asking "Would you like one of these chewy mints Ailish"?

"Trying to see through the windscreen at where I'm going would be nice" I said. She puts her head back and laughs. I glance at her and put my hand out to grab a sweet. I take more than one.

"Hey greedy, I'll have to buy some more now", telling me while slapping my hand. We're enjoying acting like a couple of kids. We need to get away from reality for a while. Just for now.

We're not far from being in the cosy B&B we chose to stay in for the next week. We can now start to smell the wonderful scent of the Atlantic Ocean. I open the window on Mams side so she can breathe it in. "Ooh, that smell is the best! Could not ask for more" she says excitedly.

We can see the ferry in sight now. Heading toward it, I slow down to manoeuvre the car into position where I am told to park. It seems that it is full, as I have the last space. Getting out, I pat the top of Dads old green car to remind myself to be thankful for the miles it has gone to get us here safe and sound. I can do without having to fork out good money to buy another one.

We stretch and walk to the lower deck. There are quite a few people sitting at the windows to take in the scenery. It's to be expected, as it is the height of the season. I hear them talking with each other. I can hear different accents. American, French and sounds like German too. (Carly flashes across my mind as I hear the German being spoken.) I'm hoping *we* can find a seat at the window. I spot a space. I turn around to Mam and quickly grab her yellow cotton cardigan by the sleeve then head toward the seats before they are taken by someone else. She gives me a startled look.

"What yer doin', yer nearly ripped me good cardigan off me back."

I reply half laughing, "Oh, *that* old thing. It's fine anyway" I get a look of disgust from her. "I was joking Ma. I know it's your best one." She rolls her eyes at me.

Sitting at the window, we settle for the next five minutes. A very short journey across, but we decided it's nicer than driving over the bridge. Enjoying the atmosphere, Mam interrupts our silence.

"Wonder how Carly is getting on Ailish. I just hope she's enjoying herself. Oh, I just wish she was here with us", turning her head while staring at the scene outside.

The sea is very calm and serene. It's as blue as the wonderful summer sky. I look at the lush green hills and my mind wanders to betters days when our family were altogether. I would say she is thinking the same. She carries on and says. "Would've been nice wouldn't it. I would have all my family with me then, apart from your Daddy of course" I'm thinking of Carly too (and Dad) but I don't want to spoil our holiday by reminiscing.

I tell her calmly. "She'll be having a good time. *We* need to have a good time too. So don't worry your head off."

As soon as we get on the ferry, it's just about time to get off! We scuttle along with all the others trying to disembark. Wishing the journey had been a bit longer, we find our car. We don't have to wait around, as we were the last one on. As I drive off, I point out the famous town clock in the village where we sailed into. Mam says that she finds the clock *very nice*, but she's more interested in going back to Skellig Michael Island. I agree and tell her we'll go any day she wants while we're here. She yawns and stretches, says she could do with a nap when we settle into our rooms.

It's been a long day as we started off really early. Mam was up at six o'clock, as I was still snoring. I've been driving for almost five hours and I can honestly say that I feel quite knackered. I know I'll sleep like I've never slept in a long time. How couldn't I with all that salty sea air to breathe in.

We arrive at the lovely quaint whitewashed stone cottage perched happily on a small hill. Standing proudly with the sun glaring across its rooftop, it looks like a monument for the weary traveller and in the most glorious location we could ever dream up. I park at the front and gaze around before getting out. I open the car door and see lush green hills in the distance and hear the sound of the sea which is only a hop around the corner. That magical sound of the waves lifts my senses to another dimension.

My look is obviously a picture of happiness as I move my legs swiftly out of the car on to the tarmac. I rub my backside to try to get some feeling back, smiling as I do.

Mam looks at me and says "God Ailish, I've never seen your face look so happy for ages. This island surely will do that to yer."

As we soak in the warm spiritual atmosphere, a portly woman appears from the solid oak doorway. She waves her chubby hand at us. I return the wave. Walking up the pathway towards her I look at the lushest green grass I have ever seen, the garden with its own veggie patch in a far corner, and the different colours of the flowers that dance in the soft breeze, welcoming everyone who comes to gaze and admire its beauty. I notice the one tree that stands to the left of the house. I look straight into the eyes of a bird who sits on a lower branch, chirping away its song as we enter the long-awaited restful holiday home.

"Hello, you must be the O'Neill's'? I'm Mary; it's lovely to see you. Come on in and I'll show you around the cottage, I'm sure you'll want to rest after your long trip."

I rudely yawn in her face and tell her, feeling quite embarrassed, "Oh. I'm so sorry. You are right, we *do* need a rest. Sorry again. I'm Ailish and this is my Mam, Kathleen. We'd love to look around first of course".

I tell Mary we think her cottage is beautiful.

As we are passing the sitting room, I see it's full of wooden beams painted white and lots of light coming through the windows showing off the surrounding beauty.

I know now that I've picked the right place for us to kick back and forget the stress in our lives.

We follow Mary with her dark shiny shoulder length hair bouncing and bobbing along as she walks. We thank her. Smiling that relaxed and happy smile, she turns around to let us know that breakfast is served up until 11 o'clock and that she'll leave us to unpack our bags. What? Not us, we'll have a nap before attempting to even unzip the zippers on our bags.

Before leaving us to our own devices, she asks what time would we like to be fed. We tell her simultaneously that we would like it at 10 o'clock. Time enough for a decent rest.

Mary told us that she lives in the larger cottage next door which is attached by a modern glass passageway (didn't notice that from the road), not that far for her to travel to make our breakfasts, just a skip and a jump. Then off she goes, hair bobbing along her neckline.

Before our bedrooms are taken over by our snoring, we investigate the premises with constant smiles on both of our faces. What a place. Mary has good taste. It is so clean and done out with bits and pieces that are all related to the sea. The wooden black and white oval clock on the wall in the kitchen is way beyond big. It's the biggest clock we have ever seen but it fits right in. The pale grey walls and the cream cupboards give it a modern twist but still leaves the character it deserves with the old slate floors covered in a bright red patterned rug covering its worn-out bits. (I took a sneaky peek.)

The living area is larger than we expected with its two

2-seater charcoal couches comfortably decorated with several cushions with seaside prints embellished on their deliciously soft bellies. We wander back upstairs to the well decorated rooms. One very large with its en suite bathroom and the other just as comfortable but not so large, which is the room I choose as I know Mam would want the en suite. The bathroom is just as tasteful. I notice that there is a driftwood piece that has been sculpted into three dolphins standing on the sink surround. I shout to Mam to come into where I was standing. She pops her head around the doorway then sighs with her hand up to her mouth and states "Oh Ailish, dolphins are very spiritual. This is the right place for us that's for sure." Reaching over to touch it, she backs out to rush into her room to retrieve her mobile phone. Before I know it she's back again, phone in hand, taking pictures.

"Maybe we could bring Carly here to recover from that horrendous nose bleed that she had Ailish."

Pausing as she casually takes more pictures, I turn away to hide the guilty hot flush glowing on my cheeks. Then adds "It's amazing how the hospital took her in when they are so busy with more serious cases, don't you think?"

She knows. The look says it all. I quickly glance and see the twinkle in her eyes and the raised eyebrows. All mothers have that apparently. That instinct to know everything their children do. But they keep their mouths shut until the time is just right.

Walking out and into the room I strip off my top layers and lie on the bed. Closing my eyes, I think of what Mam has just said about Carly. If she really knows the truth about the baby, she is playing a good game just to keep the peace. Being sent to this island was meant to be. A spiritual place where we forgive and forget.

I awake about a couple of hours later. I am deciding whether to knock on Mams door or not, as I need to eat, I'm starvin'. Obviously I don't want to leave her alone, so I tap lightly on her door. I hear movement then she opens the door. "I feel as fresh as a daisy now Ailish. I'm *so* hungry, how about yer self love?"

I answer her yawning. "OOH. Sorry, Yes I am *starvin'*. Shall we have late lunch or early dinner?"

"I think I could eat both", as she grabs her yellow cardigan off the bed.

"Let's go then" as she pushes me out of her room. I rush into my room, brush my hair and grab *my* cardigan. "Off we go then." I link arms with her and we smile at each other and rush down the stairs.

Our week on this beautiful island goes by too quickly. I take Mam everywhere she wants to go, to reminisce. *Eventually*, we get a couple of calls from Carly to let us know she is fine. We laugh, we cry and we nearly wet our pants on one occasion. Not because we can't find a toilet, we are just laughing too hard. And *then* we need to find that toilet.

Everything is going to plan, apart from one night when I hear Mam crying. I creep next door to her room and tap as quietly as I can on her door. When she opens it, I notice the red nose and swollen eyes. I enter and close the door behind me. I ask her why she's been crying.

"Been dreaming of yer Dad." When she wakes up, she

sees him standing at the end of the bed. I tell her that she was most probably still asleep when she saw him. Insisting she *wasn't* asleep, she goes on to tell me he was trying to tell her something but she wasn't sure what. Apart from that, she knew he was trying to get a message across to her. And he's warning her of problems ahead, as he looked very concerned. She remembers him saying "I will be here for you when you cry". I hug her and tell her that he's always around her anyway. I settle her down and tuck her back into bed, then quietly return to my room. I go back to bed but can't sleep.

I think about what she told me. I shiver at the thought, but I believe her, as I see him at the end of *my* bed too. Seems to coincide with the weird feelings I've been having lately. I saw a man in my dream and he told me he would be there for me all the way. When I woke, he was there, my Dad that is, but only for a few seconds, then he just disappeared. The same scenario as what Mam said. I wasn't frightened by his presence at all. I thought about that scene in my mind for ages and ages. And then I must have fallen back to sleep. But after I wake up again it feels as though it was all a dream.

The next morning after eventually getting some long-needed rest, we enjoy our most incredible breakfast that Mary had cooked for us in her own kitchen, delivered on very hot plates. I have never known my Mother to be so quiet in my life. I would put it down to three things. One, the good food she was stuffing into her mouth, Two, she was still half asleep and Three, she was still thinking about Dads visit. But most likely, all three!

After dragging our feet off the comfy chairs, feeling very stuffed, we slowly walk toward the staircase to tidy ourselves up to go out for the day.

We discovered while we were on our holiday that we have a lot in common. We really *do* laugh at the same things, cry at the same things and enjoy looking at all the most interesting historical sights on the Island.

After spending the most wonderful week I've had in a very long time, I was very sad that it had come to an end. We spent our last night chatting until it was nearly dawn. Naturally, we eventually fell asleep. Didn't even notice I was squashed, until I woke up. I felt like a child again in my Mother's arms. I looked down at myself and noticed I had slept in my clothes. What a mess! It reminded me of the times when I used to come home quite worse for wear. (To put it politely, drunk as a skunk.) I very quietly left the room as Mam was still sleeping. Mary had told us the night before, that there was no hurry to leave early, as she didn't have anyone coming that day to fill the vacancy. That was a bonus! As I cleaned myself up, I noticed as I carefully looked in the bathroom mirror a happy smile on my face, even though I did still look like I needed more sleep. I noticed the creases on my face where I had been lying. Oh well, it was worth it for the long and lovely talk me and my Mam had.

Two hours later after another one of those mind-blowing breakfasts, we were ready to leave. We left that lovely cottage at noon. Said our sad goodbyes to Mary, hugging her as if we were close friends, and telling her that we would love to return one day, then we went on our way. I think I saw a tear in my Mothers eye. I felt a few tears in mine, I can tell yer.

While travelling home we didn't converse a lot. I'm supposing we have a lot on our minds.

CHAPTER 4

Arriving home after a tiring journey, we hear the phone ringing. I rush into the house to answer, before whoever it is hangs up. I quickly grab it, unfortunately with sweaty palms. The phone falls out of my grasp. "Shit" I shout.

"Ailish, what are yer doing love?" Mam asks.

I pick up the phone thinking I had missed the call. But I can hear somcone mumbling something.

Mam is whispering behind me. "Who is it Ailish?"

"Shush, I can't hear." I tell her.

"Carly? Yes we just got home. Right, Okay I'll tell her". I turn to Mam and she frowns.

"We can't wait to see you. Be safe. Bye." I turn back around and tell Mam that Carly is on her way home next week. She lays her holiday bags on the floor and raises her voice in excitement.

"Ah, I'm so happy she's coming home soon", then turning to me with a look of concern on her face. "Didn't she say she would be staying there for *three* weeks though Ailish? It'll only be just over two when she gets back, won't it?" I answer her, hopefully with no concern in *my* voice.

"Yer, it will be. Could be that she's missing us" I laugh. "We'll find out when we see her. Sounded cheerful enough when we spoke." Oh God, no she did not. I've lied to my Ma again. She settled for my answer, so I didn't mention my sister again, for now.

After taking our bags upstairs out of the way (I know I won't be unpacking mine until tomorrow); the kettle was put on for tea of course. We sat and chatted about the relaxing week we'd thoroughly enjoyed. We bought Carly a souvenir (Mams idea, I just don't think about things like that) from the Skellig Island shop. Mam says she can't wait to tell Carly all about the *fantastic* time we had. I also mention I can't wait to find out how her holiday went. The more I think about her coming home, the more anxious I get.

I'm not due to go back to work until next week, which is four days away. I decide to spend the rest of my days off pottering about the garden. Mam comes out on occasions to sit in the sunshine as we are having one of the nicest summers for a long time. She'll stay out until she complains that it's too hot, and then slowly wander back into the shady house. This is her ritual most of the day, every day.

I think to myself I might just give the shed a bit of a clean out too as it hasn't been sorted out in a while. I decide to go into the kitchen to ask if we have any disposable gloves hidden away somewhere. I know there has to be a lot of spiders and other scary bugs in that shed that I don't even want to think about. I can just imagine all those horrible dirty critters hanging off my hands, that's why I need the disposable gloves. Mam finds some in her cleaning basket and warns me not to scream as the neighbours would be around in less than a minute. I tell her I'll be fine and that I can manage. (Lying again.) I come out of the house back into the garden and something hits me, not literally, but I've realised something I hadn't thought about before, my future. I'm still happy living in this house with my Mother and doing things for her but I wonder how she would feel if I met someone and decided to leave. Or most importantly, how would *I* feel. The way I'm feeling today, I would miss this homely house a *lot.* I think maybe it's that we've enjoyed some good quality time together and we enjoy each other's company. But I'm sure I will be around this house for a while yet though.

I come out of my daydream and consider that dirty shed again. Off I go, down the path to our sacred hideout with *so* many memories. I open the door and peer inside. I'm surprised; it's not as bad as I thought it would be. I sit down on one of the wicker chairs that Dad put in here for me and Carly when she played with her dolls and I read, or was it the other way around? She read and I fed the dolls maybe, can't remember now. I look around the happy old place and think to myself; the last time I sat in here, I was with Carly trying to calm her down. The thought of that day really makes me feel sad. I was very upset after we left the hospital. Can't even imagine how *she* was feeling. I also felt alone not being able to talk with Mam about what happened, but Carly knew it would be for the best if she didn't know the truth. Maybe it's just as well she wasn't allowed to have it, she wasn't ready to be a mother yet. (I'm a great believer in Destiny.) I'll be very happy to see her home again. Roll on next week.

I look around our rather large shed, which is more like a playroom from the past. I want to start sorting out some of the boxes that are scattered around but I notice that the light is catching something in one of the corners. I see a small tin shining so I walk over to pick it up and do not remember ever seeing it before now. I make myself comfy in one of the chairs and slowly open it.

I see bracelets and rings that Carly used to wear and then I see some paper folded up at the bottom of the tin. I open it up, being very curious as I do so. I realise as I notice the date on the right hand top of the paper, this hasn't been here for years like the jewellery, and it's dated this year, 2015. The first page states "This is the *very secret* writings of Carly O'Neill. Not To Be Opened by Anyone." I feel a smile coming. But that smile very quickly turns to tears.

I continue to read this diary of events, confused and shocked. The contents are written, I would say with a shaky hand as it looks like a bunch of scrawls. Carly describes her moods day by day.

DAY ONE *Feel a bit uneasy today. Ross asked me to continue to take the tablets he gave me when we first met. I'm unsure whether to take this tablet or not. He told me that if I take one every day I wouldn't get moody, I would feel confident and sexy all of the time. I must admit though that I did feel very sexy and wanted him constantly when I did take them.*

That first time we had sex when he gave me that first tablet, our sex was the best I could ever imagine. Sex is the best with Ross. I want him now.

DAY TWO *I have taken two tablets so far. One yesterday and I have decided to take another today. I really do want him more and more. I cannot wait to see him and feel his body all over me. He has the most desirable body and looks great naked, needing to masturbate right now. I also feel I have loads more confidence like he said I would. OH God! I love sex so much!*

DAY THREE *Soon I will be in Ross's arms. I still haven't told Mam and Ailish that I am going to Berlin with him for three weeks. He has booked us into one of the best hotels. I know he wants the best for me and will look after me, all the room service he said we'll have while we are in bed. I hear the sound of Mam outside my room now. I'm a bit worried that she will not want me to go on the trip, but I'm old enough now so she can't stop me. I don't want her to think I can't look out for myself. I will write again tomorrow as I'm hungry. Mam makes the best dinners. I will have to ask her to teach me. I might need some cooking skills if I get married to Ross. Exciting thought.*

DAY FOUR *I'm getting excited now. I really need to tell my family that I will be leaving in a month. The only person who knows I am going with Ross is Molly, who I booked the flights with. I told her not to mention it to Ailish as I was afraid I would get the third degree. Ross couldn't book them, as he said he was too busy. I didn't mind at all as I felt more grown up when I did it myself.*

As I read these horrible and very naive words (anyone could tell she's still young by reading them), I feel so nauseous I want to get my hands on this Ross and wring his friggin' neck. The rotten bastard is making her take God knows what, just for his sexual means. I am *so* worried about her; I just don't know how I'm going to deal with this when she comes home. I carry on and read the rest of it. My hands are shaking, no that's wrong; my whole body is shaking as I'm *so* anxious. I have to breathe in very deeply a few times to calm myself down.

DAY FIVE *I haven't taken a tablet today. I don't feel moody like Ross said I would. I'm happy about that. I still feel sexy but not as much as when I do take a tablet. I didn't take one as it makes me want him more. I will take one every day when I am with him. They must be quite strong, but he said there is no danger in taking them whatsoever. He told me he has known a lot of men that have taken them for a couple of years with no problem. Well that's okay then isn't it?*

DAY EIGHT *Did not feel like writing for a couple of days. I am quite happy and not moody at all. I wanted to prove that when I don't take the tablets I'm fine. But I do prefer feeling really horny. Feeling tired today so I will write more tomorrow.*

DAY NINE *I've taken a tablet every day for five days now. Oh God, have I masturbated or what! I have noticed though, that when I take them for a few days in a row I feel a bit down too. It's probably because I can't get my hands on Ross and play with him. Ooh the thought, I love it.*

DAY TEN *I have experimented a bit on putting more make-up on my face today. I know I have full lips, but feeling sexy I need my lips even fuller. I took a lip liner out of Ailish's room (I will put it back, maybe). I look in my hand mirror to put lip gloss over it and I see a sexy lady looking back. I'm very pink and delicious. I like the look, so I think I'll keep the lip liner for a while.*

"Fuckin hell Carly...why?" I shout a bit too loud. I thank the Lord my Mammy is not in the garden, as she would be in here in a nanosecond, tea towel in hand ready to swish it across my dirty foul mouth. Glancing down once more at Carly's last line whilst pushing my hair away from my sweaty forehead and thinking, I don't give a shite about that feckin' lip liner. I flick through the other days in her diary and see that the words are very similar. She stops writing the day before leaving for Germany.

I stop and put the papers back in the tin as it's making me feel even more nervous the more I read. I'm in total shock. I don't know what to think anymore, but I know I am scared for her.

CHAPTER 5

Carly is thinking very seriously as she sits on the plane bringing her back home from Berlin. She wonders how she will get through the next few months without Ross. Missing him and remembering the sex they enjoyed over the past two and half weeks. It should have been another few days but Ross had to travel to London. Business matters, he told her nothing more than that. Feeling hot and sweaty she pictures the scene in her head. Falling asleep, she dreams of them rocking back and forth, faster and faster until they are satisfied. She is awoken with a start. The stewardess announces to buckle up as they are due to land. Pulling herself up from her seat to wipe the sweat from her face and under her arms (and wishing she could include putting her hand down her pants to wipe her crotch), doing the latter very discreetly, she then fastens her seat belt.

After gathering her suitcases together from the airport carousel, Carly walks importantly towards the taxi rank. After waiting a short time, the vehicle pulls up to her. She tells him her destination then plonks herself on the seat feeling tired out. Inside the car she takes out her mobile and calls her home number. Her sister answers.

"Ailish, I'm on my way home now, I've just got in the taxi so I should be home in about half an hour." Ailish hesitates as she needs to take a breather.

"Oh, hi Carly, I will tell Mam as soon a she gets back. She just walked to the corner shop to get a carton of milk. I'm sure she'll have the kettle on as soon as you walk in the door."

"OK Aili, that'll be nice, I'll see you in a bit". Then I hear her breathing, maybe waiting for me to tell her that I can't wait to see her, and then, I think she hung up. I couldn't think of anything else to say to Carly anyway. The only thing I am thinking of is the papers I read in the shed last week, that secret sinister diary of sex and drugs. I thought of that *find,* all week. Night and day, so I'm a bit worn out to say thc least. Mam has commented on my look of sheer knackeredness.

I kept myself busy in that shed; it now shines like a new penny. In and out, back and front, top to bottom. I never stopped. Well, what else could I do to suppress my mind from the horrible thoughts going through it? I knew I could never in a trillion years, tell our Mother. She would either stop Carly from seeing that bastard, which would be the less of punishments, or would find him and string him up by his balls which seems to me more appropriate. The worst scenario would be, she was taken to hospital with a severe panic attack or worse, a heart attack.

I have to keep as cheerful as possible around Mam. I don't want her to get suspicious of what has been going on with her younger daughter. Mam now walks through the door with her bag, with more in it than what she went out for, which is quite normal for her. I tell her as I take the heavy bag.

"Carly just rang; she's on her way home and should be here in about"…I hesitate as I look at the clock on the wall. "Twenty minutes I would think." Mam looks happy and surprised. I put her bag on the table.

"Good job I bought these then isn't it" she says smiling, pulling out Carly's favourite chocolate biscuits. I help her put the other groceries in the cupboards and see something for me, my favourite biscuits too. I was getting worried as I thought maybe I was being left out. I seriously think I would have cried if she had left *me* out, the way I've been feeling over the past few days. Stressed out I am.

"Thanks Ma, you bought a treat for me too, I'll enjoy one of these with my tea." (I honestly could do with something much stronger but I don't tell her that.)

"You're very welcome love. I'm happy Carly will be home soon, I've missed her, haven't you Ailish?" I reply very carefully, trying not to have a strange tone in my voice and a suspicious look on my face.

"Of course I've missed her. I can't wait for us to sit and chat in the kitchen with our cups of tea and biscuits. Have a good old natter about what she did on her holiday." I rub my hands together showing some excitement.

"What do yer think?" I say, as I look for a cloth to wipe the table down. She smiles nodding her head, and says "Can't wait."

We then potter about for a bit. When we hear the sound of a vehicle outside, I rush to the window with Ma on my heels to the front sitting room as we hear the slam of the taxi door. I feel my Mothers loving hands on my shoulders while we both stare out at the beautiful blue sky welcoming Carly's return home.

As we now see the taxi, we walk to the front door, quickly opening it and seeing Carly walking toward us looking very different. She seems to have aged around ten years. We see her dressed in a floaty multi-coloured strappy summer dress (obviously bought by Ross) which helps to enhance her good figure. Also enhances her bosom as the dress shows off her cleavage! And the shoes, they're a Wow! With footwear like that, well, what can I say; I've seen stilts shorter than them. Her hair looks as if she has had it done at a very expensive salon. And definitely looks more mature than her usual T-shirts and denim summer shorts! Good God, she now looks like a glamour model! I glance behind me and look at my Mammy. I'm not sure whether her look is of shock or pleasure, as it is such a weird sort of twisted mouthed, actually quite humorous look. I don't know whether to laugh or cry quite frankly. As Carly walks in the door I notice she had a lovely flushed look about her, it could be the expensive makeup she has on. Her normal look with makeup is usually not much at all, apart from a bit of lip gloss and maybe a touch of mascara. I decide to comment.

"Hi Carly, *you* look different" She gives me a funny look as we kiss each other on the cheek. (I feel like a short arse, as I have to just about stand on my tiptoes to reach her face.) "No, I didn't mean that in a horrible way, God no, you look *gorgeous*." She smiles at me, then gives Mam a hug and kisses her too.

Mam says "Ooh, you do look beautiful me darlin', why don't we go through to the kitchen and let me look at you in a proper light. It's too dark in this hallway." Should have it painted a lighter colour then, I thought through bated breath. Its time she had the whole place done out quite frankly.!

Mam hooks her arm through Carly's as they slowly wander down the hallway to the kitchen. I walk behind looking at them both and thinking how life is changing so fast before my eyes and not for the better either. It annoys me that I have to act as if I don't know anything about what my sister is getting up to. But I have to decide (I know I will have to) when I am going to get my sister alone and speak to her seriously, to find out exactly what she is up to? I must decide very soon as I'm not a very good actress. I hesitate slightly before walking in after them, as I feel a bit anxious once again.

As I pass the hallway mirror, I glance and see an unglamorous me. I play with my hair a bit then I decide to give up. What the hell, much more important things to deal with than the way I look right now. I *could* do with some new make-up though.

Carly wheels her case (looks a lot fuller than when she left) across the floor and puts it against the wall. She puts her gorgeous designer handbag (new of course) on one of the chairs. Don't want to dirty that expensive accessory do you, I think to myself. I'm not jealous really, more suspicious than anything else. (Would love a leather bag like that though, who wouldn't?) Mam grabs her arm and takes her over to the window.

"You look all grown up Carly and I love your new outfit. Sit down; you must be tired after your journey love. Did you have a good time in Berlin? Tell us all about it."

Two hours went by quite quickly, hearing all about what she did and what she saw. Where he took her to buy her new clothes and the stylish hair dresser he knew, to do her hair. What she didn't tell us is all the great sex they had and the tablets they took to enhance their desires for each other. I shook just thinking about it.

Carly eventually got off her chair, had a good stretch and yawn before heading upstairs to bed. Mam stood up after she left the room and did the same stretching and yawning ritual.

I was still sitting with my head in my hands and then looked up and yawned as I watched her. The last two hours of talking about what Carly did in Berlin have been quite spell bounding. I feel like my sister has morphed into someone I don't know very much about anymore. She seemed to act as if she was tired, but to me she seemed rather moody. Mam turns to me and asks if I'm hungry. I look at her and ignore her question.

I ask her, "Well, what you think of the new Carly?" Now having her back to me as she's searching the fridge for something to eat. She mumbles from the fridge.

"Very nice but"...Turning to me with one hand on her hip.

"I do think she looks a lot older with all that new

make-up on and the new posh clothes, I'm just so used to her looking the age she *should* look." Then going back to searching.

"I agree Ma; I think her boyfriend has her twisted around his finger. But as long as she likes the way she looks then that's fine." I tell her I'll get something to eat later as I'm not hungry. I leave the kitchen and wander upstairs to my room to do some thinking. I get to the top of the stairs and hear Carly in her room, music playing softly, that's a first.

I open the door to my bedroom and hesitate before going in, as I think I see a dark shadow in the corner just hovering near my bookcase. I look again but must have been imagining it as it's now gone. I go in and lay on my bed. My mind is racing so much I feel that I'll never be able to rest properly again until I've sorted out the problems I know I have ahead of me and I feel a great burden on my shoulders, I wonder how I am going to handle *this* situation with her.

I start thinking about the last time I had to talk to her two years ago, I was so nervous. This time is more serious and very scary as I don't know what her reaction is going to be. Will she shout and scream and throw things at me? Or will she run off for a while to see her friends. Sandra Delaney moved away a year ago, so that won't be a problem. Think Ailish, think.

As I was thinking hard, I must have fallen asleep because when I wake up, I am shaking. I remember the dream I was having. I was very scared as I was being chased by a man dressed in a black suit who was shouting and coming at me with an enormous bottle of oversized tablets telling me I must take them. He said if I didn't he would force them down my throat. He caught me but I was saved by a man who told me he was my Guardian Angel. He told me never to worry anymore as he would always be there. I felt so safe with him. He took me away from this man in black and placed me back in my home so I would be safe again. I awoke thinking that I really don't know what to think anymore, but I do know that I need to talk to her and tell her that I found her tin in the shed.

Two days later things seem to be kind of normal around our home. I still haven't spoken to Carly yet. There's one thing that I *have* noticed, she seems to be getting very moody. I try to put it at the back of my mind and tell myself it could be her time of the month.

Until one day the following week. Mam mentions that she snapped at her when she was asking her about her course at Uni'. Carly had apparently spoken to her as if she couldn't care less about the course anymore. Mam had only asked her if she had bought all the notebooks that were required and if she needed more clothes that were more appropriate for the University?

We are talking in the kitchen (we seem to live in there) as I have just got home from work. Carly had left the house after the row, to see her friends. Mam said she was upset about the whole thing and can't understand why she had gotten so mad at her. I tell her that Carly will be love sick and misses her boyfriend so much, that she won't be interested in anything else right now. I have never heard my Mother get so angry and upset as she is fairly easy going, so when she gets up off her chair and flings her cup in the sink I know things are going to get worse. Walking over to the sink she recovers her china cup which is in pieces.

"Oh, Ailish look, my favourite, I've broken it" and then starts to cry. I go over to her and put my arms around her. We hug each other until she calms down and then I sit her down on the chair and make her some *lifesaving* tea. I choose a mug for her that I had bought for her one birthday a few years back. "Hope this one's okay for you Mam." She nods. I pour our tea silently, hand her another tissue and sit down beside her and say "We need to talk about Carly". I swallow some of my tea and go to grab a biscuit even though I'm not hungry, habit I suppose. I sit down again and then I go for it.

"I didn't want to tell you, but I found something in the shed that is very important." Suddenly grabbing my hand, "What Ailish, what did you find and *when* did you find whatever it is you're going to tell me!" I feel sick now, that familiar nervous stomach. I go on.

"Before I *do* tell you, don't get me wrong as I would have told you eventually." And the colour drains from her face.

"The week before I went back to work, you know that time I decided to clean the shed out." She looks at me and nods.

"Well, I was sorting through the boxes and saw a tin in the distance on the shelf. It was shining as if it was beckoning for me to come and open it. So I did."

Her face was totally distraught and I hadn't even got to the bad bits yet.

"And then what?" she asks me. "What was in the tin Ailish"? I decide then at that moment I have to lie to her, well at least modify the contents. I go on.

"It's a kind of diary that Carly wrote and started earlier on this year. It's what she's been doing with Ross and what they've been taking I'm afraid." I look down and think of what I am going to say next, as I know what is coming.

"What do yer mean by taking? Taking what Ailish"? Oh God, help me!

"She's been taking…cannabis Mam" Oh I am a big liar but I just can't tell her what she was *really* taking. When I think about it, I really don't know what she's taking.

"So that's probably the reason why she's been getting moody" I say with my mouth twitching. I'm very happy she wasn't looking at me knowing that lying twitch too well.

"What, oh my God Ailish, she shouldn't be doin' that, I don't care about him but it only leads to stronger drugs, that's what I read in the newspapers and you hear it on the telly too you know."

I watch her nervously rubbing her hands around one another. Then she says "We haven't even met this boyfriend of hers; don't know anything about him, all we do know is that he's leading her astray. I hope he never wants to see her again, which would put a stop to it. Or maybe I should put a stop to it. I am her Mother after all."

She drops her head into her hands and cries. This crying seems to be commonplace lately.

After I have calmed her down she asks me "I wonder why she hid her tin in the shed and not in her bedroom? It's as if she thinks I would look in her drawers and such when I go in to vacuum."

"No, no Ma I really don't think that at all. I would say she put it in the shed as we hardly go in there now, am I right? Would have thought, best place!" She wipes her eyes again and looks across at me.

"We need to help her Ailish. I can't let her carry on the way she is, smoking those drugs. I will worry for the rest of my days if we don't. I've heard a lot of people '*do pot*' but I don't want Carly to carry on taking it."

I tell her that I agree and that we do need to help my sister, but this is going to be harder than what she thinks.

The day turns into night and we still haven't had anything to eat. We are still waiting for Carly to come home from seeing her friends. Mam is flicking channels but not finding anything interesting to watch. I'm in the kitchen again, telling myself I should really eat something or I'll be out of bed in the early hours, starvin' of hunger. I decide on scrambled eggs on toast, it's easy. I pop my head around the sitting room door to ask Mam if she wants some eggs too. She looks at me and sighs and then gets up from her old comfy chair to join me in the kitchen. I get the eggs out of the fridge and Mam gets a pan out of the cupboard. We are silent as she does the eggs and I do the tea and toast. As we eat, the only noise is our knives and forks clicking on the plates. "Ate too much" I say when we finish and I give out a large belch.

"I feel the same Ailish. I shouldn't have eaten so much

toast, it filled me up." We stand up at the same time and I take our plates over to the sink while Ma makes another pot of tea.

"Wonder when she'll get home?" Ma says with a miserable tone in her voice and then walks lazily back into the comfort of her familiar chair in the sitting room. I follow her after I pour our teas. I plonk myself down opposite her.

"Well, it's almost ten o'clock. I'm sure she won't be out too much longer, as that one friend of hers, Eileen I think it is, she's not much of a night owl so I'm sure she'll chuck her out the house soon. Or her Mam will for sure." I yawn loudly and then Ma copies me.

"I want to go to bed after my tea but I won't rest until she's home. I'll be very upset if she comes home with alcohol in her, you know that don't yer love. Never mentioned that she would be out for the night. I wonder if I should call Eileen's Mam to see if she really *is* there, what do you think love?"

I answer her cautiously "Why don't we wait a bit yet. She *is* old enough to be over at her friends and you don't want her getting mad again." It's ridiculous to think that my sister is such a sore subject at the moment.

My tea now drank; I wander up stairs to the toilet and sit and think. Best place to think, especially when the door's locked, nobody to bother me. In reality I could easily fall asleep while thinking, but I'm *so tired of thinking*, what am I going to do about Carly? As I try to think I hear the noise of a key going in the lock of the front door. Oh God she's home and I'm not down there! Please Ma, don't say the wrong thing to start her off again especially if she's got drink in her. I try to hurry but now realise I need more than a pee. Not at this very moment when I should be downstairs! I try to hurry but that's not going to happen not when it's one of those when you sit on the toilet for ages trying to get it out!!

I hear their voices. I can only hear mumbling but no shouting thank God. When I eventually finish, I hurry to wash my hands and then rush down the stairs nearly falling as I go too fast. They are in the kitchen and when I walk in trying to look calm, they are chatting about where Carly has been all day. Mam is asking her why she hadn't taken a jacket as it is cool out now. Carly tells her she's not cold at all. Then they both turn and look at me.

"Hi Ailish, I was just telling Mam I hope that she didn't wait up for me coming home."

She then turns to Mam, "I'm sorry that I didn't call yer but I had a lot to talk about with Eileen. I didn't mean to get annoyed at you before I ran out this afternoon but I want to talk to you both about going to University."

She sighs and then says "But I'm tired can I talk to you tomorrow; would that be alright?" I look at her and try not to show my feelings and then I tell her to go to bed.

She turns to say something but I say "Carly, can we talk when I get home from work?" Mam gives me a knowing look, then kisses us both on the cheek and tells us that she's off to bed.

"Talk to you tomorrow, see you in the morning." I kiss her goodnight then Carly does the same. I decide to sit at the kitchen table as she is still hanging around looking for something to snack on before going up to bed. Turning to me as she searches in one of the cupboards, "Aren't you going to bed too Aili? You usually do by this time of the night."

"I will in a minute" I tell her whilst drumming my fingers on the table. Shall I go to bed and not say anything? Or do I open my big mouth.

I continue. "I'm just wondering what you want to talk to us about Uni'. Are you not fond of the idea now? You know that Mam paid a lot of money for that course for you." Closing the cupboard door she sits down beside me with her chosen snack then says, "Ailish, I already know this and if I *do* decide not to go Mam will get most of the money back from the University and the rest will be from myself." Ross she really should say. She continues to eat and then stands up to get herself a drink of juice. I shouldn't but I say "So you're not going then is that it?" She turns to me and gives me a look of why don't you just mind your own business.

Then shouting very loudly, "No I am not". Oh shit! Shit, shite! I can't believe what I'm hearing but I should. She goes on.

"And don't you be telling Mam, as I'm going to tell her in my own time."

Answering her, still in shock. "Thought you were going to tell her tomorrow?"

"I am going to mention that I maybe won't be going because Ailish, I don't want to upset her and I also have a better plan which is just as good. I will let you know tomorrow." She swigs the rest of the juice down her throat and then says goodnight.

Left on my own now to wonder what she will be up to next, I decide to tidy up in the kitchen and lock the doors before wandering up to bed myself. Finishing up as I double check the doors and the TV, making sure it has been turned off.

I walk up the stairs to bed wondering if I'm going to get any sleep tonight. Getting into my pyjamas, I again notice a dark shadow in the corner of the room.

I say out loud. "Who are you and what do you want, you should show yourself, I'm not scared you should know that". I am still looking at the shadow and it suddenly turns into the shape of a person. I am now starting to feel a bit nervous. The figure is still dark and gloomy but I watch it until it fades away. The feeling I get after it has disappeared is of calmness and a strong feeling of being secure. I then get into bed and read a couple of chapters of my book to help me relax. I put my book down and turn off my bedside lamp. I attempt to sleep but the more I try the more I toss and turn. When I eventually fall asleep I have that same dream again of the man in black trying to make me take drugs but I was saved by my Guardian Angel once again.

CHAPTER 6

My alarm goes off at the usual seven in the morning. I am still as tired as I was when I came to bed. I must have had only about three hours of sleep. I decide to call work at nine o'clock when they were open to let them know I won't be in today so I set my alarm for that time, call them and then go back to sleep.

After calling into work while still lazing in my bed, I drag my feet onto the floor yawning, push my arms into my plush white bath robe and leave my darkened room to get some breakfast.

I notice Carly's bedroom door is closed, I didn't really expect her to be up anyway. I am glad in a way as I could not be bothered to face her this morning. I walk into the kitchen where Mam is sitting reading the morning newspaper while drinking her tea and eating a slice of toast.

I walk passed her, grab a cup from the drainer and then still half asleep sit beside her and say "Mam you've got marmalade on the paper, look there at the top". She wipes it off with a paper towel whilst rolling her eyes at me, then licks her finger where some of it fell onto her lap.

"Do you want some toast Ailish? You still look tired, you should have stayed in bed a bit longer. Not going to work I gather. Are you okay?"

I answer her with no real interest, "Yes Mam I'm okay didn't get much sleep last night." I leave her to read her paper and go to get a bowl of cereal, don't fancy the toast. I sit back at the table to eat and start to thinking about the dream I've been getting. I turn my head to look at Ma and start to tell her about the dream.

"Ailish, how am I supposed to understand a word you're saying with a mouth full of food"? she says, quite annoyed.

"Sorry. I was saying I've been having a strange dream lately" I reply while scraping the last bit of crumbs from my bowl.

"Well, this strange dream what's it all about then?" asking, really interested. After listening to my (trying to be not too long winded and detailed) story she agrees with me, that it is a sign from above trying to tell me something. She thinking it could be Dad. I'm not as certain about that, as when the shadow morphed into a more of a figure I could make out as something more human. It didn't look like Dad as it was bigger and taller and darker skinned. I told her this and she said that it *may* be my Guardian Angel.

"We all have one although," she hesitates and I can hear the cogs working in her head as she stands up with hands on her hips. "Dreams can be exaggerated, it may be your spirit guide" then she gives me a weird look, "Oh Ailish, I hope he doesn't show his face, that's the sign that your needs are dire." I sigh and reply "Oh God Ma, it wouldn't be that bad, would it?"

Mam is a strong believer in the afterlife and I can honestly say now that I definitely believe. I know that I sometimes smell Dad's awful aftershave but I wasn't sure whether I was just imagining it. But seeing what I saw in my bedroom has certainly changed my mind. I now know it's not my mind playing tricks on me. I just wish I knew what he or she is doing there. My gut feeling has been telling me for weeks now that it may be warning me of what is to come. I feel comfort from it so I'm trying not to worry. Time will tell I guess.

I have my usual shower and get dressed in my *lazy* clothes as I have no intention of going anywhere today. I honestly believe that I've made the right decision not to go into work. I feel that my destiny is proving that today is the day I have to talk to Carly but the thought of talking to her is a bit like work, don't want to do it sometimes!

I look out of the window into the garden and hear the birds singing and notice that it is a beautiful sunny, cloudless day. I wash up the few breakfast dishes as I watch the birds hopping around. My mind wanders as I watch nature's wonders that I usually miss due to being stuck in my work environment. The garden looks lovely with the colourful flowers scattered around. They were planted many years ago when me and Carly were kids. Those days I remember were days of laughter and fun with Dad around then of course. Things have changed so much, those days now feel like another lifetime away.

I hear Mam walk in. "Good morning love, beautiful day to have a day off, just as well you couldn't sleep last night." She grins.

"Yer, you're right there" I tell her.

She gives me a kiss on the cheek and says, "I think I'll take my cup of tea out into the garden for a bit, fancy bringing yours out too? It'll be a nice change to have your company, especially during the day. I do feel lonely at times".

I turn round from the sink and look at her sorrowful face. "Ah Mam, I didn't realise you still felt like that. You know that Dad's still around you though don't you?" I put my arms around her to help her feel reassured and then I take her now older looking arm to walk into the sun-filled garden. We sit on the old wooden seat, but not before pushing some cushions under our bums. I rush back indoors as I have forgotten to grab my sunglasses and sun cream, (knowing that I will get a telling off) then return to sit back down, closing my eyes as I lean back onto one of the floral cushions. I sit for a few quiet minutes, then we both start to speak at the same time.

"When Carly gets…" we say, and then I tell Mam to go on. "When Carly decides to get out of bed do you think we should all go for a walk to the park, we could feed the ducks too? Then we could mention the drug thing to her when we get home. We should, shouldn't we?"

I sigh loudly and say to her "Just when I thought we could just relax for a couple of hours you bring up the D word…and I don't mean duck either." She laughs at my jest.

"If you want to get out that would be great. But if you like, and I think it might be best, I will talk to Carly, I don't want you getting yer' self upset." I know it will be for the best that she is not involved; obviously I don't want her finding out the truth.

We chat for a while about the neighbours' goings on and the new dog they got from the shelter. I tell Mam she should get herself a dog. She doesn't make any comment. So, I keep quiet.

I get up to get out of the sun.

"Want more tea?" I ask as I take her empty cup from her hand.

"Eh, well, maybe, but only if yer wash yer sweaty *bum hands* first though love" I look at her smirking and rolling her eyes, realising that she had noticed my poor attempt of wiping the sweat from my butt crack. Then says "I'm just going to sit here for a while to watch the birds. There's been one that keeps coming back; I've been keeping an eye on it. I think he's the messenger, I think he's been keeping an eye on me too."

Mam is a great believer in birds being messengers from God. She told me a story of when her Granny died. Not knowing that she *had* died until her Mammy had sadly informed her the following day. That day before was when she was home alone and a bird had come right up to the window and was knocking hard on the glass with its beak. From that day on, she was a believer. As I walk through the back door into the kitchen to get that tea, I am thinking, shit, if it had been me in that same scenario I would've freaked out for sure.

I go back into the cool house and take off my sun glasses then grab a towel to wipe my brow as I'm feeling uncomfortably hot. I'm wishing that Carly was up as I'm feeling quite unsettled...I'm so used to being at work I can't wait to get out of this house.

She must have read my mind as I hear the noise of the toilet flushing. Not long after I hear her coughing then yawning as she's heading down the stairs, I look at the clock on the wall in the kitchen, Christ it's still morning, I'd better watch myself as she's never her best at this time of the day.

I pop my head outside to let Mam know that she's out of bed. Mam heads indoors to ask her if she would like a cooked breakfast.

"Yuk Mam. No thanks, it's too hot to have something cooked anyway." Her attitude toward her Mother is not at all right; she is being very ungrateful but Mam just shrugs it off. Carly then goes to get some juice but nothing to eat.

Mam notices this and says to her, "Aren't you getting something to eat, we were thinking of going to the park in a bit. Not that you knew that, but I don't want us to go and you complaining about being hungry love."

Oh God here we go. Mam always thinking that food is the answer to everything. I stand there and listen to this and think I know exactly what Carly is going to say. And I am right.

"Mam I don't always eat breakfast, you can't force me to eat you know. And who says I want to go to the park anyway?"

I interrupt and say in my annoyed voice "Carly, she's just looking out for you and if you don't want to eat or come to the park with us that's your choice but don't speak to your Mammy like that, it's not right."

"Fine, I will do what I want then." She turns her head to speak. "Sorry Mam I didn't mean to be nasty to you but I'm feeling a bit down today, maybe I should come to the park, it might cheer me up. We could feed the ducks like we did when Dad was alive, couldn't we?" I look at Mam and her face is a picture of happiness. "Yes we will do that. If you go and get yourself washed and dressed we can get ourselves out and have a nice day, can't we?"

My body now relaxes with relief and I think to myself thank God for small mercies.

I smile at Ma and the gesture is returned.

"Let's get ready then Ailish" and she leaves to do exactly that. But not before packing the picnic basket.

I was the first to be ready. I peer inside the basket that is waiting on the table, filled with the usual carbohydrates. I search quickly through the kitchen drawers for the camera, think it may be good idea to have the day remembered. Making sure that Mam had put in bottles of water, I hear a strange noise coming from upstairs. I turn to move very quickly towards the staircase and run two stairs at a time trying hard not to fall flat on my face. I realise now the squealing sound is coming from Carly's bedroom. The door is already open wide so I run in unannounced. As I turn my head toward the noise, I see my Mam on top of Carly trying to hold her down, with sweat pouring from her forehead, looking like a professional wrestler would grab their opponent. Carly is still dressed in her pyjamas having not even attempted to getting to the stage of showering.

"Oh, Mother of God, what is happening to her Mammy?"

"Help me Ailish. She's pushing her legs out and kicking me in the thighs."

I grab the legs as Mam holds her hands. We seem to be in that position for a long time as my feet start to cramp. Then…silence. Carly suddenly calms down, then curls into the foetal position and sobs her heart out.

After what seems like a million hours, I pull myself off of Carly's bed and look at my sister as she sleeps. Mam had walked out when Carly had calmed down. I stop her calling a doctor as I know that would be the worst thing to do under the circumstances. I assume it had started out as a panic attack and then her adrenalin went into overdrive. Thank God I assumed correctly. If a doctor had been called in to look her over the next thing would be blood tests. Then…I don't even want to think about it. In my opinion the drug she is taking has caused her some terrible anxiety as well as a sexual high. Not a good mixture.

I leave Carly to sleep after giving her a special kiss on her cheek.

I wander in to our usual meeting place to talk to Mam, who was sitting in what seemed to be a trance. She looks up when I sit at the table. "What's going on with Carly, Ailish? Is this her way of crying out for help?" I sigh but say nothing.

Then Mam asks "Or do you think it's the cannabis she's taking that's causing her to flip out?"

I shrug my shoulders and still say nothing.

The rest of the day seems to go on forever.

Carly eventually shows her face outside in the garden, while me and Mam sit next to each other taking in the sunshine. That doesn't last long as she is still in her pjs, looking across at us before wandering back inside. All we hear is a mumble telling us that it is too hot to be here anyway.

I am worried.

Walking up the stairs I hear Carly in her room. I'm not sure whether the sound is her music or her voice. The door to her room is ajar so I hesitate and I listen. I realise now she is talking on her phone to Ross. I quietly stay where I am and I hear her telling him how she's had a good day today. What! Have I been living in a dream today? Then I hear her saying how she misses him and can't wait to be with him soon. I hear her walk toward the door so I back away but I don't leave, then it's closed. I really shouldn't but I listen in to her conversation. I wish I hadn't. She is telling him she will still keep taking her tablet each day so not to worry and asking if it is normal that her moods are changing while she is taking the tablets? Never mentioning the trauma that she has been through earlier. He is obviously telling her that the tablets won't do that to her, as she agrees and says it's most likely her times of the month are lasting longer than they should.

I want to go in there now and let her know what I found in the shed. I have to think this out very seriously so I continue to the bathroom. I can do a lot of thinking sitting on the toilet so that is what I do for the next five minutes. The problem is if I stay any longer, she might leave her bedroom and the moment will be gone.

I now hear Mam yelling that the tea is getting cold, "Anyone coming down for a cup or not?" I now get my backside up and open the door and shout down to her that I'll be down in a second. I notice Carly's door is still closed. I rush downstairs, grab two teas, look at Mam and tell her quickly that I'm going to talk to Carly. I glance at her before I go back upstairs with the mugs in my hands. She looks at me with what I thought I saw were tears in her eyes. I tell her not to worry, that's it, as I didn't have time to stop and chat.

At the top of the stairs I stop at Carly's bedroom door. I take a few deep breaths and then shout.

"Carly I've brought you a mug of tea. Can I come in?" I hear her shout back at me "Oh, Ailish, just a minute." I hear her scuffling around and blowing her nose. I feel nervous as I wait; it is making me want the toilet again. Carly eventually opens her door and takes one of the cups from me.

"Come on in." She sits at her desk and gives me a confused look. "Where are the biscuits then? You know I like one with my tea." I could have slapped her right then and there. I turn on my heel, run down the stairs into the kitchen, rush past Mam, grab the biscuit tin and quickly run back up to her room. Phew! I was unsure whether she would let me back in again or not.

My life will never be the same after entering that

bedroom. I walk in as calmly as I possibly can. She smiles as I came in with her biscuits, then takes them out of my hands as if she is going to stuff her face with the whole tin!

"Do you want one Ailish?" handing back the tin, so I casually take one and dip it in my tea. Lose half of it in one dunk, not a good start but I still drink it.

She now looks at me as if to say, get out, I would like to masturbate now as I'm taking these strong drugs which I don't really know exactly what they are doing to my body but I'm going to take them anyway because my boyfriend, even though he is not here, wants me to take them as they help me wanting sex all the time.

After I come out of my semi comatose state, I answer her.

"Just want to talk to you, to get to know what's going on in your life, you know like things that you haven't told me about that you might want to mention to me, after all I *am* your big sister. We've been through bad times before you and me, so tell me, what is going on?"

"What do you mean Ailish; I'm a bit confused at what you're trying to ask me, help me out here please."

I think for a moment as I need to choose my words and use them correctly. As normal I start to sweat with my T-shirt sticking to my back and that horrible familiar wetness under my arms. I spurt my words out, no messing about anymore.

"Before you came back from Berlin I decided to clean out the shed." Carly looks at me with a kind of half taken aback look as if to say, I'd better be careful, as what she is about to say, might not be what I think it is. I carry on. "I started to sort out boxes and I saw a tin Carly, I think you already know what tin I'm talking about?"

Our eyes meet, she asks looking very nervous, "A tin, what kind of tin?" and then she turns her head away from me to take a sip of her tea (to ease her now quickly drying up throat I would say). I didn't come into her room to try to upset her as I love my sister very much, but what I was about to say to her still had that effect.

"Carly, ever since I found the tin I have been a walking wreck, worrying my head off about you and keeping it a secret from your Mam, who I have to tell you, thinks you are taking cannabis. Which I told her, as she's not stupid, she knows *something* is up." I stop for a sip of my tea, almost burning my lip in the process.

"Oh Carly, it wouldn't be so bad if you'd been smoking cannabis, which could be sorted out much easier." Then pausing for a second, I carry on, "You know I never swear in this house but if you keep lying to me I will tie you to this *fucking* bed and never let you go back to see that man you are screwing, who it seems is using you to get exactly what he wants from you." I saw now that she was starting to get upset and trying her hardest not to cry.

I take a hold of her arm and say "At least own up and let me try and help. I've noticed that you've been very moody and that's not like you is it? And the trauma you had to deal with earlier on. It scared the shit out of your mam and me."

She looks at me with her sad face and takes hold of my hand. "Ailish, I am *so* sorry. I never thought you would find my tin. Do not know why I didn't hide it in this room though."

I reply, "Maybe subconsciously you really wanted it to be found'.

She shrugs. Then I say "Taking stuff you know nothing about could seriously harm you. I thought you had more sense than that." I shake my head in dismay.

We are quiet for a few minutes while glancing at each other waiting for who is going to speak first.

So, I go for it. "Why are you still taking them?"

"I *like* taking them. They help me to feel confident when I'm around Ross" as she fiddles with her finger nails.

I get mad again and tell her, "But he's not here is he, are you stupid or what! When did you suddenly need extra confidence, you have always been a confident girl"?

Her long face now tripping her up, she answers, "I like to have more confidence with him as he has *posh* friends and he takes me to posh places too. The tablets make me feel more grown up. I *need* them now." When she said those four words I knew I had to do something to try to stop her from taking the drugs.

I have to ask but I am scared to hear her answer. "How long have you been taking them Carly? *And tell the truth.*"

I can see her chin trembling as she is on the verge of tears.

"I took the first one that day we had sex in the hotel room in Dublin a few days after we'd first met." She wipes her wet eyes and face on a tissue I hand her from the box on her bedside table.

I take a very long breath of air into my lungs.

"So, he forced them on you that long ago and since you met again he is still pushing them on you, that's right isn't it?"

She mumbles one word very quietly. "Yes."

"Friggin' hell! You're a stupid girl." I shake my head in disbelief.

Then says, "I like taking them, you do not seem to understand that" .

Oh, I am mad now, not at her but Ross. I know why she likes taking them, apart from feeling confident and horny most of the time, she is now addicted to them. What's so sad about it all is I do not think she realises this. I reach for a tissue from the box now. I blow my nose and play with the tissue, pulling it to bits and letting it fall to the floor. I'm thinking hard now.

"Carly look at me" I say with a stern tone in my voice. "I am *so* worried about you. The thing is, I really don't think you realise the moods you are getting has anything to do with the drugs, but I do. Think about it, you have never been a moody person I know I've told you this before but it's *so* true." I let her think about this. She stands up and starts to leave the room.

I grab her arm with a questioning look, "Can't I go to the toilet now?" she says looking teary eyed. I let go of her arm and apologise. While she's gone I quietly sob.

Coming back into the room ten minutes later her face is washed and she has on her pyjamas.

"Are you tired?" I ask her.

She doesn't answer me, so I ask her another question that I had completely forgotten about. "You told me earlier that you've decided not to go to University and why is that? What else are you going to do?"

Yawning while answering "Maybe I will go to bed, I'm fed up with all these questions you're asking." She then pulls her duvet back, jumps into bed and turns her head away from me. I start to bite the skin around my nails; I'm fed up with all this too but I need to find out.

"Turning away isn't going to make this go away. You have to tell me, we'll find out in the end anyway so don't be so stubborn." I wait too long for her answer.

Starting to move, now facing me. "Ross said I can be taught architecture from his office in Berlin so that's what I want to do, and we can live together. He's bought a lovely posh apartment in the city; he said it's an enormous place Ailish. When I get settled there you can come over to visit."

I honestly think she's insane. So I tell her what I think about her plan.

I calmly say, "You don't seem to understand what you're doing do you? You are taking drugs that in the future could harm your health. I'll stand by you all the way Carly if you let me help you stop taking those drugs." I sat beside her on the bed.

"When do you plan on going over there to live?" I take hold of her hand. "Me and Mam would miss you, worry about you too, especially if you're still taking drugs."

She sits up and says "Well we decided I would leave here maybe in a couple of weeks."

My eyes pop out of my head, "You need more time than that, to get off that shite you're on."

"I'll be alright Ailish, Ross will look after me" She *is* insane. "Anyhow the two people who are going to teach me won't be available until then. Also, he gave me a key to his place so if he's busy when I *do* go I can get in without having to meet up with him."

I could carry on all night asking her questions and telling her what she should do, but I'm really tired now and fed up with trying to warn her of the consequences of what she is doing and what she *will* be doing soon.

I'd promised Mam that I would cook tonight. I wish I could just go to bed and sulk. Before I leave Carly's bedroom I hug and kiss her and tell her to think about what I have told her. She hugs me tight and tells me that she loves me. I tell her I love her too. I hope and pray that she might listen for once. I leave her room and blow her another kiss into the closed door.

I walk into my bedroom before going back downstairs to start cooking. I look into my mirror on the wall and study my face. I look older than my years; I don't like the wrinkles I'm starting to see around my eyes. When did they get there? God, I've only turned twenty four a few months ago, I shouldn't have them already. Maybe it's because I'm tired. I'll have to check when I'm not feeling like this. I sit on my bed and I wish Dad was here. I miss him so much. I know he would sort out the problem with Carly, she wouldn't even think about taking drugs if he was still here. He would have none of that nonsense going on in *his* house. I talk to him. "Dad please help me, I can't do this alone I'm not that strong, you need to be there for me. How am I going to get her off the drugs in such a short time, I don't know what to do." And then I do what I've needed to do, have a good cry. (Again.)

I wash the tears from my face before heading back downstairs. I see Mam in the kitchen, already preparing some veggies for our meal tonight. She is standing putting food into pans and hears me walk in.

She asks without turning around, "I thought you two had run away. You've been talking to her I presume? How'd things go then?"

Standing beside her I look at her and yawn in her face. "Well for a start I'm worn out".

She turns to me and says "Yer, I gathered that Ailish. Has Carly gone to bed without having anything to eat?" I yawn again and sit down at the table.

I reply, "She'll most likely be down later to eat after the sulking has stopped and realises that she's hungry. So, I'll make some for her too, it can be heated up when she wants it."

Mam looks over at me "Ailish, you're tired. I'll be doing the tea tonight. Just relax for a bit, go watch some telly or something, I can manage. I'm just steaming some potatoes and veg with a bit of chicken, not hard to do, been doing it for years now you know."

I feel bad about not cooking for her so I volunteer to make some gravy, knowing that's my speciality, she won't refuse it. Telling me she'll let me know when it needs to be done and then pushes me out of the kitchen. I do as I am told and go to throw myself into an armchair in the sitting room. As I do; I see the news is on the TV. I turn the volume up as I notice something going on in Germany.

The newsreader is saying that some of the cities have been targeted by drug dealers, one of them being Berlin. My ears prick up more now as I listen carefully to what is being said. Apparently the police have found out about a new drug that is out on the streets that some prostitutes have been taking. Some of the women have been found dead and the police are investigating their deaths. Oh my God! I feel sick at the thought that this new drug could be the same as what Carly is taking. Surely he wouldn't let her take that. Would he? I'm feeling a bit panicky now.

I'm so thankful that my Mother isn't in here with me to have watched what I have just seen. I don't know what to think. Do I tell Carly about what I've found out? Would this be the answer to getting her off the drug by scaring her? As I'm contemplating an answer, Mam walks in to ask me to make the gravy if I still want to do it. She second glances and sees me rubbing my chin looking concerned.

"Are you alright Ailish, thought you would be catching up with the news."

I tell her, "I was watching it, it's over now, nothing exciting happening. Just the usual stuff, politicians arguing and talking rubbish. I'll make that gravy now."

I don't feel like moving and I'm not hungry at all. My sensitive stomach is playing up big time after hearing that shocking and scary news. Why life is so hard at times I do not know, our family doesn't deserve any of this.

I get out of the armchair slowly, walking towards the kitchen the smell of the food makes me nauseous. I need to pull myself together as I don't want Mam to be suspicious. If she sees me acting strangely she *will* be asking questions. I start to make the gravy with Mam standing beside me mashing the potatoes. We hear the sound of Carly's bedroom door opening. We look at each other and smile.

"She could never resist the smell of roast chicken, could she? Get another plate out love will you?" We all sit down to a well-deserved meal; and I say to her that tomorrow I promise I'll cook.

I relax, enjoying their company and actually eat all of my meal after thinking I wouldn't be able to eat it at all. After clearing up the clean plates we all retire into the sitting room. Carly curls up on the couch and picks up the TV guide. She tells Mam that the news will be on in fifteen minutes. Oh God! They don't need to be watching what I saw.

I watch Mam getting comfy in her chair and settle for the evening ready to watch the news as she usually does every evening. Thinking very quickly I sit on the couch next to Carly and snuggle up to her. Feeling nervous but knowing I have to hide my feelings, I say to them both.

"Why don't we turn off the TV and play a game of cards. Remember we used to enjoy playing Uno when Dad was alive" Looking over at me I can see that she is tired, but I remember so well how she used to enjoy the days when we used to have a good laugh when we had a family game. She sits up and stretches, then stands and, taking the TV remote in her hand, turns it off. I think, oh God, what a stroke of luck. (And relief.)

We spend the next couple of hours playing that card game. What a laugh we have. It takes my mind off the dreadful thoughts that I don't want to share.

When the clock chimes midnight, we pack up the game looking at each other and yawning. Moving our tired bodies very slowly off the comfort of the old lived in furniture, I feel happy and sad at the same time. I wish our family could stay together for longer than where destiny is going to take us. I feel, and have done for a while, that destiny will tear us apart.

CHAPTER 7

I wake up the next morning feeling refreshed, ready to get on with the day ahead. Then I remember the news I heard last night about the drugs in Berlin.

I need to take more time off work to try to get Carly off the drugs. I decide to call to let my boss know that I need to take a couple of weeks off due to an emergency. I tell her that Mam is not well so I will need to take care of her. My boss understands the situation as her Mother had taken ill during a time when she should have been training staff, 'but that's life' she told me. I'm so glad she understands my *downright* lie!

I lie awake after the call into work and worry about today. I see the sun shining through a chink in the curtains and hear the morning songs of the birds outside. The sunshine is such a healer of worn out brains full of stress and worry, like my own. So, I think what a lovely day to be outside and splashing my feet in the ocean. I should actually suggest it and see what they think. It would keep Carly out of the house and keep her mind off the drugs. But I have to stop her from taking any before we leave. How am I going to do that?

I think of where she may have hidden them. If I creep into her bedroom while she's taking her shower I could look around, she would never hear me as the radio is always blaring in the bathroom.

I jump out of bed feeling quite energetic. I have a full day ahead of talking my sister out of a life that she'll regret.

Walking past Carly's room I see her door is already open, just my luck that she's decided to get up earlier than usual. I hear her talking downstairs. I pull my shoulders back in a sort of I'm feeling confident now manner. So, I walk nonchalantly down the stairs and I join them both for breakfast.

"Good Morning Mam." Then turning toward my sister "You're up early Carly" I say. I normally would have said something to take the piss as she's always lying in bed until noon or sometimes later. But don't want to set her off in a frenzy.

She replies with a tired, but much more of a cheerful look. "Yeah, and?" I still keep quiet until she decides to speak. Hard to believe what she is doing to herself when I look at her youthful face?

"If you must know I was just saying to Mam that I couldn't sleep anymore, too hot. We should go somewhere today to cool ourselves off. Especially with you taking time off work Ailish you should make the most of it." I nodded my head at that. Carly continues. "Go to the beach; get ice cream, things we did when we were kids." She waits for an answer as I am drinking a glass of juice.

Then she says with the sulky look she often has these days, "I'd like to go anyway." (Probably thinking she isn't going to get her own way this time.) Neither me or Mam have answered her yet, we are concentrating on eating breakfast, unlike Carly. One mouthful now chewed up, I answer her. "I had the same idea actually." I now turn to ask, "Can you be bothered to go Mam?" I feel sorry for her, she looks as if she hasn't had much sleep.

"Oh, not sure love, it's a bit too hot out there for me. Why don't you two go, it would be nice and I'll get a bit of peace for the day. I could have something nice for your tea when yer get back, even though you missy, (pointing at me) said you would make something special for us tonight." I had really forgotten, too much on my mind. I feel badly about it. "Sorry Mam, I will stay at home tomorrow and I will cook."

Carly is now smirking as she walks past me to head upstairs for her shower.

When I hear the bathroom door close I jump up and say to Ma "Now's my chance to look for her drugs".

I quickly discuss with Mam how I am going to get rid of her stash of cannabis. I haven't as yet told her about Carly leaving in a couple of months to go back to Berlin. I'll have to soon, I know that.

I hear the sound of the boiler as she turns on the shower. I look at Mam and she shoos me away with her hands.

"Hurry up Ailish. If you find it, bring it down to me and I'll burn it outside when you are out"

I haven't got time to tell her what I think of *that* idea.

But as I hurry up the stairs I think to myself, God, glad it's not cannabis I'm trying to find and give to Mam. We would have the Garda at the house in a minute wondering why she is burning cannabis in her garden. Her being arrested and thrown in the local cop shop until we got home and trying to explain why she was burning it in the first place! (And why she wasn't smoking it?)

I quickly open Carly's bedroom door and leave it open so I can hear the shower being turned off.

I look in every drawer, search in every bag and go through pockets in cardigans and jackets, nothing. Thinking quickly, where would I hide something like that?

I scan her bedroom looking carefully around trying not to miss anything and then I see her pillow and think maybe? So I look under it and yes, I see a bottle. I pick it up and look at it with great interest, turn it around in my fingers and see a name on it that I don't really understand. Well how would I?

I now hear the shower being turned off. I shove the bottle in my dressing gown pocket, at the same time thinking, frickin 'hell Ailish, what are you going to do when she finds out her drugs have gone?

My mind is racing, wondering whether I am doing the right thing or not. Shall I, shan't I? I decide to keep them and face the consequences of what I know will be a huge argument, but I'm at the stage now where I have to do something before she leaves the country.

I have to lie again to Mam about what I've found, she never needs to know, and I think it would kill her if she did.

I rush to my bedroom to hide the tablets before I'm found out. I close my door and think where I can hide them. Putting them in my underwear drawer for now will do. The last place Carly would look. She hates my style of undies, they are nowhere near the sexy lacy tiny bits of material she puts on.

One time I remember I had a pair ready to put on lying on my bed when she walked in and said.

"Ugh, you're not putting them on are you Ailish, you'll never get a boyfriend with them on show."

I replied by telling her that One; I don't go around with my knickers on show and Two; they're only cotton shorts, they're not *that* bad. Are they? She answered by saying that she wouldn't touch them with a barge pole. So reasoning tells me, she definitely wouldn't go anywhere near my knickers.

I hear her come out of the bathroom heading toward her room and then I hear the door closing. I'm hesitating before I go back downstairs before telling Ma that I've stolen Carly's *stash of cannabis.*

At this rate the amount of times that I have lied to her just lately, I will have to ask Him upstairs to forgive my sins several times.

I decide to get ready instead of stressing myself; I'll tell her later when I get the chance before we leave.

As I get washed and dressed my thoughts wander to what kind of day I want this to be. Obviously, I don't want to spend all our time together arguing, it needs to be a good day with good memories even though I still have to discuss her future.

I hear Carly, who's now in her bedroom, so I pop my head around the door and ask what she's going to wear. I really don't want to be walking around with her dressed to kill in heels and a posh frock just to go to the beach! She points to the very pretty shorts and T-shirt that are lying on her bed.

"Very nice" I tell her. And very expensive I'll bet by the looks of them. I don't mention that. Makes me wonder what *my* clothes must look like compared to hers; let me think, three words maybe; *cheap and cheerful*?

I get dressed in my cheap and cheerful cotton sun dress, put a bit of slap on my face and race downstairs before Carly does. Mam is in the kitchen, turns her head toward me as I walk in and says nervously,

"Well? Did you find it?"

"Yes Ma, I've found it and hidden it in my room" I tell her.

She looks at me a slight worried.

"Keep that stuff from her Ailish. If she goes looking and starts to ask for it do *not* give it back to her even if she goes off shoutin' and screamin', she'll just have to, that's all there is to it." I put my hand on her shoulder and tell her not to worry as I promise I will take care of everything. Just hope I can keep that promise.

I talk to Carly about which beach we should go to and we decide on Donabate. Not that far to drive, only about forty minutes, as we don't want to be stuck in the car on a lovely day that today has become. Now ready to leave, it feels good to get out just the two of us, getting up to mischief like when we were kids. Chance would be a fine thing these days! It would be more like us throwing stuff at each other.

Carly is quiet for the first, I would say, ten minutes then she starts.

"Ailish, were you in my bedroom this morning?"

Thinking quickly, I say, "You know I was, when I came in to discuss the clothes you have on right now" Oh God, I'm hoping this is not the start of a very argumentative day. She goes on.

"You must know what I'm on about, someone's been snooping around in my room. Ailish was it you who took my painkillers from under my pillow?" Painkillers, who is she kidding? I need to concentrate on my driving so I tell her that and will talk with her when we get to the beach.

Glancing my way and sighing, "Well, that tells me right away that you did but why, I don't know".

I again tell her what I've just told her, and then she stops talking. I glance at her. Her face is as miserable as a dark and rainy day in Dublin.

When we arrive in Portrane, I find a space to park nearest to the beach as possible and I notice that Carly's face has slightly cheered up. I tell her that we can easily walk to Donabate from here, we have all day. We gather our things together, beach towels, bottles of water and sun cream. I notice that there's not loads of people around so we can choose where we want to place our towels on the sand.

Carly chooses a spot and asks if this is okay with me. I agree that it is just perfect. Partially in the shade is good for me as I don't want to end up trying to get home with heat stroke. (One time I almost did, bad memory.)

As soon as she puts her stuff on the towel she strips off her shorts and T-shirt and runs down to the water shouting at me to come and join her. But there's only one problem, I forgot my swimsuit! Shit…but I decide to go after her anyway. I throw off my sandals and walk toward the ocean where I can see her. She sees me and asks why I'm not in the water with her, I tell her what I did and she laughs. It's so nice to see her laugh. I've noticed just lately Carly can suddenly become so solemn and it worries me a lot. She swims away from me for a few minutes then turns back. Now standing next to me I notice her showing off both her new gorgeous (pink, of course) swimsuit and her curvy, slim figure. She *is* very attractive after all. As I look at her it makes me want to do something mischievous that we used to do to each other when we were kids. I look at her and then bravely grab her waist. I then quickly and with some restraint from her, pull up the backside of her swimsuit to give her a wedgy. (No one around so I didn't embarrass her.) Then I'm off and running screaming with laughter, well, I needed to get that sudden solemn look off her face and it worked a treat.

"Aili, come back bitch, I'm going to frickin' kill yer." We both run further along the beach until I am out of breath. She grabs me by *my* waist now, puts her hand under my dress and goes to give *me* a wedgy; looking at me now with a shocked expression on her face and says, "Ailish that's cheating, you got none on." I laugh so hard. Like we used to.

I tell her that I pulled my knickers off when she was

swimming as I was too hot. So glad I did. After spending the next hour doing a bit of splashing around and sunning ourselves, I think it is time to talk.

We move our towels out of the sun altogether and get comfortable. Carly dries herself off a bit more and as I hold the towel around her she takes off her wet swimsuit to put on her underwear. I put my undies back on very discreetly. My sister is watching me and is still in shock at my uncharacteristic decision to take them off in the first place.

We sit together watching the scene in front of us. We see a couple of families with their children running around and laughing as they throw a Frisbee in the air for their small dog. In the distance we see a couple walking hand in hand looking content and relaxed. I notice the way Carly stares at them with that familiar solemn look. I wonder if she really is happy with the way her life is going. I need to ask but I push the thought to the back of my mind.

I point out a boat on the horizon and then a small plane in the air which is advertising some kind of festival on its streamer. Still staring in a world of her own, then she suddenly looks over at me then smiles that Carly smile I remember from our childhood. So, I decide to speak.

I start off a bit shaky, as my usual nervous stomach is at it again.

"We've had a nice day so far don't you think." Silence, she's staring at the children.

"Carly are you alright you don't feel dizzy or nauseous, do you? If you do, just keep sipping your water and lay your head down until you feel better." She stops staring.

"No, no I'm fine, just thinking about stuff" she says while playing with the sand flowing threw her fingers.

"Oh yeah. What kind of stuff?" I ask.

Not answering me at first she looks and says, "I feel like I'm getting miserable a lot these days and I've been having bad period pains which doesn't help." She then asks me, "Why did you take my painkillers out of my room?"

"I've wanted to talk to you about that Carly." I hesitate while I think of the right words to say without having a shouting match. "I went into your room because I was looking for those tablets that Ross is making you throw down yer throat. You need to stop taking them, *full stop*. You know that I read your diaries I found in the shed so I know what they're doing to you Carly. How come you're *that* stupid and naive? I want to help you as best I can to get you off them. Haven't you thought that maybe it's the tablets making you become moody?"

I watch as her brain is processing what I've just said.

"Those tablets you took are my painkillers though Ailish. Ross got them for me when I was in Berlin when I had bad pains." Oh God I think this is just getting worse.

"Ross got them for you!" I said raising my voice a touch more. "Ross this, Ross that, I'm sorry Carly but how do you know that they *are* painkillers anyhow? Do they help you when you are in pain?"

I'll bet they don't I say under my breath. She answers, "Well, sort of, in a way they do. They take the edge off the pain a bit." I don't want to upset her too much but my mind is racing now. I'm thinking weird things now, like these tablets could be something illegal that she really shouldn't be touching. I go on and ask her.

"Are you still taking those tablets you wrote about in your diary. Did he give you some more until you see him again?"

I wait for her answer but she concentrates on the sand under her feet, so I ask again.

"Carly look at me, did he?"

"No, no he didn't give me anymore. I ran out of them a few days ago. He hasn't given me anymore since."

I don't believe her, not for one minute. She looks as guilty as sin itself. We are silent for a moment as we sit and people watch. I decide that I don't want to talk about the ridiculous tablets anymore, just for now anyhow.

I'm becoming a bit restless so I lean over to get my watch out of my basket. I notice that we've been here almost three hours already. I let Carly know that it's probably time to make a move as I am ready to eat something. She agrees so we pack up our stuff.

Walking to the car I suggest we eat at the Waterside House Hotel. Her eyes light up as soon as I mention it. Our parents used to take us there for a treat when we were kids. We would sit outside and have to be on our best behaviour as it is a decent place to go. Mam always said it was her favourite place to eat.

We smile at each other and I tell her it would be my treat, as it's a bit more expensive than your usual run of the mill cafe.

I suggest we walk to Donabate, but Carly says she's a bit tired so we get in the car. It's still quite warm out so I open the windows to get the sea breeze in. Can't beat a car with no air con' in it. I'm fooling myself of course. Dad didn't care; he used to like the wind in his hair. (Or what was left of it.)

It doesn't take but a few minutes to drive to the hotel. I park the car and as I get out I check myself as I couldn't remember putting my knickers back on! Phew, I did! Thank God for that, my Mammy would never forgive me for walking in *her* place without my underwear.

The first thing we do is go to the toilets to make ourselves look a bit more decent. Carly pulls out of her basket a very large chiffon type scarf affair that is extremely nice. She takes off her shorts, arranges this piece of material around herself as if she has done this before. When she has completed this, it looks like she has on a summer dress; she turns to me with hands on hips and says "Tah Dah! What do you think?" I tell her that she looks very presentable and pretty. I check myself in the mirror, put on some lippy and brush my hair. Glancing at my reflection and thinking not much more I can do there then.

We walk into the Tower Bar and Bistro and I ask someone where we could order afternoon tea to have outside, overlooking the sea like we used to do. We are shown outside and taken to a table where the view is spectacular on a clear day like today. It couldn't be a better way to end our afternoon.

Carly and I devour dainty sandwiches, cream cakes and scones; everything on that three-tier plate stand is demolished. We chat through a big pot of tea then end our lavish lunch with coffee like a couple of gluttons.

During our conversation I try to talk Carly out of going back to Berlin until she gets off the tablets. Telling me that they are not harming her but enhancing her sex life, anyway Ross is only giving them to her temporarily until she doesn't need them anymore. I can't understand why. When does the time come that she won't need them anymore, when she learns to feel she wants sex all the time without them? It baffles me. I really don't think Carly understands either. Ross seems to be brainwashing her to the extent where she just trusts only him no matter what.

I don't know what else to say to her anymore I just want her to come to her senses. Before leaving the table, Carly pulls her chair out telling me she needs the toilet. While she's gone I decide to give her the painkillers back so I pop them in her bag, which is the only way to give them back without an argument. When returning she picks up her bag, turns to give me a guilty look as the rattling noise gives it away, then thanks me. I don't say a word.

I push the chair back after paying for our memorable food and feel so full I could burst. Carly says she feels the same.

We walk back to the car holding our stomachs as we go. Driving home is a doddle, not much traffic to bother us. Our conversation is over with as Carly falls asleep while listening to the classical music I had turned on. That's a first; demanding the CD to be changed when I have it on is the usual. Can't understand why!!

When we arrive home, Mam asks if we want some tea.

We look at each other and laugh.

"What have I said that's so funny, you two?" I tell her where we have been and I could have sworn she turned green with envy.

I think she is pleased not having to cook for us. She'll just pop something in the microwave for herself.

CHAPTER 8

It's been two weeks now since Carly got back from Berlin. Things are changing for the worse. She is starting to get more irritable and wants to be out with her friend more often. That's fine with me. I'm getting a bit fed up with her snapping at us for no reason.

Mam is worried about her and wants to find out what her problem is. But I remind her of the conversation I had with Carly when I went to the beach with her last week.

She sighs as we sit in our usual spot in the kitchen and says, "Ailish I don't want her to go back to Germany. I've a bad feeling that something might happen to her. If something or someone hurts her, I would never forgive myself for not trying to stop her".

I feel so sorry for Mam but the problem is that Carly is over the age of consent and there is nothing we can do to stop her, bar throwing her in the shed and locking her up. I tell Mam my thoughts. She says that locking her in the shed would be a good idea, just wishes that she could until she's off the drugs.

The next time we see my sister is the following day, she

called to say she was staying with Eileen for the night. While she is out I tell Mam about the really great day I had at the beach with my sister. I show her the pictures that I secretly took of her on my mobile while I caught her gazing into the distance in a world of her own and not paying any attention to what I was doing.

"That's a good one Ailish, she looks happy and content there." And then I show her the selfie I took when we were having our afternoon tea.

"Yer both have cream around your mouths and jam there too" pointing to our faces. "Good memories for you to keep love. Hope we'll have more in the future."

Looking at me so forlorn, and then taking a tissue out of her skirt pocket to wipe her nose as she's now on the verge of crying. I put my arms around her and hug her with all my might. I feel like I'm the Mother now as I try to comfort her. But the feeling is mutual and we're both crying now, comforting each other.

Carly is sitting on the bed in Eileen's bedroom yawning and stretching as she tells her friend that she wishes she could stay another night.

"Yer, I do too Carly, but Gran is coming to stay tonight so the bed will be hers." Eileen takes Carly by surprise telling her that she has a job interview at the travel agents in the city.

"What, the same one where our Ailish works?"

"Same one. Ailish isn't the apprentice anymore so they're looking to hiring another one, so I'm going for it. I'll find out all the gossip from yer sister, especially about you" she says pointing right at her.

Carly looks up from putting on her sandals and says "What do you mean, you already know about me. What I told you last night should last you a lifetime. And no telling Ailish what I told you, she doesn't need to know that I'm still taking those drugs."

Eileen replies "I won't be telling her because her and yer Ma would kill yer!" then went on "Ah but when you're living in Germany I'll find out what yer up to from your sister then you'll have more of us on yer back looking out for you." Eileen carries on with a look of concern, "*I'm* worried about you too Carly. I don't think you should be still taking those tablets and you shouldn't be lying to yer sister about it, she's only trying to help after all."

Carly looks at her friend annoyed and says, "You know what, I thought you were on my side after what I told you last night. You know if I told Ailish the truth then she would tell Mam and then all hell would let loose like you say, but the tablets make me feel good and I trust what Ross tells me. You forget that I'm in love with him and that's my reason for going back to Berlin."

Eileen decides not to say much more on the subject.

But Carly carries on "I've already told Ailish that when I settle there she can come over to see me, well you can do the same Eileen, you're welcome to you know."

Eileen just nods and decides to change the subject; she feels she can't do much more to talk her out of taking those drugs.

After they have both dressed and had breakfast, Carly asks for more juice and then grabs her handbag from the door handle. They talk about what they'd both like to do that day. Eileen suggests shopping in the city; Carly says she would rather just hang around the up-market cafe that has opened recently, she doesn't need to buy any clothes or make-up letting her friend know that Ross gets her everything she needs. Eileen rolls her eyes at her and laughs and accuses her of turning into a snob and a poser. Carly tells her that she's just jealous and sticks her middle finger up at her. While they talk, Carly still has her hand inside her designer leather handbag searching for her precious goods. At last she finds what she's been looking for, opens the top and pops one in her mouth. Eileen looks at her in shock as she has just watched her best friend doing the one thing she has been trying to talk her out of all night.

Still feeling quite knackered, she grabs the tablets out of Carly's hand and asks her angrily.

"What the hell are you doing you frickin' idiot, you really are stupid aren't you and right in front of my face. Trying to kill yer self yer eejit?"

"Give them back to me Eileen." Carly, getting really angry now, scuffles around her friends kitchen until the tablets spill all over the floor. "Now look what you've done", trying to hide her tears as she struggles to pick them up. Eileen doesn't help her but stands watching with arms folded, still annoyed. When Carly retrieves the last one, she puts it in the bottle and looks over at her friend.

Eileen now sees the tears in her eyes and walks over to her and takes her hand, "Don't you see what you're doing to yer self, we all want to help you. You can't see the truth, because those drugs are dimming your mind, the one thing you should care about more than your fanny! Wake up Carly, please!"

Carly runs toward the front door shouting "I don't want to see you anymore; Ross is the only one I trust now. I wish I was with *him* not you". Eileen tries to grab her and maybe, just maybe she could calm her down to tell her how much she cares about her. But Carly gets the better of her and runs out of the door and down the path and now she's gone out of sight.

Eileen wondering whether to run after her, but decides against it, thinking she needs to cool down and then she'll call her tonight. Hopefully coming to her senses by then.

Eileen walks back in and decides to phone Carly's house. While waiting for someone to pick up she notices one of the tablets still on the floor. Walking over near to the sink she sees it and picks up the drug and looks at it, carefully rolling it in her fingers.

"Hi Eileen everything okay?" "Hi Ailish." Eileen pauses for a few seconds then explains through anxious breaths what happened, while asking if Carly is still there. She's not. We discuss what to do next and I tell her I will walk to the park to see if I can find her there. I suggest that another place to look would be around the bus stops; as if Carly was in such a disgusting mood she might just leg it and go anywhere she can be alone to think things through. Eileen agrees, telling her that's where she will look.

Wondering whether she should tell me that she's found one of Carly's tablets, thinks quickly then decides against it for now as it would make matters a whole lot worse.

No more time to waste, we finish our conversation and hang up. I'm now very worried and knowing I have to tell Mam, to talk over the problem with her quickly. Before I know it, I'm being pushed out the door while being told to hurry up and find her, before it gets too dark to do anything.

Before Eileen leaves, she puts the tablet in her bedroom drawer not wanting her Mam to find it when she returns home from work tonight. As she does, she hears the sound of the front gate opening. Looking out of her window she sees me heading towards the door. Rushing down the stairs, she grabs her bag and keys before I knock. Eileen opens the door quickly, nearly pushing me to the ground as she does.

"Hi Ailish, sorry about that. I tried to talk to her. All night I tried and this morning, she just went stupid."

I take a deep breath in and sigh, "We just need to find her before she has any more stupid ideas."

Eileen quickly locks her front door then we both go our separate ways to search for Carly.

As I walk quickly up the street on my way to the local park, I'm thinking how serious this situation is becoming. The humidity in the air today is becoming a burden as it's slowing me down somewhat but it doesn't stop me from searching for my sister.

I look in the newsagents and the sweet shop (Carly still loves to go in there when she's in need of her sugar or chocolate fix) before going on. No sign of her there. I walk and walk, looking down every street as I pass, behind the trees and in doorways, everywhere I think she may be.

It's getting hotter and my feet sweat a bit as I didn't have time to change into my sandals. I'm feeling a bit downhearted but as I'm nearing the park I feel a bit more hopeful of finding her. I get to the park gates and push them open, I'm sure she's here, as the place is so familiar to her. I walk a lot slower now, searching everywhere. I even look in the public toilets as its cooler in the dark, cement surroundings. Not a soul in there. I walk on toward the lake and seeing the sun shining on the water. I sit on one of the wooden benches and gaze over the beautiful sight. Now closing my eyes, I feel rather worn out and pissed off with myself; I had no time to think about grabbing my sunglasses either. I try to think where I could look next.

As my mind wanders, I hear the sounds of youths laughing and carrying on, seemingly having a good old time. I open my eyes and look ahead to see two girls and two boys around sixteen in one of the boats. I watch for a while and notice that they are drinking alcohol. Not a good idea, as for a start it's not allowed on the boats and they are definitely under age. I wish for just a minute that it was Carly in there as I would be shouting at her to get out of there and to come home. But it's not and I need to get my tired arse off this seat and look further. As I get up, the sound from the boat seems different now. I look over and see a noisy commotion. One of the girls is shouting and waving at me to help as the two boys have fallen in the water. As I look closer I notice that they are too drunk to help themselves. I'm not a strong swimmer but I know I need to do something very quickly! Oh God,

I've got a dress on, so off it comes, and I've no time to feel embarrassed. Just as I'm about to jump in to help, I hear a loud voice shouting.

"No Ailish, don't, I will." I look around and see Carly appear before my eyes. Carly quickly steps out of her shorts and jumps in the lake to help the two people that seem to be nearly drowning. I realise my mouth is wide open as I watch in shock.

Carly is a very strong swimmer, won swimming competitions when she was at school, so I don't worry but keep a close eye on them.

I walk nearer to the edge and see my sister swim toward me, dragging one of the young idiots toward the bank as he is crying. The other one still needing help, obviously can swim as he is still afloat, but she goes back to get him. I help her get them out and then I help Carly. I pick up my dress and wrap it around my sister. I rub her down, then throw it on the back of a bench to dry off in the sun. I take her in my grasp and ask her if she's alright. She mumbles something into my hair that sounds something like 'Yes, but I'm fuckin' wet and still pissed off'. I don't really care if that *was* what she said, as I have her with me, to take back home and I'm not letting go.

We checked that the two youths sitting on the bank were okay, as they were very upset and crying. The two girls who were standing next to them, suddenly walked off rather quickly with their heads down, looking as if they didn't want anything more to do with this pretty crazy situation.

One of the boys stood, legs shaking a bit and gives

Carly a hesitant thanks. They get on their mobiles to call their parents to come and pick them up. Before we leave they say sorry for causing so much trouble, then we see the park keeper heading in our direction. He looks me up and down and I realise I'm still standing in my underwear! We explain what had happened and then I take my dress, pull it over my head and tell Carly to get dressed too before we end up being arrested.

I think if it wasn't for them Carly might have stayed here in her hiding place all night. Mam says all things happen for a reason, God, she's so right.

I again hug Carly and hold her face in my hands.

I ask, "Why did you run off, we were so worried about you. Let's go home and get you cleaned up, shall we?"

"Good job I *was* here" she answers. "Those two people could have been a lot worse off seeing as you're not a good swimmer, now are you?" I shrug and don't comment.

I say, "Come on then, let's get you home before our Mam calls the police".

Carly, shivering even though the sun is warm on her skin says "God, you'd think I was a little kid, it's not like I've been out all day and night, I'm hungry though, the breakfast I had at Eileen's was that horrible gluten free bread, it tasted like cardboard."

We both laugh and then, "Oh shite, I forgot to call Eileen and let her know I've found you". I do it right away.

When we arrive home, walking down the path toward our front door, I see Mam standing at the sitting room window looking out. She's most likely been there pacing up and down all of the time I was out searching for Carly.

In the next couple of seconds, the door is opening and she rushes out with her arms wide open.

"Oh my God Carly, you look a mess, what happened?", giving me a look as if it's all my fault.

Carly rushes upstairs to have a shower while I tell Mam what happened. She takes it upon herself to call Eileen to ask her if there's anything else we need to know while Carly was staying with her. I go to my room to get something dry to wear as she talks to her.

I hear Mam's voice going up an octave which always means something's wrong.

"What, she did what, no way Eileen, that's terrible, thanks for telling me. No darlin' I won't drop you in. I'll tell her we just cottoned on to what she was doing. Okay? Alright love we'll let you know. Bye for now". Then she hung up. I rush back down and find her sitting in the kitchen, upset again with her head in her hands. I kneel down at her feet and take hold of her.

"What Mam, what did Eileen say to you"? I pass her a tissue to wipe her face; and then she told me what she had found out.

"Why is she taking drugs Ailish and pretending that they are something else."

I knew she was lying all along and I'm thinking that Eileen has a big mouth too and should have kept it shut. Mam is still talking but I'm not paying attention.

"Do you know why? Eileen has told me that she is taking something but doesn't know what they are. Did you know about this, I thought she was smoking cannabis Ailish, isn't that what you said?"

"I did yes, but I…Oh Mam I'm so sorry. I've been trying to help Carly stop taking the tablets. I really have, I was going to tell you, I was."

I wonder if I really would have. Mam looks at me with so much disappointment in her face, gets off her chair and walks away from me. She rushes up the stairs then I hear her bedroom door close. I sit down and wonder what I'm going to do now.

Two days goes by with not much conversation between us. I'm feeling bored now with not being at work so I tell Mam this as we sit out in the garden.

"I think I will go back to work next week. I know I can't do anything more to help Carly."

Mam gives me a concerned look and says "I've been thinking, I will talk to her. The only way to stop her in my opinion and I've said to you before, is to stop her going back to see *that* man. He's the one that's caused all this palaver in the first place." I give her a disturbing look.

"Don't look at me like that Ailish. I *am* her Mother and I *will* put a stop to it, once and for all. I don't care if she shouts or runs away again; I am not having her ruin her life over this." I know I should think before I speak but I just let my loose tongue go for it on my Ma.

"Don't be so bloody ridiculous, you know she isn't going to listen with being old enough to do what she wants and she'll tell yer that too. There's nothing more I can do Mam. I told you, I've been trying since she came back from Germany. She'll have to learn by her fuckin' mistakes, won't she?". I knew I would regret what I just said as she told me "How dare you swear like that you little shite." Then she went on and on.

"If yer Dad were here he would"…, blah, blah, blah.

Then saying "I knew something wasn't right with our Carly; I've had a bad feeling ever since she came home. She will have to listen to what I say this time." I start to speak, not caring how I was going to answer, but think better of it when I notice a mad and very angry expression on her face. Walking out into the garden still with the look of a mad woman, getting a surprise when she sees Carly then tells her to come and sit beside her. I watch them glance over in my direction as I sit down. By the look on their faces I'm afraid that the rest of the day might turn quite nasty (and I don't mean the weather). We enjoy each other's company in silence for a while.

I go back into the house as I'm feeling rather hot and sweaty and decide to take a shower as I need to relax and forget about everything that is bothering me. I take longer than usual as I know that Mam wants to be alone with Carly.

As I come out of the bathroom I hear them still talking. I try to listen but the door must be closed to the kitchen. I carry on and walk to my bedroom to get dressed. Then as I'm putting the T-shirt over my head, I begin to hear their voices getting louder. Now fully clothed, I quietly go down the stairs and hear Carly shouting. I see that the door is ajar so I stand behind it cowering in the corner. She is telling Mam that Ross wants her to leave home and live with him in Berlin. I sneak a look around the door and see my sister pick up a heavy plate from the table and aim it at our Mother. Rushing into the room I try to calm her down while at the same time pulling the plate from her grip.

I shout "This has to stop *right now*".

Carly stares at me, looking quite shocked, then rushes out upstairs away from us. Mam tells me she tried talking her out of leaving and to make her see sense. I don't want to tell her, I told you so.

Two days go by with no words from my sister. She stays in her room most of the time; she doesn't even want to see her friend Eileen.

We feel sad and miserable, we just want Carly back, the girl that used to be full of life with never a word against anyone.

The next morning, we hear Carly get out of bed early which is not quite her normal routine. I tell Mam that I will find out what she's up to. I watch Carly go back and forth from her bedroom to the bathroom. I ask her what's going on and notice that she's been crying a lot as her eyes look very swollen. I then peek into her room and notice that her suitcase is open on her bed. She walks past me with her hands full of toiletries.

Then telling me, "I'm leaving Ailish, I've had enough and I've just run out of my tablets too. Can't take the way I'm feeling". She cries again while trying to talk.

"Ross told me to come over to stay with him so I can get more drugs." I put my arms around her as she sobs her heart out and then I ask her to come downstairs to talk to Mam. She thankfully agrees. As we walk down the stairs I tell her that she should realise now that she is addicted to those tablets. She doesn't answer.

We walk into our usual gathering spot in the kitchen where our Mammy is. She turns her head around as she stands at the sink doing her usual chores. We look at each other and I see a spark of hope in my Mam's eyes.

"Carly can I help you love, sit down and I'll get yer something to drink. Do yer want something to eat as well?" Carly looks up at her and shakes her head, then suddenly changes her mind.

"Can I have some toast and marmalade please?"

"Of course, yer can" she tells her. Mam happily looks after her younger daughter with a smile on her face. After the food has hungrily disappeared Ma asks her what's going on. Carly tells her she's leaving.

"But I'll come back Mam you know I will. You know I love yer and I always will." She then looks at me and says with honesty in her eyes.

"I love you too Ailish, but I need to be with Ross right now, he will look after me."

Here we go again I think, but keep it to myself.

We both agree to let her go but she must keep in touch with us. We all agree that she should return in a few months and stay with us for a weekend.

Leaving the kitchen to carry on with her packing, we realise somehow we need to get her professional help, even if she kicks and screams.

Carly leaves two days later with not a dry eye among us. Mam says she doesn't want to come to the airport. She would be more comfortable and less teary-eyed staying at home than waving her off and watching her get on the plane.

I drive her to the airport wondering why I am doing this; it feels so alien to me, a bit like a dream, (more like a nightmare) where I'm doing something I can't control.

We get to the airport and I want to find a place to park, but Carly tells me just to drop her off as she can see that it's very busy and I probably won't find a parking space anyway. I agree, so I illegally park at the front where the taxi ranks are located and get her suitcase out of the boot of the car, much to the annoyance of the taxi drivers. But I don't care at this stage so I carry on doing what I want. I can't help but look at her with my sad face as I *do* feel miserable. We hug each other very tightly and then kiss each other's cheek.

She looks sad too and says "Don't worry Ailish, I'll be okay. You're my older sister and I know you will always be there for me no matter what. Dad will be there for me in spirit if I need him, you know he will." I agree with her then let go of her but my heart is saying *don't let her go.* My head saying, this seems to be her destiny, I can't stop that. I watch as she walks away.

On the way home, I glance in the rear-view mirror to make a turn and Christ, I've just seen the dark shape of a man sitting in the back seat of the car, and then he's gone again. I'm not scared, just concerned that he may be trying to warn me of something to come again. I feel it in my bones.

PART TWO

CHAPTER 9

Carly walks into the airport with a quivering chin. She walks to the toilets to blow her nose and tidy her face up a bit. Looking in the mirror she sees the *real* her, a young woman who knows deep down what she is doing is wrong. What she didn't tell her family is her feeling of depression, on some days severe. She has to tell Ross the way she's feeling as he will know what to do. Can't wait to see him she thinks, craving sex constantly. I would have him in now, in this bathroom up against the wall if he was here. Walking into the cubicle to masturbate as she thinks of him inside of her, doing so every night before sleeping.

She sits on the plane excited at the thought of spending quality time with Ross and eventually seeing his plush, posh apartment she's heard so much about and lying in his arms in his king size bed with his king size erection inside her.

Now walking through Berlin's Tegel airport after collecting her luggage, pausing to pull out her mobile and let Ross know that she has arrived. She can't get through so keeps trying until he eventually answers.

"Sorry Carly I am *so* busy right now, I should be there soon, and I'll call you when I'm out of the meeting?"

He waits and hears her sigh and then she answers him, "Well I suppose, but you won't be too long will you? I can't wait to see you Ross."

"I know sweetheart, I need to see you too. I'll be as quick as I can I promise. Okay?"

"Oh. Okay then, talk to you soon, I love you." He doesn't answer her and hangs up quickly. She looks at her phone and thinks that's a bit weird, not telling her he loves her. Most likely because he's just too busy.

Putting her phone in her deep coat pocket she wanders around passing the time until he calls back. Sitting down as her bag is quite heavy, she waits. Only ten minutes pass and then he calls.

"Carly, I can't pick you up I'm too busy, get a taxi and tell him to take you to The Hotel de Rome and tell the receptionist you want the key for my rooms. If you get bored go to La Banca Bar that's in the hotel, they have great cocktails there, I won't be too long alright."

She thinks, can't wait and then answers "Yes I'll do that, but why a hotel and not your apartment? I'm a bit confused."

"Yes, I know, I'll tell you when I get there Carly. See you soon."

Then she quickly asks "Which hotel did you say; sorry I'll write it down this time."

He tells her again and then he hangs up his phone, Ross secretly thinking 'Is she stupid or just hard of hearing?'

Arriving at the hotel she pays the driver and is greeted by a man in uniform who opens the door for her. Looking around this tasteful interior, she walks to reception and asks for the key for Mr Carmichaels' rooms like he told her. While waiting, she thinks Oh my God; this hotel is for the well heeled that's for sure. A porter is called over to help her with her luggage and he says he will take her to the Suite. She enters the elevator with him and he presses the button for the Bebel Suite. A suite, wow, she shouldn't expect anything less from Ross.

When they arrive at the suite the porter opens the door for her and takes her luggage into the sitting room. Her eyes light up with astonishment as she takes in the beautiful surroundings. Before she takes a tour, the porter asks if she would like him to unpack for her, she tells him no, gives him a tip and then he leaves.

She has never seen anything like this before.

It's like a turn of the century apartment with high ceilings and a lot of light pouring in. The rooms are done in a yellow and grey theme with a mix of modern and antique furniture. She walks into the bathroom and notices a lot of marble, it's amazing. Then she finds the bedroom and jumps onto the huge bed laughing while stripping off her clothes. Walking around naked she feels very sexy and finds some music to put on. Noticing the balcony, she walks toward it and looks through the window to see a long seat with cushions, each one placed at a particular angle.

She runs into the bathroom, grabs one of the plush white bathrobes, then opens the door to look at the view outside, seeing the beautiful Plaza below. It is early evening now and the sun is still out, shining brightly onto the roof tops. Gazing out watching the people, especially the couples below, she feels a bit lonely. The track on the CD changes to a sultrier slow-paced song. Now moving toward the bedroom placing herself on top of the huge comfortable bed. Caressing her body with her smooth hands, she moves them down toward her genitals, placing them in-between her legs.

Now masturbating even harder, thinking of Ross wanting him right now so she can place his hard erection deeper than where her fingers can reach. Pleasing herself several times and then starts to feel lonely again. She hears a knock on the door and thinks its Ross; he must have known I need him now. Walking to the door still naked and opening it, only to see a hotel porter with a bottle of red wine in his hand. Noticing the colour of his face change to match that wine, thinking poor man. She apologises and tells him she'll be back in a second. Closing the door and smiling, she grabs that same robe, wraps it around herself then walks back to open the door and tells him again.

"Sorry about that." Then noticing the bottle in his hand asks him.

"Is that for me?" He tells her it is, a welcome bottle for her to enjoy. He also lets her know that if she wants breakfast in her suite in the morning just let reception know and they will be at her service. Thanking him she takes the bottle from his sweaty hand. Skipping back into the bedroom giggling, she decides to take a shower as she wants to find out more about the La Banca Bar.

Feeling very confident, she walks toward the bar and notices someone sipping a *very* pink cocktail. Walking up to the lady with that pretty drink, noticing that there's a vacant seat next to her, she sits on the brown leather bar stool, asks what she is drinking as she wouldn't mind one herself. Carly now takes a bit more notice of this woman, who she would put at maybe in her mid to late thirties. She is dressed very colourful in a beautiful fitted lemon dress with a gorgeous cerise flower print all over which shows off her curves and accentuates her long dark shiny hair. God, she smells divine too. Carly knows she's somewhat attractive but this woman is very beautiful with an Italian look about her and more experienced in many ways, she's sure.

Replying to Carly's question, she tells her the drink is a Rose and Pomegranate Martini garnished with rose petals, how lovely. Carly orders the same and discover that it's delicious. They exchange names, "I'm Maria, pleased to meet you", putting out her right hand. Carly also discovers that this beautiful woman is alone and staying at the hotel for a couple of nights. She asks Maria how she has such an exotic look about her. She answers that her father is Italian and her late mother was German. Carly enjoys her company and they have a few more cocktails. She is feeling slightly tipsy now and hears that her tongue is getting looser too, they go on chatting. Maria tells Carly she has recently bought an apartment in the Wilmersdorf area of Berlin. Work was needed so it affected everyone who was supposed to move in two days ago.

Stating louder than expected "Which is very unprofessional, as to buy a place in that building cost me over two million." What! She's a female version of Ross. Carly asks her more about what the building looks like, letting her know she's really interested in how she's furnished the interior. During their conversation Carly had explained her intention of becoming an architect. Maria describes the building and the architect who designed it, Sebastian Treese she says. Carly wishes she could live in a place like this. Then thinking, Ross is staying here and has an expensive apartment, wonder if it's the same building. If it is, she can't wait to move in. Maria gets carried away, which Carly doesn't mind, when she describes the furniture and the way she has her apartment decorated. Carly feels Maria is talking a bit too much as she has had a few more drinks, and is getting a bit bored.

Wishing Ross was here now even though she is enjoying Maria's company, she really would rather be having several orgasms. Excusing herself, she walks towards the ladies, trying not to fall over on her rather high stiletto heels. Discovering she's alone, hurriedly pops a pill, swallowing it down with a gulp of water from the posh taps. Already taken one this morning but wants to feel extra sexy for him when he eventually gets here. She redoes her luscious lipstick then checks herself in the full-length mirror before leaving, seeing a sexy woman with a gorgeous flowing grey and pink full length (almost see through) dress covering her body. She does look older than her almost nineteen years which makes her very happy. Walking back to the bar she smiles as she notices that Ross has arrived and he is sitting in *her* seat. Is he flirting with Maria? Now trying to control a pang of jealousy, she doesn't want to look like the immature one around here. As she moved closer to them, Maria looks in her direction and that signals Ross to do the same. He smiles his big smile at me and says in his sexy throaty voice.

"Hi Carly, I've missed you so much."

They embrace and he says, "I hear you've met Maria. She tells me you've been having a few drinks together."

(How does he know this woman? Carly thinks he knows everyone, he's always on the phone to a ton of people.) She tells him they have and she's got her drinking one of the best cocktails ever.

Maria says they'll be seeing a lot more of each other. Carly frowns while looking at them, first Ross then Maria. She wonders how they'll be seeing more of each other. She's just about to ask them, then Ross asks if they would like another cocktail as he is ready for a drink after the stressful work day he has had. The three of them chat and Carly hears a lot about the night life in Berlin and eventually discovers how Ross and Maria met…

Eighteen months ago, she walked into his office asking for the best interior architect/designer he has in the city. They've been friends ever since. Ross gave her the best of what she wanted and the story began.

Ross laughs and says "She had come to the right place, not only did I give her Christina, our best interior designer, but also I wanted to buy a decent place in the city as you know" he says looking at Carly. He continues.

"Maria was in the process of buying a fantastic place in the Treese building and she mentioned that there was a penthouse duplex still for sale. So, I went to have a look and fell in love with it immediately. I can't wait for you to see it Carly, you'll love it too." So, that's why I will be seeing more of Maria, we'll be neighbours.

They all have one more drink and then part company, promising to meet up with Maria again.

Feeling very sexy and gagging for it, Carly grabs Ross by the arm and they head up to the suite. She drags him into the elevator; thank God there is no porter in it, and when the door closes pulls his face to hers and sticks her tongue down his throat hungry for his love. She jumps up on him and throws her legs around him feeling his throbbing erection wanting *her* love.

When they arrive at the suite, he struggles to open the door as she's still partially wrapped around his body. They eventually get in the rooms and almost rip each other's clothes off. Throwing themselves onto the king size bed they caress each others faces. Carly feels his hot body all over her as he caresses her breasts, licking her nipples with the tip of his tongue as they harden. She feels the wetness in between her legs as she's so hot for his hard lovemaking. She manoeuvres that still throbbing hard erection toward her wet mound and feels it enter. Oh my God, her legs almost around his neck, they move up and down feeling the extreme desire of their bodies close to each other, enjoying the best feeling in the whole world. They go on and on until they are both screaming with satisfaction. Spent with exhaustion they fall asleep for a while. Carly needing a drink is the first to leave the bed. Walking back into the bedroom, noticing Ross is now awake, she lays beside him and they kiss again.

Whispering in his ear "I've missed you".

She wants to make love again but he tells her he's had a long day and needs to sleep. But he surprises her before sleeping by letting her know that he will be spending the whole day with her tomorrow. He said he will take her to see his penthouse as he needs to check on it to see when the work will be done so they can move in. Carly tells him she can't wait. All she really wants to do is have one part of his body in her all day, but she doesn't tell him that. Letting him sleep, she walks out onto the balcony with her drink to watch the world go by. She wraps one of the hotel's luscious blankets around her body and watches the lights of the buildings below twinkle in the darkness. They hypnotise her into thinking seriously about what she is doing with her life. Really wanting to stop taking the drugs he gives her, she wants a normal life with him without the need for them. Wishing now she had listened to Ailish telling her she needed help. There is only one problem; Ross still wants her to take them. If she talks to him and lets him know how she feels he might understand. But will have to do it when the time is just right. That time has not arrived yet. Carly plans to stick around for a while.

The next morning, she is woken with a knock on the door. She turns over and stretches her naked body to see Ross walk out of the bedroom to answer it. She hears him thank the porter, close the door then walk in with a trolley full of the most scrumptious looking breakfast goodies that she's ever seen. Carly sits up and he serves her with a tray of coffee and asks what else she would like.

"I would like *you*" telling him in her sleepy voice.

He laughs with that sexy sound he has and she wants him even more. She decides to put her coffee on the side table and surprise him by jumping out of the bed to grab him. He doesn't stop her, they wrestle around and she feels the wetness in between her legs wanting him to enter her again. They make love passionately with such force and hunger and she climaxes several times. Now hungry for her breakfast, she feasts on one of the best she has had in her life. There is everything anyone could ask for. Carly sees special coffee and tea, fruit and toast, posh cereal, a whole lot of wonderful and colourful delights she has never encountered before, right before her eyes. She loves him being her slave for the morning as he feeds her, with several sensuous gestures thrown in. Feeling around under the sheets to find out if he is excited again but he moves away, Carly is *so* disappointed. She wonders, am I turning into a nymphomaniac? She feels like she is, but enjoys sex so much she can't keep her hands off him. Would she feel the same if she wasn't taking the drugs? Carly really doesn't know anymore.

Ross has a private driver who comes to his beck and call anytime he wants him. His name is Matthew and Carly liked him immediately they met.

He is an Englishman which surprised her; she was expecting an old fart with a German accent. But he has kind brown eyes and is quite young. She was going to dress up for the day as she wasn't sure where they were going but Ross told her to dress casually as they would be *slumming it* today. The definition of slumming it to Ross, is going to stay in a four-star hotel, so Carly doesn't mind. As it's a bit cooler today, wearing her navy-blue Chanel pants he bought her with a white three-quarter length sleeve fitted T-shirt, also Chanel. Still wanting to look good, she ties her flowing long blonde hair into a flirty up do.

They are in the car, Carly not knowing where they were going so takes in the sights of the city. She didn't see much the last time, as all they did was have sex and eat great food.

It seems she is getting a tour of all the museums and touristy places as they pass quite a lot of them. Now she sees the zoo, the entrance looks like something from a Chinese restaurant. Carly is getting bored so yawns and yawns again. Ross puts his arm around her and tells her they'll be there very soon.

When they do get there, *there* is the most beautiful place she's ever seen. Matthew opens the car doors for them then seeing in front of her this large and elegant white building with a style and flair of Paris boulevards (seen them in a magazine).

"This is it" Ross tells Carly, pointing to the building.

It is where she will be living with *her* Ross. "It's gorgeous I can't wait to see inside." Ross tells Matthew they won't be too long and they walk towards their future home. It is a gated entrance which is not the usual but a fantastic large ornate gate with its beautiful French style design. They enter the elevator and kiss each other.

"Wait until you see the rest Carly, you'll love it, it's perfect." Carly is so glad she met Ross, as at times like this she feels *so* happy.

When they arrive at the main door, noticing that it's not an apartment but a duplex penthouse, it's enormous with three bedrooms, a private patio, a courtyard garden and a private roof terrace. This is where she goes to sit when Ross deals with the contractor who is there, apparently to finish off the work. Carly thinks she will love living here and won't want to leave. Having Ailish and Mam visit in the future will be a thrill to say the least. They won't want to leave either.

As Carly sits contemplating her new life here in Berlin, she looks around this magnificent place and wonders if in the future she'll be famous for designing a building as good as this one.

Carly gets off the seat and looks down at the street below where she sees Matthew standing outside of the car smoking a cigarette. Wondering what he does when he's not driving Ross around, maybe married a German girl and going home to her loving arms? Or maybe he lives alone. She continues watching him and it's as if he knew, he looks up and sees her looking at him. She feels a bit embarrassed. He pretends he hasn't seen her and looks around at the sky as if watching the birds. Carly smiles and walks away to go inside to look for Ross. Removing her mobile from her bag she takes a few photos of this wonderful place to send to Ailish. The furniture Ross has chosen is in such good taste, trendy but comfortable as she finds out when trying out every chair in the place.

Naturally trying the bed out, Wow, what a room; she could spend all day and night in here. She takes more photos of the bathrooms and the kitchen. Another Wow! Carly sends the photos to Ailish with a text message saying, *I have to pinch myself to realise that this is my home too. Isn't it gorgeous? Send more soon. love C xx*

Ross shouts that he is ready to leave so she picks up her bag, runs into the living area where he is and grabs hold of his huge soft hand.

Back into the elevator he asks "Well do you like it?"

"What, of course I do, who wouldn't; it's the best place ever. I feel so lucky to be here." Ross tells her they'll be living in it tomorrow. Carly kisses him with more passion than before.

They walk out of the elevator through the gate and back onto the street where Matthew is waiting for them. He opens the car doors for them, but just before getting in Carly takes a photo of the front of the building, another one to send to her family.

As they sit in the back seat Ross tells Matthew to go somewhere Carly didn't understand. She nudges Ross and looks at him as if to say well where are we going. He quietly laughs and apologises.

"Sorry Carly I thought it would be a good idea to take you to my office to let you meet the people who will be training you soon. That okay with you"?

Ignoring him for a moment, she digs in her bag finding first an unopened bag of Irish toffees (shoved in there by her Mammy to remind her of home). Replacing her sweets, she pulls out her mirrored compact opening it to check her make-up. Noticing Matthew glance at her in the rear-view mirror as if he was saying don't worry, you look fine. She secretly smiles at him, then carries on checking to see if she *did* look okay.

Carly looks at Ross then tells him "Yes of course it's okay, I'm looking forward to meeting them. I am bit nervous though".

He reassures her like he usually does. Strangely, she feels nervous as the drugs normally give her a huge boost of confidence.

Arriving at the offices of Carmichaels Architects Carly alights from the car and notices how big they are, looking like a building you would see somewhere in New York. Upon entering she looks around the vast reception area, you could get lost in this area alone, it would be a good place to play hide and seek. They are greeted by an attractive woman with sleek red hair pulled back off her glowing bespectacled face.

"Good afternoon Mr Carmichael" in her perfect broken English accent, half smiling. Ross smiles at her and replies. "Afternoon Naomi, are Thomas and Karolin in their offices, not out for lunch, are they?"

She answers him without blinking it seems. "No not at all, they are both in their offices ready to see you and..."

"Oh sorry, this is Carly who will be working here with us, most likely next month."

Naomi makes Carly feel like the new kid on the block with her stern but professional attitude. She puts out her hand and Carly takes it.

"Nice to meet you Carly" she says, friendly but sternly.

Carly suddenly wants to laugh as it feels so surreal. Feeling like she's on a film set and Naomi is the bad actress. Carly could see right through her, she fancies the pants off Ross!

Carly smiles at her and walks with Ross toward the elevator of this massive place. She can't grab him in this *contraption* as it is all glass everywhere. Everyone can see inside and they can see every floor as they go up. They stop at the very top of the building. Ross lets Carly out first and what she sees takes her breath away. The panoramic views are just out of this world. Stopping in amazement to look around while Ross walks ahead. You will be able to see for miles as it's such a beautiful clear perfect day out there. No wonder this floor is why the top architects have their offices here including Ross. Carly has her mouth open in amazement as Ross walks back to get her and whispers "Looks like you're catching flies Carly".

He then closes her mouth with his hand. He laughs and then Carly sees other people looking at her, Oh God, now she *does* feel embarrassed.

Carly meets with Thomas and Karolin in their very swish offices. She gets on very well with both of them and now feels excited about the day she starts her training. They have coffee and tea brought in for them by a young man. He seems even younger than Carly but it is obvious by his look (determined, excited, but trying hard not to act like a dickhead) it's his first step into his dream coming true to become an architect.

They talk about what she would be learning and the only thing she wasn't thrilled about the volume of work she would be doing on a computer (she nearly threw one out of a school window years ago). They told her they could do that if that is what she would prefer. Carly confirmed she'd prefer that (thank you very much).

Carly still feels like she's on a film set as for some reason, her gut feeling is telling her that she won't be doing this training after all. She just hopes it will be for a good reason. She can't get pregnant again as she started taking the Pill a few weeks before coming to Berlin. Her mind is racing as she hears their voices talking around her but is really not aware anymore as to what they are saying. Carly decides to get up off her chair and walk towards the window. Her strange feelings are making her nauseous and nervous. She hears Karolin stand then walk toward her. Touching her shoulder she asks if she's feeling alright.

Carly answers, her feeling a bit dazed, "Sorry, I just felt a bit hot and dizzy for a minute. Could I get a glass of water if you wouldn't mind?"

Karolin hands her a glass from the table and she takes it gratefully. Ross now looks concerned and he makes the decision for them to leave. He says that they haven't eaten lunch yet and that could be the reason for Carly's dizzy spell. She agrees, then thanks them both for their time and leaves with Ross. Heading toward the car now she feels relieved that they will be going for lunch as her stomach is rumbling.

As they travel, Ross's mobile is ringing, he answers but can't get a signal. He asks Matthew to pull over at the first opportunity. The roads are quite busy so Carly wonders when that will be possible. Then Matthew suddenly spots an opening down a side street and finds a space to park. He must know this city very well. Ross then gets out of the car to make a call.

Silence for a moment then Matthew speaks, "I know it's none of my business but you look a bit pale Miss O'Neill are you alright?"

Carly looks at him and giggles and then says to him "I am *so* sorry Matthew but I'm not giggling at you as such, but it's when you called me Miss O'Neill that did it".

He looks at her with a confused look on his poor face.

"Matthew, I wish you would call me Carly that *is* my name is it not?"

She adds "I'm okay, thanks for asking, I'm just hungry that's all and I felt a bit dizzy for a while. Can I ask you where *are* we going for lunch?"

Hopefully it won't be a place where it's heaving with people as she'll only start feeling hot and bothered again. He lets Carly know that they are going to a private members only diners club. He must have sussed out that she wants some peace and quiet as he tells her that it is a quiet and comfortable place to eat. He goes on to tell that he recently picked up Ross from the club and went into the dining area which he thought was very nice. Carly thanks him, then sits silent in the back waiting for Ross to finish his call. After checking her mobile several times to see if anyone still loves her, Ross eventually returns.

He sighs and says "Sorry for the delay, we need to eat now, off you go Matthew".

He then continues to send text messages on his phone. They arrive at the dining club about ten minutes later as

Matthew knows all the short cuts.

As they sit and order their lunch in this *very nice* place (Matthew was so right) Ross tells Carly he has to go to London on business in a couple of days, that will still give him time with her, to move into the penthouse tomorrow. He goes on to tell her he'll be gone for about a week. Carly sighs and tells him that she will miss him as she's just arrived, would feel very lonely. He holds her hand across the table and kisses it.

Ross tells Carly in his ultra sexy voice "Just think of tonight and the next, in bed together feeling each other, kissing each other..."

She quickly tells him "Stop, you're making me feel I want you right now".

He suddenly stands up and takes her with him towards the other end of the room, around a corner and down some stairs and then sees him taking a key out of his pocket. He opens a heavy wooden brown door, pulls her in and locks it behind them. Up against the door now sweating and kissing and licking his neck, he pulls down her trousers and panties and opens the zip on his pants, pulls her legs up around his waist and enters her. He spins around so he has his back to the door then Carly hears the heels on her shoes clicking against it. They both climax within a matter of minutes. She wants to do it again so caresses him until he becomes hard again. They lay on the floor this time, on a very thick carpet. She gets on top to feel him even deeper. Her fantasy now fulfilled, they both tidy themselves up, then go back to have lunch.

Now feeling tired and full as a fat pig after enjoying

a superb lunch (and great sex) they decide to go back to the hotel for a siesta. Ross says he'll need the rest before leaving for London and it will be good to spend some time alone with her. Carly certainly doesn't object to that. Ross tells Matthew to take them back, then he tells him to have the rest of the day off as he won't need him until tomorrow morning.

When they get back to the suite they undress and continue with more lovemaking. Afterwards Carly sleeps for almost two hours. When she awakes, unable to talk to the sleeping Ross, she texts Ailish to ask how she and Mam are doing. Texting back and forth she lets them know she's okay and doing the touristy stuff. The chats finally end.

She wanders into the walk-in wardrobe (very large one at that) to look through her clothes, deciding what to throw on. She fancies a drink so decides to order some coffee. While waiting, Carly notices some glossy tourist brochures; they should give her an idea of where to spend some of her spare time.

Ross must have smelt the coffee as it arrives, he wakes up with a loud yawn as he stretches. He gets out of bed to help himself to the hot drink and sits on the large chair still naked. Carly laughs at him sitting there as even an attractive man can look stupid with his willy just hanging there waiting for hot coffee to spill on it.

He asks while looking at his large member, "Hey, what's your problem, just because it's not hard; it doesn't look that bad does it?" Carly is still smirking as she answers, "No but I'm imagining you spilling your coffee on it, that wouldn't be a nice sight to see".

He laughs too and agrees as he walks into the bedroom and comes back dressed in a pair of casual shorts and a T-shirt.

He looks at Carly over his cup and asks "Where are you thinking of going while I'm away?"

"Well" she answers, whilst flicking through one of the brochures, "I like the look of the museums and I could go to the zoo and there are plenty of cafes where I could just people watch."

He then tells her with a slight concern in his voice, "You don't have to walk to these places Carly, Matthew can take you anywhere you want to go. I will tell him to be at your beck and call. I'm sure he won't mind driving an attractive blonde woman about the city instead of me."

He laughs at his own comment then says, "As long as he doesn't get too familiar with you".

She looks at him and says "That is a bit naughty to say that about him, he seems to be a very respectable young man who will look after me very well".

He then shouts, quite loudly, "My God Carly, I'm not asking him to look after you, I just want him to drive you around". Feeling quite shocked at his loud behaviour, he had never raised his voice at her before, she walks away from him in disgust to sit out on the balcony. He follows her out a few minutes later and apologises. Carly accepts his apology. They start chatting about the best places to visit in the city and then he changes the subject.

"I keep meaning to let you know that Maria will be living just below us. I thought that if you need some company, I will leave her mobile number for you just in case you need a friendly face. I've talked to her and she said that would be alright with her."

Carly casually thanks him for looking out for her but tells him that she would be okay. Ross continues talking, changing the subject again.

"Carly, I've been thinking that it would be great if you started taking two tablets every day instead of one as they would make you feel even more confident and willing."

And as he said the word *willing* he did that raising and a wiggling of his eyebrows. It left Carly feeling like she was some kind of a frigid woman instead of giving it to him whenever he wants it. Telling him she's feeling *willing* enough as it is.

He continues as he put his arm around her shoulders. "Ah, I know but I noticed your confidence slipping a bit today, thought it would help you with that?"

Carly doesn't say anything, just thinks about what he has just asked her and feels a bit upset that he noticed that her confidence was not what it usually is. She leaves her coffee and disappears to the bathroom.

Looking at her reflection in the mirror above the huge marble sink she asks herself, do I really want to take more of those tablets? She loves Ross so wants to do everything he asks, but has to think about it. He has already told her they won't harm her so maybe she should just do as he asks without causing any arguments. She brushes her hair, sprays herself with Coco Chanel then decides to tell Ross that she will take more, if that's what he really wants.

Later that evening Carly takes another tablet and they go out on the town to enjoy the city. The night goes by in a blur as Ross takes her from one bar to another, then to a club where she is now feeling ready to dance the night away. Ross doesn't dance too much, instead some people he knows sit with them and he introduces them to her. Carly doesn't pay attention to their names as she just wants to dance. Ross doesn't know the women but the two men he seems to know very well.

As Carly weighs up the scene in front of her it seems to her that, either these women are on their first date or they are high class hookers. She would guess the latter. While listening to the male conversation, which is mainly business matters, Carly hears the two very good-looking women talking in German and reminds herself that learning the language would be a good idea as she would love to know what they are talking about. She feels pretty pissed off now, left out of the whole scenario. Still wanting to dance she interrupts the men by nudging her boyfriends' arm and standing up moving her arms around as she was seriously hinting, *hey dumb ass I would like some action here.*

Carly says to him, slurring a bit, "I would love to dance Ross, isn't that what we came here for?"

He doesn't look very pleased so Carly looks at the women and asks them if they want to dance. Ross now looking annoyed tells her to sit down. So, Carly also gets annoyed and tells him she *will* dance if she wants to. That does it. He grabs her by the arm, pulls her towards the door and takes her outside. Carly is shaking now, so frightened she wants to cry. He takes her face in his hands and says in a hateful voice, "Carly, you don't know anything about the people who come in this club and one thing's for sure I don't want you to either. I don't want you dancing with these women and I don't want you talking to them. Is that clear?"

After that speech Carly feels like a small child being scolded. She really wants to leave this place now, and tells him so. He tells her that he's staying for a while longer then he gets out his phone and calls Matthew to come and take Carly back to the hotel. He then places his arm around her waist, which makes her feel like she wants sex and then he takes her back into the club. He speaks to a guy who looks like door security and tells him to look after Carly until his chauffer arrives.

Maybe he owns this place the way he treats everyone around here. Carly cannot believe he has left her here on her own to twiddle her thumbs with no drink in her hand, Oh My God; she is so annoyed she wants to scream!

The security man takes Carly into a side room. As he leads her in, her first thought is the need for alcohol, she's shaking so much with anger, wanting to scream very loudly. He closes the door behind her with a hard slam. Taking in the weird environment, it looks like a high-class brothel, well not that she's ever been in one, but this is very over the top with bright red couches and black and red chaise longue of a very high quality. A very large dark oak drinks cabinet stands in the corner looking very much an antique. As she's the only one here she helps herself to a drink. Why not, Ross has just treated her like shit, she might as well take advantage of the situation. Carly pours herself a large glass of expensive looking red wine and explores this *special* room. Noticing three doors leading off to somewhere she doesn't want to know (curiosity checked them, all of them were locked), so walking around admires a cupboard which is also a beautiful antique piece. Bravely opening it she sees piles of sexy underwear, all of it very sheer. She picks up this black and red (obviously the theme around here) teeny tiny thong. Even she wouldn't wear this; it would cut her in two. She looks carefully, not wanting to disturb things and then it hits her, oh my God this place, it *is* a call girl hang out, it must be. Carly feels sick now, wishing Matthew was here so she can get out of this horrible den. No sooner has she thought it, the security guy comes in to tell me that Matthew *is* here. She pushes past with her drink still in her hand and quickly gets herself into the car, probably looking like a serial drunk with wine in hand. Carly must look pretty upset as Matthew notices her grim expression and sighs, thinking to himself, wish I could help her. She gave him her pouty miserable face as she watched him glance at her several times in the rear-view mirror and tells him this time, that she's not okay.

When they arrive at the hotel he walks around to open the car door for her. Carly would love for Matthew to come up and keep her company so she could tell him all about what she saw tonight and how Ross treated her. He looks concerned as she swings her legs out of the car and on to the pavement still holding her drink. She then swigs it back in one go and hands him the glass.

"Sorry it's just that I don't want to keep any memories of tonight."

He answers her in his quiet polite manner, "That's alright. It's just a glass after all. Do you need any help with anything else before I leave you?"

Carly knows what she wants to say but thinks better of it. Walking away from him she hears the car door close. She turns towards him and sees him watching. She turns back and goes into the hotel.

Carly is in bed when hearing Ross come into the room. She must have nodded off for an hour as the clock says 4.30 am. Christ, what has he been doing until this time of the morning and then she thinks of Matthew, he has to be available for Ross 24/7.

She hears him getting undressed and then quietly getting into bed. The first thing Ross does is put his arm around her waist so she pretends to be asleep. She doesn't expect herself to want him, but she does. Always feeling sexual and she knows it's because of the drugs but doesn't care anymore, she enjoys it too much.

She feels his erection against her back so makes him aware of her desire by groaning. Then feeling that moment of him entering her from behind she moans more and more. Her desire becomes greater, feeling him getting even harder. They end up in a hot and breathless state lying beside each other, her wanting him again as usual. They don't speak, Carly just looks at him with the lights from outside the window leaving a glow on his face. She kisses him with so much passion. Realising she is addicted to him, as she once again wants to satisfy herself and keep him happy. He turns over to sleep and Carly thinks tomorrow he'll most likely apologise for what happened at that club. She tries to sleep but her mind keeps wandering to Matthew. She ends up dreaming about his caring face, touching it then kissing him on the cheek, wanting him to kiss her back.

CHAPTER 10

Carly is awoken by the alarm on Ross's mobile. He's propped up on one elbow looking down at her with a grin on his face and of course they make love and then he orders breakfast. Ross reminds her that they are leaving today to move to the penthouse. Carly tells him she is excited and *will* get a move on after showering.

Whilst eating, she asks him "What happened last night? I don't want to start an argument with you but you made me feel like a child, why Ross?"

He sighs and says "I really don't want to talk about this Carly, you wouldn't understand, it's all to do with business anyway".

Deciding to keep her mouth shut she shakes her head in disbelief. Then he steals a slice of toast off her plate obviously to try to amuse her.

"Hey that's mine you bastard, give it back" Ross jumps out of bed and Carly chases him around the room. He does make her laugh, sometimes.

Ready to leave the hotel after making sure that she'd packed all of her stuff, Carly sees Matthew waiting. She walks towards him and smiles. He returns the smile, then takes their bags, opens the doors and off they go. Carly sits and watches the city go by and thinks a new life is waiting for her out there in this vast metropolis.

Sorting clothes out and putting them away is not her favourite thing to do but Ross is a clean freak and likes everything in its place so she has to get it done. Carly wonders, with all his money why he doesn't just hire someone to do this sort of boring stuff for him. He must enjoy unpacking his things and hanging them up as she hears him singing while he does.

Later that afternoon they are about to get some lunch before jumping into their new bed, but he gets a call to say he has to go into his office for a couple of hours to sort something out and to sign papers. Carly feels miserable and upset now and makes sure he notices. She sits on one of the chairs, arms folded in front of her and sulks. "I'm *so* not hungry now" telling him in her put-on childlike voice.

She continued, "I was so looking forward to having a whole day with you. You promised me you would show me around the city. Well we can't do that now can we".

Carly feeling pissed off now and showing it, big time. She knew he felt bad about it, his face told it all, while glancing at him several times. He picked up his briefcase, walked over toward her then sat on the arm of the chair and told her "I'm so sorry." Then he kissed her pouting lips.

"But we should still be able to go out its only..." he looks at his watch and then we hear his phone ring again, he answers it. "Yes, I know, I'll be there as soon as I can. I can't help that, it's not my fault" and he hangs up.

He holds her hand and kisses it.

"Carly, I'll be back as soon as I can, I promise"

He then calls Matthew. Poor Matthew, does he have another life?

Ross walks toward the door to leave. Carly doesn't bother to say anything to him, just lets him walk out.

The penthouse has views at each side of the building which means there is the lovely scenery of the garden at the back and at the front Carly can people watch, it's the best of both worlds.

After Ross closes the door behind him, she rises from her chair and walks towards the front to look out of the window. Feeling really down she didn't want to be alone as this was supposed to be a good day where she could find out more about her surroundings before Ross left for London tomorrow. Carly could walk out onto the balcony but she didn't want Ross to see her. Not sure whether he would look up anyway. She waits until she sees Matthew open the car door for him; then wonders how the hell Matthew got here so quickly. Does he live close by? If so Ross *must* be paying for his accommodation as there is no way he could afford to live around these parts. Carly would love to find out more about him.

She waits at the window until the car pulls away then turns to take in her lush but lonely surroundings and then wonder what she should do with herself. Sitting back down in the same chair she was sulking in, she can't help but still feel miserable. This is not like her, she used to enjoy her own company. Carly remembers what Ailish told her, noticing how she had changed and how the depression had set in. Not having had the chance yet to talk to Ross and tell him that she would prefer not to take any more tablets. But she desperately needs help to stop.

Carly misses him so much now and is stuck in this beautiful place with no one to share the pleasure. She's eaten lunch, texted her family to let them know she's alive and living here and sent Ailish the address.

It's now early evening and she is still alone. She's already taken two tablets today so needs sex *so* bad. Wandering into the bedroom deciding to enjoy the king size bed, she undresses and gets underneath the crisp white cotton sheets. She closes her eyes and thinks of Ross with his hands exploring every part of her body. Feeling very aroused, she hears the door opening. She decides to stay put as she wants him so bad now. She hears him walk in and he shouts out. "Carly, I'm back, where are you?"

"Ross, I need you in here now" Carly replies, moaning.

He walks in to watch her groaning and wriggling around now on top of the sheets. He smiles at her.

"Don't dare move" he states, quite commanding.

Carly watches him as she continues pleasing herself. He undresses quickly then enters her immediately. Oh God, she feels that she wants him all of the time now, never leaving her and feeling his erection inside her every minute of every day. Afterward, he leaves her to go to the bathroom; maybe this is her chance to talk to him to tell him she would still want him without the drugs. Ross returns to the bed where they cuddle up to each other.

She feels a bit nervous now, wondering how to start the conversation.

Carly swallows hard, gets a drink of water from the side table and says, "I want to say something, but before you answer I want you to listen first. Okay?"

"Oh no, are you leaving me?" he says looking down at her with a smirk on his face knowing that she wouldn't. Carly plucks up the courage and tells him how she feels.

What happens next was something Carly could never have predicted. The look on his face says it all, but she has no choice but to hear it come out of his mouth.

"I do not want you to stop taking them Carly" he shouts. "They are not harmful so it would be best for both of us if you kept taking them for a while".

Carly feels really scared as she's never seen him behave like *this* before.

This time it is different. "You don't know what it means to me, if you came off them you may think different of me." Carly was confused now so asked "I don't understand how I would feel any different as I do love you, you should realise that, so what is the problem?"

His face changes to the look of a saddened boy. Carly could see he was deciding whether to tell her or not but he did. "I've been married before and she left me." Christ almighty what's coming next.

He continues. "It all happened ten years ago when I was twenty-five". Oh, now he lied to me about being twenty-eight when they met. This means he is…an oldie as far as she's concerned.

"Go on then" Carly says to this older man!

"Her name was…well you don't need to know that. She left me because I was not good enough for her in the bedroom".

Carly felt really shocked, as he's dynamite in that department. She wants to hug him but lets him continue with his story.

"She met someone better who satisfied her needs, so I was thrown to one side like a piece of shit. I was devastated so I looked for something that could enhance my performance." He paused for a minute as Carly watched him quiver.

"It all started in London where I found someone who could help me out, he got me onto the same drug that you are taking. He said it would help me get hard all the time but also it would help me to look and feel good. I think I do," as he looked over his tanned and toned body.

"Before I found this drug I felt drab and sexless. My ex pulled my confidence down, so it changed my life, I found you, didn't I? I wanted you to get that same high from sex as I do."

Carly steps in at this point "I take that as an insult. You're telling me that if I hadn't taken this drug I wouldn't have been good enough for you in bed. Did you not think I was sexy enough when we met?"

She feels like he's some kind of a Jekyll and Hyde.

Feeling very annoyed she tells him. "So, I was your little experiment to find out if it worked on *me*. Who are you right now, Jekyll or Hyde? I know your game. What you don't seem to understand is there's one good fucking reason I do need to get off this drug and that is the depression that's bringing me down." She paused for a breath. "I cannot go on one-minute feeling up, then the next minute I'm right down in the gutter. I feel like I'm a victim of manic depression."

She puts her head in her hands and cries like a baby. He goes to hold and comfort her but she pushes him away in disgust.

So, he says "I know you hate me now but I have to leave tomorrow and I don't want to leave you alone like this. I was thinking that Maria could sometimes come around so you won't feel lonely. I would like to ask her so I wouldn't be worried about you."

Carly stops crying then says to him, "Why should you be worried about me after what you have been putting me through every fucking day taking those drugs. I'm addicted to them and I need some help to get off them but you insist I need to stay acting like a nymphomaniac, which I have become just for your sexual needs. I want to be *me* again."

Stopping as she's on the verge of tears again then says "I also need a normal relationship where we can love each other for what we are and not just for sex all of the time. Do you understand?"

Carly shouts, "And if I want to see Maria I will ask her *myself* if she wants to come up for dinner…or whatever".

Now Ross looks very sad and humiliated, which he deserves but Carly still feels bad for him as she does still love him. Things between them were not the same for the rest of the night. They did the usual, had dinner, he cooked, and watched some TV. He goes to bed as he has to be up early for his flight to London. Carly stays up for quite a while and just sits and thinks through what had been said earlier. Wanting to be in bed with him and make love, as that is what she does. She's his sex robot. Deciding that she will try to get off the drugs while he is away, she will ask Maria if she knows of a doctor in the area that could help her get off a prescription drug; she does not need to know what she's really taking.

When Carly does eventually go to bed, she wants to snuggle into him so bad but doesn't. She tries very hard to keep her hands off his body, instead she masturbates with pleasure.

When she awakes he has gone but she notices one of his letterheads propped up against her bedside lamp. She plumps up her two pillows to sit up to read it...

Dear Carly, I am so sorry about last night but I hope you understand what I said. I do love you and want what is best for you. I do think that your depression may be caused by something other than the drugs, it may be genetic, and does anyone in your family suffer from depression?

Bastard, how could he think that. She goes on reading.

One day we will come off the drugs but for now I think it's for the best. We are happy, aren't we?

Carly is beginning to think that he *is* mad, what she told him last night obviously went right past his stupid head...

I hope you don't get too lonely while I'm in London. I told you to tell Matthew to take you out, I wish you would. Please don't be too mad at me as I would love to come back with you in my arms again. See you in one week. I love you, Ross xxx

She lay for a while just to think and decide what to do before getting out of bed. What she really wants is some thick American style pancakes. She picks up the phone book that Ross left with several important numbers in it and then decides to call Matthew, feeling quite nervous while waiting for him to pick up. He answers in his polite way.

"Oh, Hi Matthew, it's Carly, I was wondering if you could pick me up in about an hour so I could get some breakfast, would that be okay?" He tells her of course it's okay.

She's quite excited about going somewhere different. Quickly rushing around to get showered and dressed, she doesn't want to look overdressed so puts on the usual jeans and T-shirt. Checking out her reflection in the full-length mirror before hearing the knock on the door.

Shouting "Be there in a minute."

She pulls out her favourite lipstick, quickly paints a bit over her full lips, grabs handbag and keys. Opening the door, Matthew is there, patiently waiting.

"Hello Matthew" she says, feeling quite shy.

He greets her in his professional way by calling her Miss O'Neill. Carly smiles at him and tells him (again) to call her Carly. She notices him blushing slightly. They walk to the elevator; he acts like a gentleman as he lets her go in first with no words spoken, until they arrive at the car.

Carly feels like a film star when he's around as he takes care of her like a bodyguard would do. He asks where she would like to go. She asks him if he knows the best place that does American pancakes. He thinks for a few seconds then pulls away from the kerb. Carly wants to talk to him but is lost for words, for once.

It takes almost fifteen minutes to get to the Pancake House as the traffic is quite insane this morning. He turns into a quiet lane and points to where it is. Carly puts her hand on the door handle to get out, but before she does, wonders if Matthew's had the chance to eat anything decent today. He took Ross to the airport early this morning so maybe he hasn't.

Carly feels quite carefree today so asks him with her hand still on the car door, "I was just wondering if you've had any breakfast yet".

Before he had a chance to answer, she quickly said "If you haven't, we could eat here together; I could do with some company".

For a split second Carly could see Matthew was a bit embarrassed and that is not what she wanted to achieve here. He still looked a bit uncomfortable.

He turns his head to face her and carefully says "Well no, I haven't had the chance to yet but I don't think Mr Carmichael would approve of me *eating out* with you Miss O' err sorry, Carly".

Carly feels sorry for him so she says "Matthew, I would like you to join me to have some breakfast. Ross is in London so he won't know".

Now she feels brave so says "So come on, it's on me as *I'm* inviting you" He looks ahead, staring out at a young couple who are laughing and heading to the same cafe.

Then he says "I will then thanks. I'll park the car and I will join you." Carly feels very happy and smiles at him as she gets out of the car.

"See you in a bit then" still smiling at him like they were a couple.

Carly eventually finds a seat near the back of this large buzzing restaurant. She takes the seat facing towards the entrance and pulls the other seat nearer for Matthew, as in this country the custom to share is not frowned upon. She hopes Matthew can find her so keeps an eye on the door, as she glances over the huge menu. Their pancakes come with everything you could ask for so she decides to order one of these. A waitress comes over with a jug of water and one glass, Carly asks her for another glass, telling her she was waiting for someone else. The waitress told her, with an attitude, she would return when the other person arrives. Eh? Do I look like a serial liar?

Almost ten minutes go by before she sees him walk in the door. He has removed his chauffeurs hat. As he gets closer Carly notices he is good looking. Not only can she see more of his face, she can see his lovely thick dark brown hair that matches his long eyelashes. Lifting her hand up to give a little wave. He acknowledges her and walks casually but slightly nervously towards her, looks down, then smiles as he sits down next to her.

"I'm so pleased you brought me here, it's very nice and the smells coming from the kitchen, wow!" Carly tells him.

"Can't wait to eat" she says, looking around and picking up the menu. He looks at the menu and tells her "I got to know this place when Mr Carmichael had a meeting with an American client who seems to know where all the American Pancake Houses are in every city he travels to." Carly laughs and say thank God for American pancake lovers. She couldn't think of anything else to say…felt a bit stupid.

After they have eaten their enormous and very filling pancakes, they sit with coffees, both feeling stuffed.

As Carly sips her hot coffee she tells him, "I'm pleased you decided to have breakfast with me. I would have hated to think you would be sitting waiting for me in the car most likely dreaming of having a good meal."

He kind of laughs at her comment and she thinks (and hopes) he's enjoying her company. She is *so* dying to discover if he is married or not but feels nervous to ask. When she thinks about it she would be a bit disappointed if he was. Carly feels she should just make light conversation with him to start off with.

Placing her cup down she asks "How long have you worked for Ross, Matthew?"

He thinks for a minute and says "Oh it's been about eighteen months now. I worked for him in London for six months and then he told me he would be based mainly here in Berlin. He knew I would be out of work when he came here, so he asked me if I wanted to come with him."

He takes a drink then goes on "I thought well, maybe I could as I don't have anything to keep me in London". He stops to take another drink, and then says, "But he tempted me when he said it would come with a flat with extra money in my pocket. I had to do what the cabbies do in London".

Carly asks quickly, "And what's that?"

He says "Learn where *everything* is."

"Wow, that's cool." Carly thinks now is her chance to ask. She sits back in her chair with her body away from the table saying "So…if you wanted to take your girlfriend *anywhere* in this city you would know how to get there?"

He shakes his head and with a smile says, "No, no, I don't have a girlfriend".

Carly is very surprised with his answer as he is so attractive, but she doesn't want to look *too* pleased.

Thinking for a moment she then asks, "How old *are* you?"

Her stomach flutters slightly.

"I'm only twenty-three, just a young punk I guess."

"Older than me Matthew. I'll be nineteen next month, I'm the young un' here, not you."

Matthew with a blank look thinking that she was a lot older.

They both fiddle with their cups as they finish their coffee. Carly doesn't want to leave yet as she's just starting to enjoy herself so orders more coffee.

"Hope you don't mind me wanting to stay here a bit longer, I'm enjoying your company."

He kind of goes a bit shy on her and fiddles with his hands.

"I've been told to be at your beck and call by Mr Carmichael while he's staying in London."

Carly feels she wants to give him a hug and tell him thanks, but that would be the wrong thing to do.

So instead tells him, "There is one thing I won't do and that's call you early in the mornings, I'm definitely not a morning person. You wouldn't mind showing me around the city this week, would you? I'd really enjoy that." She catches a twinkle in his eye.

"I would be fired if I left you alone to wander around the city, he also told me to keep an eye on you."

Bloody hell what does Ross think I'm going to get up to, does he control my life? Not wanting to make a comment to Matthews's last remark, just sits there and observes him, wanting more than he realises.

Carly's still on the drugs and still has that sexual urge, it's annoying but she can't help what the drug is doing to her. Her problem is she doesn't know how to control it. Is she going to have to go to the ladies all the time to masturbate? She really needs to get with Maria very soon to find that doctor.

They stay drinking coffee for another half hour than Carly tells Matthew she must get back as she has someone to see. They drag themselves up very lazily to leave, hearing their chair legs screeching along the floor and then he takes her home. She tells him before getting out of the car; she may call him tomorrow to arrange to pick her up to visit a couple of museums. He says of course whatever she wants to do; he will always be a call away.

Carly doesn't like the way she feels when the car pulls away. Rushing up to the gates to get back to her lonely surroundings, she closes the door behind her, walks through to the bedroom, throws herself onto the bed and cries.

When eventually pulling herself together, she lies there and wonders why she is crying her heart out. She discovers there are several reasons. One is obvious, getting off the drugs, the others feeling lonely and homesick at this moment and feeling so confused about the way Ross treated her last night. Depression kicking in, she just wants to stay in bed all day and hide from the world. She pulls the sheets over her head and cries again, then falling into a deep sleep, she dreams about Dad. They are walking through the clouds and she's looking down on everyone. She's holding his hand like she did when she was little and felt happy and safe. They see Mam and Ailish at home in Ireland, they both look sad. She asks Dad why they look so unhappy. He says that sometimes life can be like that, but we have to be strong and get through those times. Because our life on this earth is just for a short time, we have to make every second count. He kisses her head and then she wakes up. Missing Dad so much now.

What the hell, why did she have to dream about him? It's made her feel worse in a way but she remembers him telling her that life is too short to waste. So she jumps out of bed and runs a bath, filling it with bubbles and scented oils, feeling she wants to make the most of today. The sun shines in through the bathroom window quite brightly, but decides to light a few smelly candles anyway. Wanting to be presentable for her visit with Maria, she picks up the expensive 14 carat gold razor that belongs to Ross. She certainly doesn't want nicks all over her skin, remembering the days when she bought the supermarket's own brand.

Maria looked so perfect when they met, she's the type to be always groomed top to toe, a younger version of Joan Collins. Carly laughs to herself. She spends almost two hours shaving, trimming, buffing and just relaxing. And the smells of the candles lift her spirits somewhat. Happily skipping out of the bathroom to choose an outfit, Carly hopes Maria's at home. Should she pick up the phone or just chance it and knock on her door? Or, wrap a thick white towel around herself and look to see if she is out in her garden sunning herself. From the balcony Carly can see part of her garden so going out she stretches her neck a bit to see if she is there. Hmm, she doesn't see her but just as she's about to walk back in Maria's wide brimmed hat appears. She looks as if she has a cocktail in her hand. (Carly could do with one herself.) Knowing what to wear now, shorts and a strappy top. She's ready to have a cocktail and loosen up a bit; she needs female company, so this hopefully should be a bit more fun.

Her depression lifts somewhat when she sees Maria, it gives her a chance to talk without looking like she's just about to self harm.

Carly doesn't want her asking too many questions. She takes a basket with sun cream and water and grabs the sunglasses and *her* wide brimmed hat and heads for the sun and the alcohol.

Carly knocks on her garden door, then Maria appears before her looking as stunning as ever. She has on a beautiful strapless bright red swim suit that shows off her amazing curvy body. Her glossy dark hair is tied back and with that large glam' hat placed carefully on top of it, she looks like something out of Hello magazine, and having that holiday smell about her, the smell of the Med' Carly calls it. She looks as relaxed as when they first met which helps Carly with asking questions. Greeting her with interest, she asks her to come in and if she would like one of her cocktails. She tells Carly to take either a sun chair or laze in a lounger; she chooses the chair while Maria pours her a drink from the cooler device sitting on the table. She hasn't asked, as yet, why Carly's decided to come and join her, she's too cool. It seems she takes it all in her stride and is waiting for Carly to speak. She thanks her for the drink and tell her it's just what she needs. She senses Maria watching her as she sips it slowly. Her gut feeling tells her that she's been expecting her company.

They spend the next ten minutes talking about the latest fashions while flicking through several up-market magazines that are on the table. Then she asks Carly about Ross. Is he treating her good enough, with love and respect? She answers with a little bit of restraint, not wanting to give anything away.

"Oh, yes of course we are the perfect couple, I love being with him, he treats me very well."

Maria looks at Carly as if she is waiting for the real reason why she's here. Then asks "How are you finding your first week here Carly, don't you just love this magnificent place?", gesturing with her hands.

"I love it Maria who wouldn't, it's nothing like my family house in Ireland."

"And so, what is your family home like. Do you not miss your home town and your family?" she asks, getting up to pour herself another cocktail and then walks over to refill my glass.

"Well my home town is quaint, not far from Dublin and the house is a lot smaller. I do miss Mam and my sister Ailish but Ross is my life now, so here I am."

She takes a drink and says quickly with, Carly notices, a motherly look "Do you love him?"

Carly hesitates and that is Maria's signal to dig a bit deeper. Carly touches her hair and flicks it back before answering; she's been around too long to know all the signs of pretence.

"Yes of course I do." And that is all she says.

Then there is silence while they take in some sun and have their drinks.

Then it came out. "Maria" Carly said nervously, "Do you know any doctors who could help me to get off a prescription drug. I would have gone to a GP in Ireland but I didn't want my family to know that I've become addicted to them."

Maria puts down her drink then swings her long, tanned legs off her sun lounger and walks over to pull the other sun chair beside Carly. She takes off her sun glasses to look at her more clearly and then asks why she was taking a prescription drug in the first place. Carly tells her she had hurt her back a few years ago so kept taking them. Oh God, the look on her face was of a woman scorned as if she knew what was going on. Carly sits holding her breath waiting for Maria to answer. Getting back up to retrieve her glass, she takes a sip of her drink then asks.

"Carly" she says with concern in her voice "I would like to help you with your problem. But first..." She continues in her beautiful German accent, "Can you tell me what drug you *are* taking, as the doctor I know will need to know the exact details before he can do anything for you. Do you understand?"

Carly feels like she is being interrogated by the Gestapo, thinking now what should I say and do? Will I have to end up telling the truth? So asks "Do you really need to know before I see the doctor Maria?"

Carly looks her straight in the eye and realises that she probably knows she is keeping the truth from her.

"Yes, I do in a way because I want to help you but you don't have to tell me." She stops to take a quick sip of her cocktail, lifts her eyebrows up and says "But if you really want to keep the truth from me, well, that is up to you."

She knows. But how, that's what Carly would like to know.

She swallows her drink in one and asks for another. Maria obliges with such a calm attitude it disturbs Carly as she feels just the opposite. Maria is waiting for her to speak and to tell her the truth.

But surprisingly she speaks again, "I want to let you know that I know Ross very well, much more than he realises. I have a good idea what you are addicted to and it is not taken from a prescription. Am I right?" Carly drinks more of her alcohol and swallows hard. With a huge sigh she answers.

"Yes Maria you are right. I'm sure you know which drug I'm taking and what it's doing to me." Carly gets upset now and tries to hold back her tears but Maria comes to her like her Mam would have done and hugs her. She *does* cry now. Maria holds her until she calms down.

When Carly stops trembling, Maria asks again whether she does truly love Ross. Sitting quietly for a moment, she tells her how he treated her last night, it has made her feel that she's really not sure anymore. And then carries on to let her know about this morning with Matthew.

Maria smiles and comments "He is a lovely young man, just your type" she says, raising her perfectly groomed eyebrows, and then she changes the subject back to what is important.

Then she continues to tell Carly, "The things I know about Ross you would never have thought possible of him but my information is one hundred percent the truth."

"You are a young woman Carly; I think you should know about him before things get worse for you. He is a dangerous man when it comes to women. I don't want you to be that woman anymore as you are too young and naive to be involved."

She then told Carly that whatever she tells her will be in total confidence. She continues to ask more questions. "Have you started getting depressed whilst taking the drugs?" Carly tells her she has and now feels really scared. Then her tears well up again.

"I will try to help you as much as I can but it may take a while. I would suggest you move in with me" Maria says importantly.

Carly is very shocked as this is all happening very quickly. She says with her body shaking, "But he'll be back in a week and wondering why I've moved out. What will I tell him Maria"?

She looks at Carly with serious concern and says, "What I am about to tell you, I don't think you will care so much about what he thinks my love".

Carly is scared to listen to what she has to say, but sits back and listens very carefully.

CHAPTER 11

Maria fills her glass, then tells Carly the story of Ross.

When she met him in his office, thinking right away that he was very good looking and felt rather attracted toward him. As he spent most of his time in London she had to call her contacts to find out more about him. Her reliable *special women* she called them (not knowing who they were yet) went on the prowl to seek out some information to see if he was trustworthy. Maria said she never got involved with men who are found out to be dealing in anything criminal such as drugs. It didn't take long for 'her ladies' to find out that he was involved with very serious drugs.

Carly feels as if she is about to throw up at this point, then asks about these ladies that Maria deals with.

She tells her that she is a high-class Madame and has several ladies on her books throughout Europe.

Oh my God, Carly feels like she's in a dream, knowing now why Maria is so wealthy.

She goes on to tell her that Ross was found out to be dealing in drugs and selling them to mainly pimps that handed them out to their street walkers. On the streets the drug is called *Higher Love* due to the fact (as Carly knows) it gives you the best sexual high you could ever have. A lot of these prostitutes have been known to commit suicide over the past few months due to severe depression. They couldn't get help as if they did, they would have been in really big trouble from the dealers. Carly knows she could be in great danger of going down that road if she doesn't get help fast! When asking Maria if she knew any other background on him, she answered quickly "A lot". Carly asks her if he had been married before as he told her last night that he had. Maria's answer comes back as that it's all lies, he has definitely not been and has no children either. Carly now tells Maria the story he told her.

She throws her head back and laughs in disgust, "The lies he tells most people is just so unbelievable. He tells them that all his wealth comes from his Architectural business, Ha" she says as her head is thrown back again.

"That is utter rubbish." Going on, annoyed, "Also, he is not taking the drugs he sells and obviously now he's giving them out to girlfriends" she said pointing to Carly. She sits with her hands on her chin feeling the more she discovers about him the more depressed she becomes. Needing another drink she helps herself, past being polite.

"So" Maria says, "Do you want to be with him any more after what he is doing to you? Or would you rather live with me so I can try to help?" Carly is so lost for words through all the crap shit lies that she's heard about her now-ex-boyfriend. Eventually coming to her senses, she agrees to stay with Maria.

She starts to think about Matthew and tells Maria that he would be wondering why she's not staying in Ross's place.

"Matthew never needs to know Carly, you just need to tell him to wait outside when you want him to take you anywhere."

Balancing on the edge of her seat, Carly anxiously says, "But when Ross comes home to find me gone I won't be able to see Matthew anymore as he does work for Ross, not me." The thought of never seeing him again is a sense of sadness, she confides in Maria.

"Don't worry, I'll think of something darling, trust me." Carly does trust her as she has now become her friend. They both sit quietly and Carly takes in all of the seriously troublesome things Maria has told her. She wonders why Ross had to put her on the drugs when all the time he was lying. Was he just getting his kicks to experiment his sexual needs on her? She wishes she'd never met him. Fucking hate him, the moronic creep that he is.

Now wanting to get back to being normal and then go back home to her family, she shares all of this with Maria. They embrace and then watch the clouds come over the sun, time to go back in. Carly hears her mention having some lunch, but that makes her want to retch.

Carly tells Maria she will pack all her things together and then will help her with lunch, even though she still couldn't eat.

When entering the penthouse she would have been sharing with Ross, she feels very sad at what her life has now become. She was so excited about her new start here in this city. After finishing packing she wonders whether she should write a note for Ross. She walks to his desk and opens the top drawer, pulls out a notepad and pen. Carly sits down and writes.

Ross, I have left you because I've realised I do not love you anymore, probably never did. Don't try to find me as I will never come back. The drugs you have been forcing down my throat are causing more depression but you should already know that. You never wanted to help. Why Ross, why me? You have made my life a misery. I never want to lay eyes on you again. I hope you never hurt anymore women like you've hurt me. If you do, you should be locked up, permanently. So, fuck you Ross. Carly.

I leave the note on his desk, take one more look around and then grab my bags and leave.

Maria had left her front door ajar knowing Carly wouldn't be long. Giving a small knock she enters then shouts, as Maria is in the kitchen, and asks where she should put her bags. Maria tells her to put them in the second door on the left down the corridor. Her place is more to Carly's taste than what Ross did with his, a woman's touch of course. But none the less Maria has a good eye for very tasteful furniture, it is beautiful.

Carly does as she is told and goes into the bedroom. Wow! Now this *is* a bedroom. She leaves her bags in the room and heads towards the kitchen where she hears Maria chopping something. Maria is dressed in a full-length halter neck dress the same colour as her swimsuit, the gorgeous bright red which shows off her olive skin. Maria asks Carly to sit down as the salad she is putting together will soon be ready. The smell of this salad would make a stuffed pig hungry, it is so good. Maria then apologises, asking Carly if she may want to wash first. Carly, deciding just to wash her hands for now, walks down the corridor to where Maria points and closes the door on one of her very large and also beautifully decorated bathrooms. Carly looks at herself in the vintage style mirror above the sink and sees a young woman who has lost her way. She is so grateful that Maria is here for her.

Going into the kitchen, she places a bowl of the food on the table and then they sit and eat. Maria tells her that the bread is homemade but laughs and points to a bread maker.

"Very easy with one of those." Carly laughs and takes a piece of the delicious smelling crusty loaf full of olives. Thinking that she hated olives, but these are no comparison to the cheap version she used to eat. It is the best salad Carly can honestly say she has ever had. Maria stands up to rinse the plates and then makes coffee. Carly begins to feel a bit more relaxed now. While Maria has her back to Carly, their conversation takes up where they left it.

Carly starts, "You know I can't stay here with you when Ross gets back. I would never go out, I would be too scared." She finishes with the coffee and turns to Carly.

"I know, but I will sort something out for you. I will help you out until we get you off the drugs but we'll talk about that later.""

Carly is worried now, thinking who she is going to live with after staying with Maria?

"Don't worry; I will make sure he never finds out where you are" now changing the subject. "Here, drink some of my delicious Italian coffee, I know you will want more than one cup".

Carly takes the large white cup from her hand and knows already by the smell that she will be having more than one. Maria helps Carly to smile even though she's finding it harder as each day goes by. They drink the coffee and relax. Maria says she has already been in touch with the doctor who will help Carly. She nods her head and wants to cry again. This is happening more often that what she would like. Maria notices but carries on talking.

"Would you like to go out somewhere tonight with me as I would like to have your company?" Carly doesn't know if she should as she doesn't want to cramp Maria's style with her crabby face in the way.

Maria reads Carly's mind and says "We would go somewhere quiet and exclusive". She is looking at Carly waiting, getting slightly impatient, then goes on to tell her "Actually I *do* want you to go as the doctor who will be treating you will be there. I thought it would be better to meet him in a social environment before going to his office".

Carly frowns at her as she's thinking, oh God this is going to be great, seems a bit of an odd way to meet the doctor.

As if reading her mind again Maria says, "I know it

seems strange to you but he is very good and he'll tell you tonight when he will want to see you, just relax darling and we will get some rest before going out" She's right, Carly *does* want to rest on the bed as she feels *so* tired now, so after the coffee they both lie down for a siesta.

Carly wakes up to the sun shining through the crack in the curtains. She turns her head to look at the clock on the table; noticing it's just after five pm. She has told Maria she will go with her tonight but now really doesn't want to. All she wants to do is stay in bed. She can't go on feeling like this anymore, she feels like she's getting worse. Laying back down, wanting sleep to come immediately but hears Maria wandering around. How Carly wishes she could feel so full of life, enjoying her own company most of the time. She wonders if Maria has a boyfriend. She feels selfish as she has never spoken much about her life or asked many questions, it's all been about Carly. Beginning to cry again, she is trying hard not to let Maria hear her sorrowful sounds. But Maria is near the bedroom and pops her head around the door. Christ, she must have bionic ears. She sees Carly crying then walks in.

"Oh Carly, I am *so* sorry you feel like this, that is why I'm trying to help you. But you can't lie here, it will make you feel worse off."

Sitting next to her she says "Please come with me and I will give you one of my great massages I learnt from a special friend a long time ago. Come on, up".

She passes Carly a Kleenex to wipe her eyes and blow her nose. Still feeling like shite, she removes herself from the comfy bed just to please Maria, then plonks herself on one of the large yellow comfy chairs. As soon as she does Maria brings her a drink.

"What is this?" looking at it suspiciously. But she takes a sip anyway. "OOH, I don't care what it is, it's lovely". Maria tells Carly it's her secret recipe and that she would never tell. Having the same drink in her hand she throws it down her throat in one.

She laughs and says, "You should do the same then I'll pour you another one" So Carly does.

"I told you, that is one of the best pick-me-ups I know of." She walks out of the room to get that promised other one. Carly still feeling that she doesn't want to go out tonight.

Maria returns with another drink and pulls up a foot stool next to her. She has a small bag beside her and takes out some foot cream. This, she pours on her hands and starts to rub in Carly's feet. They look at each other and Maria says, "It's your lucky day I don't often do this to many people anymore."

Now is the right time for Carly to ask, "Do you do this to your boyfriend Maria?" She watches her face change to being more subdued. She doesn't speak. Carly has hit a sore point. "I'm so sorry if I've asked you the wrong question, I just think that you are *so* beautiful you could have any man you want."

She answers slowly, "Except the person I wanted, it's a long story. I may tell you later but this is your night my love, so I want you to be as calm and relaxed as possible so you can enjoy having a fabulous dinner on me."

Carly doesn't want to disappoint her so just closes her

eyes to enjoy this wonderful foot massage; the smell of the cream alone sends her into a trance. While relaxing she decides she should go with her tonight. Calling Matthew to pick her up early would be an option.

Two hours later they are both dressed and made-up to perfection. With Maria's help, Carly looks stunning.

"There, I have finished, you look beautiful. Now go into the bathroom, check yourself out and spray some of my perfume on yourself. I would recommend the Chanel Mademoiselle, it will cheer up your senses, it was made for younger women but I love it, give it a try."

"You *are* young Maria."

Maria laughs "If you think forty-two is young".

Carly was shocked. "What! I thought you were about thirty-two, you look so young for your age."

Maria smiles at her then poses with hands on hips. Carly strolls to the bathroom to look at her own reflection and when she does, is pleased at what she *does* see. Looking through the bottles on the vanity she picks up the perfume Maria suggested and sprays some on her neck and wrists, she loves the smell, it does change her mood a bit. Walking back into the living room she sees Maria is on the phone calling a taxi to come to pick them up in five minutes.

When she hangs up, turning to pick up her clutch bag she is aware of Carly seeming curious. "I don't have a driver like Ross because the taxi service I use is for a certain type of person like me, the wealthy. They have a special deal with us as they are paid a lot extra to keep their nose out of everyone's business. They don't go around letting others know where they have taken us. So, it's ideal for me and my business." Just as she stops talking, the door buzzer sounds, she picks up.

"Okay we'll be down in a second", then "Come on Carly, grab your bag and we'll go".

Carly is feeling nervous as they travel in this glamorous large black car, not knowing much about cars guessing it may be a Bentley. She feels like she's going to a film premiere or something like it. It only takes about fifteen minutes to get to the destination as the driver is like Matthew; he knows all the short cuts through the city.

As they get out, they are right in front of the door of the restaurant. When they walk in, the smell makes Carly salivate; it takes her back to Dublin where she used to eat a lot of seafood. The maitre d' greets Maria and takes them to their table in the far corner tucked into an alcove. Carly sees a slim quite good looking bespectacled older man stand up to greet them at the table for three. He puts out his hand to shake hers and tells Carly his name is Peter Kircher. She likes him immediately; he has honest grey eyes and is dressed immaculately in casual but smart expensive looking clothes.

Their conversation is the normal small talk at first, him telling them they look beautiful and them complimenting him. Carly can tell he is weighing her up which is what she expected. There is one thing she could never usually hide until tonight, the dark shadows under her eyes due to the drugs, but Maria has done a great job of covering them up with her expert hand and the best make-up on the market. But Carly is sure the doctor knows better. If he is the drug expert that Maria says he is, he will see right through that.

The meal is ordered and Carly actually eats a lot of it, much to her surprise. She devours the shrimp. They drink more wine after the meal and then there's silence for a moment.

Peter turns his body more her way and asks."Would you come to my clinic in the morning around eleven? We will have a lengthy talk and I will take some blood which I will test within the hour of taking it. I want to help you Carly and I am the only doctor who has the treatment to do that. I have found that there is only one more doctor who uses the same procedure as me and he is in America. So, you are in the right place for now. My aim is to have them out of your system within the next month. I will show you in the morning what I will do".

Carly had the most terrifying look on her face but both he and Maria put their hand on her arm to calm her.

"Don't be scared Carly "he said quietly and calmly "I am known to be the gentlest doctor when it comes to needles. You will find out in the morning."

Carly breathes out with a huge sigh. "Oh, and take this." He hands her a small white pill. "Take it before you go to bed, it will help you sleep".

Carly thanks him and places it in her bag. She can't wait to go to bed and to get tonight over with. It has been an interesting night but wanting tomorrow to be here as soon as possible, even though she's scared shitless. Maria senses that Carly is ready to leave so makes her excuses to her friend.

When they get back, Carly wants to talk, realising that she is very nervous thinking of the outcome of tomorrow. Walking into the kitchen where Maria is making herbal tea, asking her if she would like a cup, Carly feels slightly nauseous but nods in response.

Maria carries the tea on a tray into the sitting room where she places it onto the table next to the couch.

"I'm a bit worried about going to the clinic tomorrow" she states. "Come and sit beside me" Maria says as she pats on the seat next to her. Carly walks over and snuggles up to her as if she's her Mother.

"Would you tell me the story now about who that special person was in your life?"

Maria looks at her, feeling a bit uncomfortable about bringing up the past but she did say she would tell her. Maria takes a deep breath in and tells her the story.

"I met a man twenty-five years ago who I thought was my life partner. We met in a quiet country pub in Oxfordshire where I was on holiday with my parents, they loved the English countryside. He was from London and very good looking. He came over to our table and asked if he could buy a round of drinks. My Dad, being Italian was a bit shocked as that isn't' the way a man would try to get a girls attention when she is with her parents. But he had the gift of the gab as the British would say and my parents took to him. He acted very polite and well mannered so we chatted with him for a while. Two nights later we met again in the same place. I fell in love with him just like that." Clicking her fingers she continues.

"I asked Dad if we could invite him to our home here

in Germany and he agreed which took me by surprise. Six months later we were married." Carly is now in a trance, as she listens.

"Our life began in Oxford as he wanted to finish his degree so my parents were a bit sad about that. We rented an apartment near to the university. But he became very protective of me and his jealousy turned scary as I learnt not to look at other men as he would accuse me of wanting them and not him. I told him that he was being ridiculous so when we got home he hit me and then it got worse. I ended up one day being covered in bruises and that is when I ran home, back to my parents."

She stops to take a drink and then inhales deeply.

"My Dad cried when he saw my body and my Mother told me that their hearts were broken and that I have to come home. But I loved him so I gave him one more chance. Dad told me that if he harmed me again he would kill him. They begged me not to go back to him but I did. Big mistake, I should have stayed where I was."

Maria stands up to get herself a proper drink, arranges her body to get comfy again and continues.

"Things got worse when he threatened me with a sword he had hidden in a cupboard. He beat me instead of killing me, for no reason at all, I was so scared. I realised then he was a bit mad, maybe schizophrenic. The next morning before he left he locked me in the apartment and so I called Dad, I had nobody else. My parents got on the first plane out and got to me as quickly as they possibly could."

Maria stops again and takes another long drink. Carly

sighs and asks if she could have a proper drink now. Maria nods and then Carly helps herself. The story goes on.

"When they did arrive, Dad broke the door down, he is a strong man. I was in a state when they arrived. I couldn't stop crying. I knew my Mother was very worried."

She now stood up to use the bathroom, her body lightly shaking. Carly is in a state of shock as she's never heard a story like it. It is *so* keeping her mind off tomorrow. Maria walks back in to get herself another drink. And she sits back down. "Hope I'm not boring you."

Carly says "Not at all Maria but if…"

"No, I'm fine" she then continues.

"My Mother and I were very concerned when we went to book in at the hotel without Dad. But Mother told me not to worry so much even though she looked as if someone had just died."

Maria then stops and looks at me. "Oh Carly I am so sorry, you should be in bed as you have to be up earlier".

"No, It's alright I'm not tired yet anyway." So, Maria tells her "Carly it gets a bit upsetting I don't want to give you nightmares."

"I'm fine Maria, carry on."

How could she not. "Okay I'll go on then."

A small pause then, "Dad is a very stubborn Italian man who gets his own way when he knows he is right. He said he would call us when he had an idea about the time he would be at the hotel. He also told us he would wait in the apartment until my husband came home. That is when my Mother broke down; she knew what he was capable of when someone upset him.""

Maria looking very sad now, takes another deep breath in. "Carly, not to go into any detail…my father killed him." She stops herself, then "He killed my ex".

Carly immediately puts her hand up to her mouth as she pulls in a short intake of breath.

"He said it was in self defence. He called the police and told them what had happened but he was arrested until they had found all the evidence. Dad felt he had done his duty by getting rid of that cowardly scum, *vigliacco schifoso* as he preferred to call him. We thought he would spend a very long time in prison but he got out after five years due to the evidence of what they found. It was either him or N, I will call him. It broke my Mother's heart while he was put away. She was no good without him by her side; she ended up dying of a broken heart. It seemed that way anyhow. It was all the stress that took her away. That was the reason Dad went back to live in his home country, Italy. I couldn't go near another man, I never trusted another one again. I went on to meet a woman a few years later who was my soul mate. She was beautiful and the time I spent with her was the best time of my life."

Getting upset, she grabs a tissue from the box on the table. Carly puts her arm around her and kisses her cheek. She thought that would be the end of this horrific story but Maria wanted to tell her what happened.

"My lovely Angela killed herself due to an accidental overdose of a legal drug. My life turned around after that. I met more women who had had a similar experience as mine and who had also gone off men. So, they felt that by being a call girl, they were using the men just for their bodies, and so I started my business dealing with only *high-class* call girls. I have twenty girls in each country in Europe and they are the most beautiful women inside and out you could ever want to know."

Carly takes her hand and snuggles into her body again.

She looks up at her and tells her "Maria you are a very brave woman and I love you."

They embrace. Now looking at Carly.

"Carly, I love you too. I want to help you as much as I can. Now off you go to bed and take the pill Peter gave you, okay?"

"Yes Mother!"

She laughs and says, "Goodnight, I will see you in the morning."

CHAPTER 12

They arrive at the clinic. Maria is so supportive, Carly couldn't have done this without her, she needs her badly. Peter comes out of his office greeting them with his kindness and then sends Maria into a very comfortable room across the hallway, before taking the very anxious Carly into his office.

When walking in she notices some strange looking equipment lying on a table. Peter asks her to sit. She does while still shaking. He calms her by asking if she would like a glass of water. She nods. He gives her a few minutes to relax then asks her if she is ready for him to take the blood samples. After he does, he takes the sample into the room next door where someone will test them.

Peter talks to Carly about the contraption on one of the counter tops, taking it in his hand to explain how it works. She listens very carefully as he tells her. The moderately thin tube will be placed into her arm and will constantly put a substance into her body that will gradually help the drug weaken and then hopefully she will not want to take it again.

He then tells her that this could take more than a month, it all depends on the person and how long that person has been taking it. He went on to say that he would do it here and Carly would only have to be sedated. The only thing to do now is to find out the results from the blood tests. She feels more relaxed now. Peter excuses himself as he walks out of the room. She feels nauseous thinking not eating much this morning hasn't really helped.

Carly waits another ten minutes, then he walks in to ask if she would like anything to eat or drink as the tests aren't ready as yet. He tells her that it would probably be a good idea if she joins Maria in the more comfortable room to have their refreshments together. Carly agrees and so Maria and her enjoy coffee and pastries. As she waits with her friend, Carly can't ever imagine being without her in her life now as she has been like a second Mother to her. She thinks about Mam and Ailish now, realising that she hasn't been in touch with them for a while with all this mess going on. It is hard to remember one day from the other at times. Mentioning this to Maria who tells her she must call them as soon as they have finished here. Carly confirms she will do that, feeling a lot more confident now about getting better. They wait another thirty minutes and then Peter walks in to ask her to come back into his office. She doesn't like the look on his face, he looks quite pale. She does as he asks, sitting in the same chair as before.

He hesitates and then says, slightly nervously, "Carly, the blood tests have taken a bit longer than I expected as there was something that came up that I wanted to double check." He looks down at his hands and then looks her straight in the eye.

"The test has told me that you are pregnant, did..."

Carly could not hear the rest of what he was telling her as she must have gone into a state of shock. Her head starts to swirl around then she could feel her body slump toward the floor.

The next thing she knows she is lying on a bed with Maria by her side, with a strange lady sitting in the other chair who Carly presumes is a nurse. She turns her head toward Maria and takes her hand.

"Oh Carly, Peter has told me the news."

Her face tells Carly that this is not the usual *congratulations you're going to be a mother* look. The nurse gets up off her chair then checks her pulse and blood pressure. She looks at Carly and says she will be back with the doctor. As soon as she leaves she's almost screaming with distress.

"Maria I'm really scared now and how I got pregnant I don't know as I'm taking the Pill."

Maria's face just drops as if she already knew the answer. Carly wants to hide away and never come back. It feels like hours not minutes before Peter comes into the room. Carly watches him walk toward her with a calm but solemn look about him.

"Hello Carly, how are you feeling now?" She didn't know how she *did* feel.

She said "I really want to know what I am supposed to do now." while shrugging her shoulders. He says "I have to let you know..." Then he looks at Maria. Carly quickly says to him, "I want Maria to know everything you tell me so I want her to stay with me."

He sighs and then pulls up a chair. He then starts to tell Carly what she was not looking forward to.

"Well to start with, the pregnancy means that you can't go ahead with the treatment. If you have it terminated we could go ahead and still do it, which means you may have a chance" He pours himself a glass of water and continues. "The thing is, the drug you are taking is not good for a foetus which in the end could cause a miscarriage, but I have seen a baby born with this drug in its system..." He hesitates once again "A lot of times I've seen this drug cause a baby to be severely deformed. That is the chance you take if you want to try and have the baby."

Carly has to tell him, "I've been pregnant before while taking this drug, now I know why I had a terrible time with the miscarriage. But I'm on the Pill. I don't understand *how* I got pregnant?"

He tells her that the drug stops the Pill from working. She hates Ross even more now.

She's afraid and Maria sees that. Carly cries out loud and can't stop; she's shaking like a tree in the wind.

After trying to come to terms with what she has heard, Peter Kircher advises Carly that she should have the foetus terminated as it would be in her best interest. In the same breath he tells her to go with Maria to have a good meal and a decent night's sleep. He says he wants Carly to stay here first until she has calmed down and gives her some sleeping pills to get her through one week. At the end of that time she will have to decide what she is going to do. She pulls a forced smile, he moves towards the door to leave the room. Maria stands up to leave with him telling Carly she'll be right back. Maria can be heard crying as soon as she closes the door.

Carly lays here in this room thinking how depressed she feels. Looking around at the strange unfamiliar surroundings, thinking now about Mam and the way she and Dad brought us up to believe in life over abortion, and wondering what the hell she is going to do now. If she had one wish right now she would be lying in her bed at home in Ireland waking up from this nightmare.

Carly has one week to decide on her destiny which seems to her like she has only one week to live and cram in everything like a bucket list. She needs to write her feelings down to help herself when she feels at her worst, so is going to go shopping today on her own, not wanting to burden Maria with her moods. She wants to buy a journal, a large one.

Maria has just told Carly that she has to meet someone this morning and take them out to lunch. Being very concerned that she will not be able to cope on her own, Carly tells her she would rather be alone today to get her head around everything that is happening to her. Before Maria leaves she wants to be sure Carly calls her in case of any difficulties.

When Maria eventually walks out of the door Carly runs to the bathroom to vomit. She knew this was coming with feeling nauseous earlier. She really does not need a reminder of what is happening to her body but has to deal with what has happened to her. She takes her drug now knowing she won't throw it back up. Damn drugs, she hates them so much the way they make her feel, destroying her mind but still needing them so bad.

Whilst taking a shower, Carly's mind wanders to Matthew. She closes her eyes as her hands wander over her body as she washes, imagining it is him that is caressing her nipples. Leaning against the shower wall with her legs apart to satisfy herself as she masturbates. Wishing she was with him for real which makes her think maybe she should call him. She's sure he won't be doing too much as his boss is not here. Also, it will give her the chance to be with him before Ross *does* get back from London. And then Carly thinks about her erratic moods, she doesn't want to be a burden on him either.

Sinking into one of her bad ones now she tries to find something to wear that doesn't stand out so she can blend into the crowds. Can't find much, as when she bought these bright clothes she wasn't at this stage of depression. She finds a pair of semi boring looking jeans and a plain black T-shirt, they will do. She leaves her blonde hair flowing around her shoulders as she can't be bothered to style it. As far as make-up is concerned a bit of lip gloss is all she wants. She thinks, I don't deserve to look stunning any more as I chose to take the drugs in the first place. Carly is now facing the terrible consequences of losing another baby or possibly even herself.

Trying to call Matthew but still waiting for him to pick up. Just as she is going to hang up he answers.

"Hello, Matthew speaking." Carly swallows hard. "Oh, eh, hi Matthew it's Carly I was just about to hang up."

"Sorry I've just got back from getting the car serviced. Ross wanted it done while he's in London. Do you need to go somewhere?" Carly answers, her hands trembling.

"Well if you're not busy I would like to go out to do some shopping for some books. Would that be okay?" asking him nervously as if they were going on a date.

"Do you want me to come and get you now?" he asks with his lovely calming voice.

"Yes please, I will see you at the front of the building."

"See you in a bit then." They both hang up.

Carly realises how much she's missed him. Picking up her expensive leather shopping bag, it makes her think that she wouldn't really care if this bag was an old canvas thing that she'd had for years. As the most important thing to her now is not wealth but having herself a normal life.

While walking into the elevator she thinks Oh my God, what would I have done if I hadn't received that inheritance from Dad. That would be it, no shopping trip. Mam said that he wanted Carly and Ailish to have ten thousand pounds put into their accounts, if she didn't have that she would be totally screwed. (She was supposed to get it when she was 21 but circumstances changed that idea.)

She is getting a new feeling of excitement thinking about seeing Matthew, but how long her good mood will last she doesn't know. It's a terrible feeling trying to get through the day wondering how she can cope with how her life is right now.

She walks outside and sees the sun is shining and it's quite warm which helps her to smile. She only waits about two minutes before seeing the car coming towards her in the distance. Suddenly a feeling of regret hits her. She feels guilt and anger and her mind's getting confused. "Oh God I don't want to get in the car and feel like this. Am I getting a panic attack? I don't know, my mind is spinning, I'm sweating, and I need to calm down." She quickly opens her bag and takes out a small bottle of liquid that Peter gave her at the clinic in case she felt like this. She puts it to her lips and swallows a few drops, hoping it will work before she sweats to death and has to change her clothes. She sees him getting closer, but God is on her side, a large fluffy cloud covers the sun, phew, she can cool down somewhat now. Matthew now pulls up next to her then helps her into the car as usual. Carly tries to act as if nothing happened but can tell he notices, as she's sure her face looks flushed. She's feeling calmer now but when she got in and settled herself he speaks. "How are you Carly? It is really nice to see you." She fans herself with her hands then he turns on the Air Con.

"Oh, thanks Matthew, quite warm today I should have dressed for the summer not autumn, my own fault." Then makes a sound like a fake laugh.

Carly eventually says, "Oh sorry, the answer to your question you asked me, I'm, eh, fine I suppose" She hates lying to him. He probably thinks she's missing Ross.

"It is nice to see you too" she tells him, at least she's not lying to him now.

Matthew drives Carly to the shopping area then tells

her to call him anytime that she wants to be picked up. She wants to ask him to come with her to help choose the perfect journal to write down her sorrows. But of course, she doesn't. Getting out of the car she feels really sad.

He always seems to pick up on her moods as he says "Carly?" She turns to him.

"If you need me, just call, no matter when okay?" Carly nods, and then closes the car door. She watches him pull away much to her dismay.

Walking slowly, she takes in the nice shops that she passes with their windows full of summer clothes, then turning a corner she sees gift shops with lots of touristy items for them to take home to their families. Carly thinks of hers and knows she should call Ailish. She doesn't want to think about that right now and to worry them; she'll do it when she gets back. She turns another corner and sees some books and card shops. Staring in the windows first as there are quite a few dotted here and there.

This street is not as crowded as the other busy and sometimes noisy walkways, which is better for her; Carly doesn't feel quite as overwhelmed as she does with all those people around. She walks into a nice quiet shop which is a cross between Waterstones and the village library in her home town in Ireland. It has two sides to it, one is modern with a small cafe and the other side is quite quaint and old fashioned which seems to cater for all sorts of different types of people. Carly loves the look of it; it draws her in like an old friend. She browses the shelves looking for that perfect book before spotting the area where the journals and diaries are. She looks at one and picks it up, no not for her and then notices a journal that looks really lovely. Pulling it off the shelf she knows straight away that she wants it. It is covered in black velvet with a small silver threaded oak tree on the front with a white dove and a white angel in each top corner. She opens it up and it tells her who made it. It reads in the top inside cover that this book was made by "The Peacemakers" who are a group of ladies who have lost their children either through war, drugs or crime. It also states that the funds go to the charities who deal with these causes. This book is perfect; she pays for it and puts it securely in her bag. When she turns around Carly notices where the cafe is as she sees a sign pointing towards a set of stairs into a basement. Deciding to go down the steps to have a look, she feels like an excited child exploring an old-fashioned toy shop.

This unexpected quite large bright space is just the place for her. She sees small tables for two in the four corners. It's not very busy so Carly decides to have a peaceful cup of coffee.

Taking a seat, she arranges herself to a position where she feels more comfortable. The waitress walks over. She orders coffee and a pastry. It is so nice to sit here where no one can bother her and where she can sit quietly and go over her thoughts very seriously. After eating the delicious strudel, she wipes off her hands, retrieves her pen and writes down her thoughts in her new precious journal.

This is the journal of Carly O'Neill.
TUESDAY AUGUST 25TH 2015.

DAY ONE *I sit in this lovely cafe which is downstairs in the bookstore where I bought this lovely book, in this shopping district of Berlin, just off the main street, (Matthew said it is Kurfurstendamm) thinking about my future. I want a normal life again and I want to look forward to my future but the way things are going in my life I may well not have a future. I would never tell my family that I am feeling the way I do. I have to decide soon whether to get the treatment for my drug addiction which will kill my child as I would have to terminate my pregnancy or, not get the treatment and take the small chance of having my child. But what good would that do as I would still be a drug addict. I think I could be looking at this through rose coloured glasses because what Peter my doctor told me, doesn't give me one hundred percent chance either way. I am scared. Being alone at this moment surrounded by strangers is comforting in one way as I need ME time but in the other it is scary. I need the company of others I can trust like Maria. She is my second Mammy. Ross has let me down big time. He lied and cheated and used me as his experiment for his own sexual desires. I hate him with a passion. He should be jailed but I am not going to get involved with his illegal business. Thank God Maria let me know what he has done to me and the kind of person he is.*

I want to be friends with Matthew. He is a lovely man who I find is very kind and honest. I wish it was him who I met and had fallen in love with, that would have been very easy. I miss him when I am not with him which I now know is a different feeling I had with Ross. Ross is or I should say was my sexual partner thanks to the drugs. I still desire his body, but when and if I get off the drugs that feeling will hopefully end.

The cafe is filling up a bit more now I will relax for a while and then I might just walk around to find a museum or something that might interest me. I might call Matthew later to ask if he would have some lunch with me as he is on his own too. But then again do I want him to get involved with me, as I'm not the woman he should be getting involved with. I need to think that one over. I've already thought, I would not let him get involved with me sexually as I just want him as my friend. Oh god, who am I kidding.

Carly lazily steps into the sunshine, wondering where to go now to fill in her day. She could find a tourist information centre so she can get to know more about this city.

Wandering aimlessly in this heat with her jeans on is making her feel truly shitty. Her crotch feels like a sweaty arm pit. She needs to buy something cooler to wear before she passes out. She walked passed a few clothes shops earlier so heads back that way. Feeling lonely now, she walks through these crowds of people, wishing Ailish and Mam were here so they could chat and have some laughs. Why does she have to be here, it's not her home?

Carly stops to walk into the nearest shaded doorway to calm herself and try to control her breathing. She puts her head down and her hands on her knees thinking that she may pass out very soon. But she concentrates on her breathing to overcome this awful experience that she was told could happen quite often when she's not expecting it. She hates herself right now. Wanting to be someone else and forget her real self. But at this moment she wants to take off her fuckin' hot jeans so she can cool down. Going in to the nearest clothes shop to buy herself a skirt was one of her better ideas. Thank God she can now be at peace with herself for a while, instead of trying to pull her panties out of her sweaty vagina.

Carly eventually comes across the shop full of tourists and glossy leaflets. Opening the door she feels the cool air hit her. She browses the shelves and looks for some places that take her fancy. She finds it surprisingly calm in here; it's not a bit of the hustle and bustle that she thought it would be. Picking up a leaflet she then sees him or at least she thinks it's him. She walks nearer and taps him on the shoulder.

"Matthew what are you doing in here?"

He blushes and says "I thought you might turn up in here eventually so I had a coffee..." he says to her pointing at the cafe, "So I waited as I didn't want you to get lost, remember Ross told me to look after you so..."

Then she thought, of course, he doesn't know does he. Matthew went on to say he would take Carly somewhere to visit. (Up to her though.) She doesn't want to be alone anymore and the panic attacks scare her.

"Matthew you are so nice, I would love to have your company especially when you have sat here waiting for me to turn up. But what if I hadn't come in here though you would have been still waiting drinking coffee 'til it come out of yer ears." He laughs and Carly smiles at him. She is so pleased he has turned up, she needs him today.

Wanting to go somewhere special before lunch she tells him she would love to go the Aquarium as it's not too far to walk. Also, it's becoming a stifling heatwave outside, perfect day to spend the day indoors. (She would rather be spending the day in bed with Matthew but that is *her* secret.)

Matthew offers his arm to her as the streets are getting busier, he vows he won't lose her as he likes his job too much.

Eventually they get to the Aquarium but she feels a bit like wanting to throw up, wondering if it's because of her pregnancy. As soon as they pay the entrance fee she wants to find the nearest toilet. She must look like shite as Matthew has this *Oh God what am I going to do with her*, written all over his face.

Carly throws up just after she goes in the toilet and locks the door. When she finishes she cleans herself up as having vomit in her hair is not a good look. As soon as Matthew sees her walking out, his demeanour changes to calmness.

The time they spend there, almost two hours, has bonded a good friendship between them. Carly knows Matthew feels the same. It is so reassuring to have him to rely on.

Her stomach starts to grumble.

"Good God I'm starvin', do you know somewhere nice to eat that's not too far to walk?" Matthew suggests a nearby restaurant which he thinks Carly would like a lot.

He was right, She loves the place as soon as they walk in. It is on the tenth floor of a building which houses a hotel. She has never seen anything like it. The views are breathtaking; they can see the city from this exciting high point through the vast number of windows. There is a mass of green trees through some windows and tops of buildings through the others. Matthew asks for a table at the far end which is a bit quieter. Carly has a craving for *anything* so when they sit down and pick up the menu she has already decided to have three courses, which means more time to spend with her friend. They order their food, then just look at each other.

Holding his hand she quickly tells him before he mistakes the move for passion. "Thanks for bringing me here, I love it. You're a good friend Matthew, I am so glad we found each other."

He smiles and tells her "I feel the same too", he states with wanting written all over his face.

She really and truly does want more than friendship too but this is the wrong time.

Wiping her face after eating the first two courses, they have talked about nothing much, just taking the piss out of some of the people who have walked in. Some with strange short pants looking like they've shrunk in the wash and others who Matthew thought are weird, the women who carry very large handbags that look like they are carrying suitcases. Especially when one woman in question was only about four foot nothing!

Dessert is now served and it looks wonderful. They demolish it in a couple of minutes. Carly holds her stomach, feeling over stuffed. They relax with cold drinks and now she wants to tell Matthew about her life, as they have had a good time getting to know that they are in sync with each other. She feels very nervous and as always, he senses her mood.

"Well, what now, you may as well tell me."

She gives him her best smile and in between the waitress coming and going to clean their dishes away, she begins, "I have a lot to tell you and I really do not know where to start".

"At the beginning Carly."

"Ha ha funny, yes, I know." She breathes in very deeply then says "I have left Ross and I'm living with Maria, you know who Maria is?"

He says, "Christ what the hell, yes I know who she is but why have you left him?"

Carly tells Matthew the whole story. He is silent for a while. Then he tells her quietly "I must tell Ross I'll be resigning."

He sighs and says, "There's one only problem, I have nowhere to live. But who wants to work for a criminal, I don't. But never mind about me what are you going to do Carly. You know I'll be there for you any time you want."

She had thought about something before trying to sleep at nights so tells him.

"What I *would* like to do…" She looks down at her hands as she's not sure how this will turn out.

"Well, you could find another job here in the city and we could share an apartment. I can't stay with Maria with Ross living in the same building. We could just go for a six-month lease while I am being treated but if..."

He puts his hand out to stop her.

"Hold on a minute do you realise how much apartments are in this city. I could never afford it Carly." He now looks worried so Carly carries on with her idea.

"I have enough money in my account to pay six months' rent up front so that wouldn't be a problem, what do you say?"

Just as Carly was about to hear his answer, her mobile phone starts to ring. She quickly pulls it out of her bag looking to see who it is, expecting it to be Maria.

With a shocked look she whispers, "It's Ross" and answers it, "Hello Ross."

He tells her that he will be gone another week maybe two. She smiles, looking at Matthew while she tells Ross she's okay, as obviously she doesn't want him to know anything. Hanging up she sighs with relief and immediately deletes his number.

Telling Matthew, the good news she says "That will give us time to look for a place and to rid myself of that man. He will never know where to find me, thank God."

She immediately removes his number from her speed dial.

They sadly leave this one of a kind place, with a satisfied stomach and vow to come back soon.

CHAPTER 13

Lying on her bed after showering, Carly thinks of the good day she's had with Matthew. Maria has not returned from her lunch meeting yet so she stretches over to the bedside cabinet and pulls out her journal to write;

Back at Marias after my wonderful day spent with Matthew. We went to the Aquarium and had a good two hours there. We also had lunch at a great restaurant which overlooks the city as it's on the tenth floor. I am in love with him but it makes me sad as I can't get involved. I have told him everything that is going on with the drugs and my pregnancy and he still wants to be with me, that is being more than a friend. He knows I could get worse and have severe bouts of depression, but he wants to help. I cannot wait to look for a place to share with him, just hope it will work out for us. I will see him tomorrow as we are going to an estate agent. I hear the door opening now, Maria is home I have a lot to tell her.

She jumps off the bed and walks into the living room.
   "Hi Maria, have you had a good day. I have."

Carly grins at her, feeling as if nothing is wrong.

"Well Carly, you look different, glowing and happy like you should. Tell me all about your day as you don't need to know about mine" Maria says with a turn down mouth.

Carly sits in her bathrobe feeling more content than she has in a long time. Maria takes of her jacket and walks into the kitchen to pour a drink. "Would you like one?" asking with a large bottle in her hand. Carly frowns at her.

"It's only water silly" she tells her.

Carly takes a glass. "I have something to tell you" she says excitedly.

"I can see that, I am waiting patiently" Maria says, sitting at the kitchen table.

Carly pulls up a chair opposite and talks of her plans with Matthew. Maria smiles as Carly talks. Maria tells her that they don't need to look for a place to live as she owns a few apartments around the city. "And I have a 2-bed ground floor that is available."

"Oh Maria, that is just amazingly good news I can't wait to see it and we could move in together quite soon too, yer a great friend to me" Then Carly puts her arms around her neck to let her know how grateful she is. But Maria reminds her that she will have to decide soon.

The expression on Carly's face changes when she says "I am sorry Carly, but the longer you take to decide, the worse it will get and you know that, don't you?"

Carly feels downhearted. It's not her fault but she is right, she does need to decide. They are silent for a while. Then when Carly moves to get a tissue from the counter top to wipe her tears away, she feels the wetness between her legs and then…she is overcome with horrendous pain, looking at Maria, eyes wide and in a state of disbelief. She runs to the bathroom and sits on the toilet screaming. Maria runs in after her with her phone to her ear calling for an ambulance.

After passing out with the pain, then coming round again, Carly looks around and sees doctors. She now sees Maria, who is crying. Carly puts out her hand to her and she takes it. "Carly, Oh Carly they will take care of you my love. Try to relax, I won't leave you".

Her head spinning, Carly knows this is worse than what she's experienced before.

Woken by a nurse hovering around her, checking her pulse and the drip that is in her arm, she doesn't see Maria, presuming she must have been told to leave. Carly wants to know what has happened to her so opens her mouth with a groan as she still feels pain, but nothing is released from her voice box.

"I shall get the doctor to come and see you" the nurse tells her in her broken English.

As she leaves Carly tries to move around to get a bit more comfortable but she hurts too much.

She starts to drift off to sleep but then the doctor walks in causing her to stir. He sits on the chair at the side of the bed and seems quite confident.

"Carly, do you have any family living here?" She tells him she doesn't but that Maria is a good friend. He carries on. "What happened is that a small part of your womb ruptured, obviously you lost the child but…" Carly feels really worried now. "We couldn't save the ovaries as they were damaged which means you will never be able to have your own children, I'm so sorry."

He's sorry why is he sorry? It's Ross who should be sorry. He is the one who damaged her life. She bursts into tears and can't stop shaking as she's totally devastated.

The doctor eventually leaves and minutes later Maria walks back into the room. They embrace and cry together. When Carly pulls herself together she looks into Maria's sad tearful eyes and asks.

"What am I going to do now?"

Looking at her sympathetically she answers. "You are going to rest, that is what you need to do," as she gently strokes Carly's hair and then says, "Do you know how close to death you were? Obviously not, but you've been very lucky."

Carly quietly says, "I wish I had just gone, I have no life now."

"Do not say that, of course you do. Just think about what you *do* have Carly. Your family in Ireland for one thing and you will always have my friendship and I have let Matthew know what has happened to you. He said he would be here as soon as he can. I will look after you until you're well enough to go back to your *well*-deserved life. So, I don't want to hear anymore about you having *no* life, as you *do*."

She goes on to tell Carly that the doctor had said she should be up and about in month. As Carly is young she will heal much quicker. As Maria is talking Carly watches Matthew walk in. He looks very sad and worried; she did not want to do this to him of all people. Maria turns around to him as she sees my eyes wander to the doorway.

"Hello." Then turning to Carly, "I will see you later," kisses her cheek, then she walks away.

Matthew sits down and looks so distraught. Carly wants to tell him she'll be okay but would be lying.

"You were fine earlier today, what happened?" he says wiping his forehead.

Carly tells him what happened to her and sees a tear roll down his cheek.

Then Matthew speaks, "Don't you think you should let your family know?"

Carly answers immediately, "No I don't want them to know, they don't even know that I am, was, pregnant. So, no, don't want to worry them. I'll text Ailish when I get out of here just to let her know that everything is fine." Matthew looks at her with his head to one side with eyebrows raised.

"What?" she asks.

"Nothing Carly, I just thought you might want to let them know that's all"

"Well I don't. The doctors saved me so there is no reason to tell them."

She feels very tired and he realises that she should be left to sleep. "I will call in to see you tomorrow; you need to rest, okay?"

He takes her hand to kiss, then kisses her forehead. Then he leaves. Maria enters the room to tell her the same. Carly is now left alone to brood and cry a lot, until she falls asleep.

CHAPTER 14

TUESDAY SEPTEMBER 1ST 2015 *A lot has happened since I wrote. I have lost another child and nearly died. I have been out of hospital for one whole day now and I am living with Maria again and she is so good to me. I was told by the doctor that I can't have babies now as they had to take away my destroyed ovaries. That is what the drug I take does to women who are stupid enough to take it in the first place. Me, I take it, so I am stupid, very stupid. I want to go out on my own and I do not want to be a burden on anyone. I am supposed to rest for another week but I don't care about myself anymore so I will go out if I want to. I lay here on my bed and look at magazines, tons of them that Maria gets delivered for me or I just mope. I don't want to eat much even though Maria tries to tempt me with her home cooked meals. I never want to hurt her feelings so I try to eat some. She lets Matthew come and chat with me. I don't want to hurt him either but I am not interested I don't listen much anymore. I lay and think about Mam and Ailish and wish I was well enough to go back home, so I could get away from this city of bad memories. Maria has told me that Peter, the drug doctor, wants to see me to help me get better.*

He is almost sure that I could have the treatment now. I don't want to go back there, not yet anyway. I just want to be alone. If he can't understand that then he's not worth going to at all. I will do as I frickin' well like anyway. I want to visit museums and look at the architecture of the buildings. I wish I could still become an architect but that seems out of the question now. Who cares, I'll probably end up being one of Marias call girls, if I get off the drugs. That's how I feel about myself now. I am so tired.

Two days later Maria tells Carly that Ross has been in touch with her to ask if she's okay. He has told her that he can't seem to be able to get through. She tells her that she made up an excuse and told him that Carly had dropped her phone and it has been destroyed. Carly asks her if he calls again, can she please tell him that she had to go home as Mam is not too well. Maria said she would do that. Carly embraces her and tells her she's the best friend anyone could ever have.

Carly is feeling restless now and is ready to go out on her own. She finds that just getting ready slowly is the trick, as she's in no hurry. Maria notices that she is dressed to go out so makes a regretful comment. "Where are you going dressed up like that, don't get me wrong but your face tells me differently. You need to rest Carly."

Carly feels like her confidence has just been zapped by the comment about her face so she lets Maria know.

"Thanks for the bloody put down on my face but I can't help the way I look," she says looking right at her, then sighs, saying quietly, "Anyway I thought I looked ok".

"You do Carly but I worry about you and I don't feel comfortable about you going out by yourself"

"Why not, I'm quite capable, anyhow I want to." Carly feels like she's becoming a right bitch. Maria sighs heavily after her comment then adds.

"Where ever you *are* going please be careful and don't overdo it by walking too much, take lots of rests, which is not too much to ask now is it?"

Carly mumbles a *yer whatever*, and then picks up her bag to walk out of the door.

She doesn't want to be with anyone at all today. Wandering out onto the streets she walks in the direction that Matthew took her before she became ill. The area she went shopping is really not too far from the apartment. It's a lovely sunny day and she's dressed appropriately this time, no clammy knickers today.

Her mind takes her to the time she walked around the city with Ross when he invited her over here for the first time. She remembers the zoo and wanting to visit; but he talked her out of it because he wanted to sit in a bar and show off his arm candy (being Carly), to some of his older friends Yuk! Nasty bastard, she can go everywhere without him now.

Carly walks slowly for about twenty minutes as it's quite humid today. When arriving at the zoo entrance she recognises it from when she was with Ross, then she stands and looks. Good God it does look like the doorway of a Chinese restaurant, bright red and yellow with two elephants on either side. Getting out her phone she takes several photos. The queue to get in isn't too bad so she'll wait, but the noisy kids in front of her are a bit annoying. They are becoming a bit too loud so she blurts out a cheeky comment to their Mother. (Something like her Mam would have said to her.)

The shocked and annoyed look Carly got from her was not a surprise really. She didn't say a word to her but eventually said something to the kids in a foreign language and they were quieter. Carly realises as she stands there that she is becoming a different person. She wouldn't have harmed a fly before today but God, she hates screaming children anyway. Her messed-up hormones are playing tricks on her. At last, at the front of the line now with a view to getting in very soon.

An hour later she finds a seat and rests as she's worn out after having seen most of the animals so is not bothered about walking anymore. Resting her legs, she holds onto her abdomen as she can feel a bit of pain. While looking around to find signs for the toilet, she pulls out her water bottle to take a drink, then is suddenly pushed to one side by some youths who are acting like they have drank too much. Coughing with embarrassment, the water has gone down the wrong way and has also splashed all over her dress.

When she finally stops choking she shouts, "What the fuck are yer doing you idiots".

They laugh at her as if they couldn't give a shit. Carly stands up now to confront them but one of them tells her that he is so sorry whilst flashing his big brown eyes at her. She notices that he is very good looking *and* speaks with a sexy accent. Her sexual hormones start to kick in and she feels that familiar wanting between her legs. She was hoping that would have stopped when she was left barren, well at least for a while but no, the drugs are still in charge of her body. His friends wander off when they realise he has his eyes on her body, as Carly watches him give her the once over. She doesn't mind, suddenly feeling confident again. He asks if she's okay, then says "I feel very ashamed of myself".

Carly could listen to him all day. French maybe? Then "Would you like to join me, I was thinking I could apologise over a cup of coffee? What do you say?"

He takes her hand (very French), Carly wants to say no but the ache in her panties says yes.

"Okay yes, I was heading there anyway" Needing to feel headstrong in case she does something she shouldn't.

As they walk she thinks so much of wanting to be alone, things have changed suddenly since meeting this hunk. He pulls out a chair for her, Carly loves this. She watches him as he strolls to the counter to get their drinks. He is around her own age twenty or maybe a bit older. Nice tight bum with nice pants covering it, very trendy. God, what is she doing? Strange man buying her coffee, oh well, what the hell won't do any harm, will it? He sits opposite and asks her name afterward telling Carly he is Luc. He asks why she's here alone. Carly tells him as much as she wants him to know. She finds out that he is here on a short break with friends from a small town in eastern France. Not that she's *that* interested but he wants to talk. His voice is very hypnotic with pure sex in it. Carly obviously attracts him, he asks her what she's doing this evening. Christ, he wants sex doesn't he.

Not wanting to continue so she tells him "I really do have a boyfriend. I think he would be a bit pissed off if I was seen out with you".

But he sees right through her as she's not a very good liar, and again takes her hand.

"But I would love to as I would just to take you out for dinner and only as friends? And I'm only here for one more day."

Carly swoons at the look on his sexy face as he flutters his long eyelashes at her and puts on a fake sulky look as he pushes out his lips in a pout. She laughs and tells him okay, but she would choose the restaurant. He starts to speak French excitedly waving his arms around. She can't understand a word of it.

They arrange to meet at the lovely place Matthew took her. He says that's rather a coincidence as he is staying at the hotel right there in that same building. Well that's good isn't it, letting him know sarcastically. He looks down on her (he's very tall) licking his bottom lip in a provocative manner. They finish their coffee and Carly tells him that she's going to leave. Luc gives her his mobile number. They embrace and say *au revoir* until seven thirty this evening. As she leaves the zoo she thinks, it's just dinner nothing wrong with that. Strolling back with a *bit* of a spring in her step even though she's looking forward to a nap, Maria was right, she shouldn't overdo it. But she has.

When she gets back she opens the door to see Maria rushing toward her and giving her one of her tight embraces. She notices that she is looking more cheerful.

"Oh, Carly you look much better than when you left, where did you go, somewhere nice?"

Carly hesitates, then partially lies to her "I went to the zoo, saw most of the animals until I needed to sit down and then I bumped into Matthew so we had coffee together. We arranged to see each other again tonight, who would have thought I would see him there" Carly gives a little laugh.

"Oh that's nice" Maria says cheerfully and then, "Where are you going tonight?" Carly tells her truthfully where she's going.

"I'm sure *you've* been there before?"

She says she has then "I was thinking of going there myself."

Oh God!

But Maria goes on to say "But I have to meet someone tonight, business again, It's just not right for my kind of business, I need somewhere a bit more exclusive if you know what I mean" she says giving me a sly wink. Phew, close call.

Carly is now feeling very guilty lying to her but certainly doesn't want Maria to know that she's going out with a strange man tonight; she would demand to be her chaperone. She tells her that she's going to have a nap before starting to get ready for her night out. Maria blows Carly a kiss in her motherly way and off she wanders into her bedroom.

Carly lies on the bed and props up the pillows to write in her journal.

THURSDAY 3RD SEPTEMBER 2015 *I took a walk down to the Zoo today and I enjoyed having no one to bother me. I saw most of the beautiful animals but then I tried to have a rest and met a Frenchman called Luc who is very sexy and made me laugh a lot. He took me for coffee and we chatted. I am going to see him tonight at a lovely restaurant (where Matthew took me). I would love to have sex with him as he makes me feel very sensual but I should only have dinner with him. I still feel a bit weak after having surgery but give me another week then I would be begging for it. I think I might end up giving in to Matthew as I really do love him. Being with a strange man tonight will give me a chance to just have a bit of fun. I miss having a girlfriend to talk to. I stopped texting Eileen a few days ago as she never answers anymore, wonder why? I text Ailish now and then, she and Ma are fine. I tell her I'm fine too. I will take a nap now.*

Chapter 15

Maria looks for something suitable to wear for her meeting this evening. Throwing several outfits onto her bed she can't concentrate on the task in hand as she's worried about Carly going out tonight. Picking up her phone and wishing she was going with them, Maria decides to send Matthew a text.

Hi Matt so pleased u and Carly getting together tonight. Wish I could be there with u I need some fun. M. xx She then presses send. Two minutes pass, then she receives a text. It's Matthew's response.

Maria not sure what u saying not seeing Carly tonight, have not seen her today. Call me. Matt x

Maria calls him. Matthew confirms he hasn't seen Carly at all today. She tells him where Carly is going tonight so Matthew (with Maria's agreement) decides to go and see if she actually is there. They both wonder what is going on but he reassures her that he will find out as much as he can and not to worry. He tells her that he'll text her tonight one way or the other. They hang up and Maria is left with a weird feeling that Carly is up to no good but what? What could she have got up to at the Zoo of all places?

Carly wakes up a good two hours later feeling a lot brighter and then her thoughts go straight to her evening out with Luc. Stretching and yawning she swings her long legs out of the bed, then having a quick look in the mirror to fix her hair before going into the kitchen for a cold drink. Maria is there with her back to her, searching in one of the cupboards.

"Hi Maria, I feel a lot less tired, that nap has done me good."

Opening up the fridge to get her drink, Maria stands up straight to face her then feels uncomfortable as she cannot look her in the eye, she knows now that Carly has been lying to her. Carrying on pretending to be busy looking for *something*, Carly tries to make conversation with her but senses that Maria is far away in her own thoughts so she gives up. Deciding to take a shower, she soaps herself up with the fragrant and luxurious bodywash and wonders why Maria doesn't feel like talking; maybe she has a lot on her mind?

"Maria" she shouts, "I will see you later, have to go as my taxi is here."

She suddenly appears in front of Carly with a strange look on her face and says "I have my taxi coming to pick me up, why don't you decide to come with me?"

Carly changes the subject and tells her that she looks and smells gorgeous, hoping she looks just as nice. Maria doesn't say a word but gives Carly a smile. Not answering Carly's question, they both leave. Nothing else is said when they get into the elevator. Carly thought Maria looked rather upset but didn't question it. Both their cars where there and Carly got into her taxi feeling that her best friend didn't love her anymore. She'll have a few drinks to cheer herself up as Maria has just put a bit of a downer on a night that she was really looking forward to. She watches as the car in front pulls away at a screech as if it was her who was doing the driving. Carly suspects Maria will end up having a bit too many. Oh well, her choice.

Carly arrives at the door to the restaurant, walks into the elevator, pressing the button for the tenth floor. As she walks out she stands looking around for Luc. It doesn't take long for her to see him as he waves at her. She walks towards him very carefully as she has on her sexy high stiletto heels. Oh God, he looks sexier tonight than when she first met him earlier. He greets her with a kiss on each cheek, then they sit down to look at the drinks menu.

"Oh God I'm so ready for a good drink" Carly tells him.

"Good, so am I, what would you like?"

Carly says "Mm, maybe just a glass of red wine to start off with I think". She pauses then "Oh I will go half with you for the meal, only fair don't you think?"

"NO, no my treat Carly I asked you to come out to dinner with me so it's on me. Okay?" he says.

"Well if you insist" Carly says, giggling like a schoolgirl.

They enjoy their evening eating and drinking and at one point one of Luc's friends came over to say hello. The drinks still keep on flowing and Carly is feeling she's had enough as her head is spinning slightly but not enough to stop her from walking in a straight line. Well that is what she thought until she stood up to go to the toilet. "Hey, are you alright?" Luc said half laughing as he put his hand on Carly's arm to steady her.

"Yer, of course just going for a pee" she answers, giggling again.

As Carly passes the bar little does she know that Matthew is sitting there keeping a close eye on her. He has made sure that she wouldn't recognise him by wearing a baseball cap to partially cover his face. He notices that she has had a few to drink which always makes a woman more vulnerable. He thinks he'll stay until just before she leaves as he has the car parked very close.

When she walks back to the table skilfully dodging other people's tables (those heels again) Luc has more drinks on the table.

She states "I couldn't drink any more, I feel like I've *definitely* had enough but I will have some coffee, but make that black please."

"Okay" he answers and then swigs back one of the drinks sitting on the table.

Carly's coffee was brought over and as she sips it she notices another one of his friends walking over. They say hello and then Luc gets up from the table and takes his friend to one side so Carly can't hear what is said. She doesn't think anything of it as she feels calm and relaxed. (And horny.) When they have finished whispering at each other, Luc sits down right next to her and touches her leg.

He says "What about instead of you finishing that coffee, why don't you come up to my room and have a coffee there?" Carly watches his adorable face looking at her with his *come to bed* eyes.

"Well" she says, not thinking straight, "I will, but just for a coffee."

"Of course, Carly whatever you want."

So, she puts down the unfinished coffee and then Luc calls the waiter over so he can pay the bill.

Matthew notices them getting up to leave but stays put. They pass behind him and he waits a minute before he moves. He slowly walks towards the door and then enters the elevator to leave. When he gets to the ground floor and walks out onto the street he doesn't see them. He looks around but still they're nowhere to be seen. Hands on his head pushing back his hair he thinks Oh shit, she could have gone to a room with him and he could be staying at this very hotel. He looks back thinking what he should do next. He decides to walk to the car, parks it outside the hotel, (chauffeurs parking space) puts on his chauffeur's hat so he won't get a ticket and waits. He thinks I will wait here for as long as it takes, so I know that she is safe.

Carly sits on the edge of the bed patiently waiting for her coffee.

"Still want it black?" he says.

"Yes please" answering him with a glazed look in her eyes.

Oh, I *have* had too much to drink she thinks. Luc places her coffee on the table next to her and then sits beside her on the bed.

"You smell beautiful my darling" he tells her as he

kisses her neck, speaking to her in his ever-sexy French accent.

Carly closes her eyes but seconds later she feels the room spinning. She decides that wasn't a good idea so keeps them open. He continues kissing her then pulls her back onto the bed. She can now feel that wetness return between her legs. His hands are all over her body, now putting them underneath her dress looking for her delicious wet sex mound. He pulls her panties off then goes down on her as she groans with ecstasy. She feels the room spinning again but doesn't care this time as she is getting what she really wanted. He comes up to kiss her mouth again while caressing her breasts. She then goes down on him seeing how huge he is. They both now groan with sheer pleasure. He now pulls off his jeans then she notices his large erection is coming toward her for some eager action. She realises that she can't have that huge cock inside her as it would cause her great pain. Now knowing she shouldn't have come up to his room, she feels panicky and pushes him away. His reaction soon changes but he tries to kiss her again asking her why she pushed him away.

"I can't do this, you will hurt me." He laughs and says he knows his penis is big but he will be gentle. Carly then stands up to push her dress back down and tells him that he wouldn't understand. Luc now starts to get angry as he wants her so much. He pushes her back on the bed and pulls up her dress again. Carly now feeling very scared, tells him.

"No, I need to go, leave me alone" she sobs. But he is

determined and tries to push his self into her with force. She pushes him away but he is much stronger and tries again to enter her. Now screaming, Luc slaps her across the face. She stops crying now as she is shocked and scared by the way he has just abused her. Pushing him and screaming louder, realising the louder she screams the more scared *he* gets as someone might hear what's going on. He lets her go, then she takes the opportunity to run to the door.

He stops her and says "I will walk you down to the street to make sure you get in a taxi."

Carly then says, to his surprise "Do you think I am going to call the police to report you?" He shrugs then puts his jeans back on.

They get outside and he looks around then pulls her along the street. She feels as if she is in a nightmare. Finding it very difficult to stand as the fresh air is making her head spin even more, he turns the corner and pushes her into a back lane then punches her hard in the face. She goes down onto the hard ground and cries in pain, feeling as if any minute she will thankfully lose consciousness as she is in so much agony. He opens the zip on his jeans and pisses all over her telling her in his language that she is nothing but a cock teasing bitch.

She hears him shouting." Teaser de penis." Over and over several times.

As soon as he turns around to leave, leaving her alone lying there dirty and upset, he suddenly feels a fist come to his jaw and he goes down hard with blood pouring from his mouth. He spits out a tooth, pulls himself up and sees a man he does not know with his fist ready to hit him again. Carly slowly tries to pull herself up off of the hard and dirty ground, after hearing the commotion, when she sees Matthew standing there looking very angry.

She watches him staring at Luc telling him, "You had better get the fuck out of here or I will knock the fucking shit out of you."

Luc wipes the blood off his mouth with the back of his hand, pulls himself up and runs out of the lane. Matthew picks Carly off the ground and takes her in his arms then puts her safely into the car. She tries hard to tell him something then shouts as loud as she possibly can.

"My bag, my bag, it's still lying in the street." Matthew runs back to retrieve it and dusts it off before putting it in the back seat.

Carly finds herself sitting in a strange large room with Matthew rushing around. He sits on the floor at her feet putting ice on her face and bathing her lips with some sort of antiseptic, it seems like it is, as it stings. She feels like she wants to die as her body hurts everywhere. He sits a while until she speaks.

"Oh, Matthew I am so sorry I didn't expect the night to end up like this."

Then Carly throws up in the bucket he has sensibly placed next to her. He doesn't say a word but stays with her until her stomach has been emptied.

Then he says "I've called Maria, she told me that her doctor will check you over tomorrow. But you're going to stay here tonight".

He then asks "Who was that man you were with

anyway? I wish I had called the police on him but you must realise why I didn't".

Carly answers him, shaking, "I wish you had, he should have been locked away for the way he treated me".

She cries her heart out, feeling a lot of pain in the process.

"Carly if I had, they would have interviewed you and taken blood samples and they would have shown them what type of drug you are taking, that would have started a very huge crime investigation and you would have been very much involved."

She tells Matthew how meeting Luc reminded her of wanting to start a new life and just have a bit of fun.

"But now I will never trust another man." He looks at Carly wondering if she meant him too. She reassures him by hugging him tightly.

"I was *so* scared Matthew, what would have happened if you had not been there I don't know"

Carly is sobbing like a baby, Matthew puts his arms around her and holds onto her shaking shoulders. When she has calmed down he suggests that she should get some sleep. He helps her out of the chair.

"Oh, I hurt so much" she groans.

"That's why you're seeing the doctor tomorrow" he says and slowly takes Carly to one of his bedrooms.

Helping her into this well needed comfy bed he says "Try to get some sleep; if you want me I'll be right next door to you."

She nods her head and he leaves her to rest. Closing her eyes she suddenly hears him quietly pop back in.

He places her handbag on the floor and whispers "Thought you might need this".

He smiles and leaves, closing the door behind him. As Carly feels herself drifting she thinks about her family, especially her Dad, dreaming about when she was a small child again, he is reading to her as she sits on his lap. It's her favourite book about a Robin that comes to visit and sits at the families' window waiting for food. He tells her that the Robin is really him in disguise and she should look out for him soon as he will be watching her. He pulls her head toward him, kisses her on the top and says he will be waiting for her.

Carly wakes up feeling ill and scared, looking around this strange room she tries to recall why she's here. But where am I?

It suddenly dawns on her and she shouts, "Matthew, Matthew I'm scared."

Then groaning, "Please".

Crying in pain and shaking she's just about to shout for him again but he runs in and kneels down and asks.

"Carly, why are you so scared I'm here now and the doctor is due here in about..." He looks at the clock on the bedside table and says "Ten to fifteen minutes so you don't have to be worried." He looks scared himself as he hasn't a clue what is wrong with her and neither does she.

The next fifteen minutes go by very slowly. Before then, Matthew brought Carly water which she managed to drink then he tried milk, that didn't work very well as she hates it at the best of times. While asking for a bucket to throw up in, which she does, violently, she shakes even more now and thinks this is it, I'm doomed. He holds her until Peter, (the doctor) arrives and Carly sees Maria come in the room after him. She approaches and puts her arms around her and says that Peter will do everything to help her.

He looks in her eyes and tells her "You will need to come to the clinic with me, you need to be on a drip."

While taking Carly's pulse he tells her that she is severely dehydrated and the constant vomiting has drained her body of the addictive drug, the reason for her shaking. He and Matthew leave while Maria helps Carly to get into clothes which she had the sense to bring with her. Maria hugs her and says she'll be fine once Peter has taken care of her. Once Carly is dressed she opens the door to the room and tells both the men that she's ready to go. Matthew comes in, picks her up off the bed into his arms and down they go to the car. He puts her carefully and gently into the doctors' car and says he will see her soon. He kisses her head and then she sees the tears roll down his cheeks. Struggling to look at him she whispers "I love you" then closes her eyes.

10TH SEPTEMBER 2015 *I have been through hell and back. I will never forget the horror that I went through after I had spent the evening with the Frenchman Luc. It was like being in a nightmare. Why he hit me I cannot understand. I will never trust another man apart from my lovely Matthew. My wounds are healing now and Peter the doctor has told me I have to stay on the drug I'm taking for a while longer. If I stop taking it again my body will go into shock. The bad news is I might have to stay on it longer than what I thought. The other problem is the drug is also helping me become more depressed as he had warned me it probably would. I can't take anti depressants they will not do any good either. I feel really miserable as I don't have a proper life anymore. Matthew has told me that Ross is due back next week and that is why I'm back at Marias. Maria has arranged for me and Matthew to move into her empty apartment before that happens. But how can I do that to poor Matthew? He does not deserve being with me. But he has told me he loves me and wants me to get well and then we will have a proper life. He has told me that he has a new job in a hotel working behind the bar. The money isn't great but Maria said we don't have to pay any rent until everything is sorted out. That will help a lot. I have been told off by him and Maria as I've not been in touch with my family yet. I still wouldn't ever tell them what is going on. I will text Ailish asap. Hope Mam is okay. I do miss them both and want them to meet Matthew in the future if I ever get better. The look on Peters face when he was letting me know what the drug is doing to my body has made me think I will never be the same again. That is one thing I will keep to myself.*

I hear Maria heading this way as she is insisting that I have to eat something.

CHAPTER 16

Hoping for a bit of relaxation in the next few days, Ross arrives home in a *fucking uncomfortable taxi.* (His thoughts.) Being used to the comfort of his chauffeured car, he can't wait to get out of it. He pays the driver and slams the *Goddamn door.*

He enters his home and carefully and quietly closes the front door, thinking Carly will be in bed, then throwing his briefcase on the floor he walks to the bathroom to run a bath. He pulls off his clothes then wanders into the kitchen to get himself a cold drink. Wondering why Carly has been ignoring him for the last couple of weeks, he's sure he'll find out when he talks to her in the morning. Enjoying his drink, he casually walks into his office and over to his desk to check for any mail that he has missed. Noticing a letter propped up he takes it and sits naked on his expensive leather chair. He looks and studies it thinking it's obviously from Carly as it's her hand writing.

Opening it slowly, dreading the contents, he reads it and shouts out loud, "You fucking bitch" then rips it up into small pieces to let it rain all over the floor.

Crying is not usually his thing but at this moment he breaks down, not only because Carly has left him but he hates the thought of being alone.

He sits in his chair until he's starting to feel cold. He looks over himself and realises he is still naked then wipes the snot falling from his nose. Shivering uncontrollably Ross stands up quickly to rush to grab a bathrobe from the back of the door in his bathroom. He sees the water still running in his bath, turning off the taps just in time before it came over the top. He jumps in anyway not caring if the water goes everywhere and lays back thinking how he can get Carly back; he suddenly puts two and two together.

"Well just maybe" he says out loud.

With a smile on his face but feeling annoyed he thinks, Matthew has resigned and Carly has left me, seems too much of a coincidence. In his head he plans his next move to find out, *what the fuck is going on!*

Today is another day. These are the carefree thoughts of Ross as he rises the next morning. Feeling more relaxed than he has done in the past few weeks he slips back on the bathrobe and checks his phone messages. There is nothing that he has to sort out right now, so he calls his dealers to check if everything went to plan when he left London. He left when he made sure that all the work he did there was taken care of. Also to make sure his group of people who are put in place to get the drugs to the correct companies and private individuals, which give him the best deal. Some of these businesses deal with hookers who want them to enhance their sex lives just as he did with Carly. The pimps and the madams get more clients when their women take the drug, as they are always rampant with more sexual needs. Ross is making a lot of money from this drug and he knows in the near future it will be global which will then welcome him into the billionaires' club. The other group of people *are* the billionaires who want something new to try on their frigid wives, with reports of successful encounters.

He is very pleased with his call to London as the reports came back as *job complete,* which means he can now concentrate on the whereabouts of Carly. His work here in Berlin can wait a few days as he pays his staff more than enough to deal with any problems that may arise, which is very rare as he has the cream of the crop when it comes to good architects. His business in Architecture is now becoming his hobby as he is more interested in the exciting thrill he gets when dealing with this recent drug.

After doing the usual routine, shower, breakfast and calling his office, he now thinks about the letter he found last night from Carly. He feels annoyed more than upset thinking about all the money he has spent on her to make her look really good. He thinks that she has taken him for one long ride and just used him. He knew she wanted to stop taking the drugs but he also knows that would be very difficult. He thinks, fuck it, I don't care anymore, I just want to find her and tell her I want her to stay, so I can have her back in bed with me. He walks out on to the balcony and watches the people below. Some arm in arm, others taking pictures with their mobile phones and some alone. *He* doesn't want to be alone, he would go irrefutably insane. Walking back into the room, he decides to call Maria, she might know something. Picking up his phone he looks up her number and calls. Waiting for her to pick up he suddenly feels anxious knowing how well Maria knows him, she might just lie to him anyway so he decides he will talk to her face to face. Or maybe not, it could be a waste of time as she is a very clever woman, poker face is her forte, but I'll give it a try.

She picks up "Hey, Maria how's things? Just got back last night, yes, I'm good; been very busy, you know how it is with me. Would it be good for you if I came down to have chat? No, thought we could have a cocktail together just to catch up, what do you think? Okay, see you in a minute. Bye."

He hangs up thinking shit; she always has the last word on everything. I'll just take it slowly and maybe, just maybe if she has a few drinks they might loosen her tongue up enough to let me know where Carly is.

17TH SEPTEMBER 2015 *I am happy at this very moment in my life. I will not think about my future as things do change very rapidly for me. I am now living with Matthew and we are about to have one of his cooked breakfasts, can't wait. The sun is shining and I am for once in a few weeks feeling proper hungry. I hear him shouting it is ready now, so I will write soon. x*

Carly and Matthew are enjoying their breakfast sitting out on the small patio overlooking a courtyard in the bright sunshine of their apartment. Thanks to Maria who made sure they got in before Ross was due back from London.

"Oh, look there's my Dad" saying excitedly with her mouth full of food, pointing to a robin looking up at them sitting on the fence.

Matthew nearly choking on his food, said quite shocked "What are you talking about".

"Sorry I didn't mean to scare you" she said.

Then she told him about the dream. Telling him that she believed in dreams and spirits and that bird most likely *was* her Dad.

They both went on to talk to each other about their lives from their childhoods up until the present. They loved every moment that took them back to stuff they did that upset their parents. The times they played hooky from school but also the good stuff that made their parents proud. Matthew told her he really wanted to be a train driver; he has always been a train fanatic. Carly told him that he was still young so he could still fulfil his dream. But Carly was fearful that she would never get to be the Architect that she always wanted to be. Getting to know each other they feel closer than ever. Matthew lays back into his chair and looks over at Carly who now has her sunglasses on. That's annoying, he thinks. He can't see the reaction in her eyes when he brings up the subject of going to the clinic to get her treatment. He sighs and goes for it, hoping for a reasonable answer.

"It's about time you went to see that doctor again. You know I'll come with you. Pick a day where I will be working nights but it will have to be soon."

Carly stands up looking at him feeling really pissed off.

She takes off her sunglasses. "I was hoping you wouldn't bring that up" she wants to forget about the treatment, so continues to be annoyed.

"I would rather just forget about it and take each day as it comes but is that too much to ask.?"

She waits for his reply. Matthew is scared to mess things up for the rest of the day.

He calmly tells her "Well it *is* up to you what you should do but you have to get off your drug addiction and you know that."

"Do I, do I really? The way I've been feeling today I want to put it in a jar, put the lid on it and every time I feel depressed take that lid right off and pour it all over me like magic fairy dust. But I can't do that can I?"

She puts her head in her hands, feeling overcome with sadness. Matthew comes over and tries to comfort her but he realises she isn't interested. She continues, trying to hide her discomfort.

"I know I should go and try the treatment but you know what Peter said, that it wasn't guaranteed." Walking off the patio, throwing her sunglasses as she does then hears them shatter into pieces.

"Oh shite, I really liked them, I don't have any now" and that is when she gets really upset.

She cries liked she's never cried before. Matthew doesn't try to help this time and walks away, through to one of the bedrooms and flings himself on to the bed. Putting his hands behind his head, he wonders what the hell is he going to do with her now.

"Hi Maria you are looking very beautiful and sexy as

always." Maria closes the door behind Ross, feeling quite sick at his slimy comment and also thinks no way will he get any information out of me.

"What would you like to drink Ross?"

"Oh, maybe a Bloody Mary yes, that's a nice way to start the day, with a nice stick of celery with it too if you wouldn't mind."

"Coming right up" she says, sticking her middle finger up at him as she enters the kitchen.

Bastard, I know quite well he's only here to find out where Carly is.

They sit with their drinks.

Silent for a moment then he speaks "I won't beat around the bush here Maria. I'm sure you know why I wanted to see you."

She wasn't going to mess around either. "Ross, I know that Carly has left you. And she has told me the reason why." She sits right opposite him crossing her long legs and continues, "You should realise I know what your game is and that I would never let on where she is but…"

He interrupts her saying "I know that you know about my business in drugs Maria but why should I believe what you are about to tell me."

Getting slightly annoyed she says "Ross I was about to say I think you should leave her alone. She is young and you have messed up her mind. You should keep your drugs away from girls like her. I don't and would never have *my* girls on drugs to keep them going, that is not my way of working in this business. But you start messing with lovely girls like Carly you're asking for trouble".

She takes a drink and says "So I will not help you at all."

"Are you going to cause trouble for me?" he says.

"Oh Ross you are being very immature, just think about what will happen when her family get to know what you have done to her and they *will* find out one way or the other" she stands up to refill her cocktail and sighs "If it comes from my mouth it will be only if she contacts me and asks me to tell them, but that would be only in a dire situation which I hope, for your sake Ross that that event never happens."

Ross realises he is going to get nowhere so he finishes his drink and says,

"Thanks for the drink. If you change your mind and decide to let me know where she is, you know where to find me." She leads him to her door and just about pushes him through it, telling him that will never happen. After closing the door, she leans against it thinking and hoping he'll never find Carly, wherever she goes.

Carly feels hot as she lies on the couch. Rubbing her eyes she looks around for Matthew and then remembers how upset she was before falling asleep. Oh God, I hope he hasn't gone out and left me on my own as I don't feel too good. She stands up and feels a slight bit dizzy. Walking toward the bedroom she hears him moving around. She walks in and tells him she is so sorry but she doesn't feel very well, could he help her. Just after asking him she puts her hand to her head and then passes out right in front of him.

The next thing she knows, recovering consciousness, is the stark white walls of Peter's clinic again. Matthew has already talked to Maria to let her know the situation. Peter tells him that she was severely dehydrated again which can sometimes happen considering she is taking two of the illegal drugs every day. He also tells him that he has taken more blood tests and the chance of him getting any good results from the treatment would be very low now. Maria walks in to be told the same. They both sit silent now knowing that the drug could eventually end up killing her.

Maria thinks she would see Ross put in prison in a heartbeat for murder, if that turned out to be the case. She and Matthew both break down, holding each other for comfort. Before leaving, Maria puts Matthew in the picture about Ross trying to find her, but not to worry as he has never known that she owns more apartments in the city. He would never know where to look.

Two days later Carly sits alone in their apartment waiting for Matthew to return from work. He didn't want to leave her but she insisted and told him that she'd be okay.

Turning on the TV she finds nothing that interests her so takes out her journal and writes.

22ND SEPTEMBER 2015 *I sit here in this apartment waiting for the man I love to come home. I feel more depressed now but I try to keep it to myself. I try so hard to be cheery and happy as much as I can but it can be really hard to do sometimes. I feel like that song my Mam used to listen to when Dad died 'Tears of a Clown.' She used to listen to it in her bedroom; me and Ailish would hear her crying. So we knew she was putting on the happy look and pretending just for us. But that's what Mothers do I guess. I will never be a Mother and that hurts a lot. I would love to have a child with Matthew, why I did not meet him earlier I do not know, just my fate I suppose. Sometimes I need to be alone to get away from pretending. I will text Ailish now to let her know that I have broken up with Ross but I have met someone else my own age. She will love him and I know Ma will too. But now I am getting confused as I how can I get them over here when I feel the way I do? I don't want to feel like this anymore but what am I supposed to do? Maybe I will just text her to tell her that I am okay and nothing else right now. I wish I could get help. Oh Dad, please help me, I'm still scared. VERY scared.*

Matthew told me to make something to eat and plenty to drink so I had better do that so I don't get ill again. X

Chapter 17

Carly is once again alone. With Matthew working again, she *hates* being on her own. Picking up her phone to call Maria she suddenly abandons that idea, throwing it back down. Pushing her hair out of her eyes she walks out on to the patio and sits to enjoy the sunshine.

Thinking out loud she shouts, "What will I do now, I am fucking fed up".

She feels like jumping off the nearest tall building to stop the unwanted feelings of hopelessness. But then thinks that Matthew would be in a state of shock seeing her body splattered all over the place. So, she decides to venture out instead to buy herself a pair of sunglasses to replace the pair she damaged in anger.

Not knowing this end of the city she calls for a taxi. Changing into a skirt and brushing her hair, she looks into the mirror and sees her greying skin and the bags under her eyes, thinking she looks much like an older woman. Checking the rest of her skin very carefully and feeling disappointed, the tears roll down her face.

She remembers the day when she and Ailish went for

afternoon tea after being on the beach on that lovely summers day. Changing clothes in the hotel toilets and looking at the reflection of an attractive woman. My God what has become of me? She wipes off the tears and gets on with tidying herself up then walks to the front room window to look out for the taxi.

As soon as the driver picks her up, getting inside the car she hears her phone ring. It's her sister. They discuss how she is and how sorry that she hasn't had the time to come over to visit them. Ailish tells her that Mam wants to speak to her.

Her Mam spoke. "Carly how are yer love, we have been wanting to see yer so you can tell us all about yer training". Carly wants *so* bad to let her know how she is really feeling but she stops herself and says "Mam I've missed you too, I'm fine and I'm working really hard".

Her Mother sighs and then asks "How are yer *really* Carly, I want to know how you're doing with those drugs yer taking and how long will it be until you have stopped. I worry about yer and I would love to see you soon love."

"Don't worry Ma, I am seeing a doctor here, he's nice and taking care of me to make sure that I'll be off them as soon as possible." Silence, then,

"Okay, I'll put Ailish back on. I love yer Carly, take care love."

"Love you too Mam, bye."

Carly feels the tears stinging her eyes again, tells her sister how much she loves her too and then she is gone. Staring at her phone she feels that she may never see them again. Shaking her head to get the horrible thought out of her mind which scares her so much, she wipes her eyes once again and then the taxi stops. After paying the driver she steps out onto the street feeling somewhat self-conscious. That feeling only lasts a few moments then she thinks...*whatever.*

She wanders around the shops to find a replacement pair of sunglasses looking for the darkest and largest pair she can find to hide her face. After trying on several pairs and really getting fed up with the whole process, she eventually goes for the first pair that she tried on.

Mumbling under her breath "God, and after all that time deciding".

Then after that stressful event she comes across a shop that sells hair accessories. Pushing the door to go inside she sees different coloured wigs. While carefully taking her time to choose, she asks if she could try a few on. Looking in the mirror she likes what she sees, an improvement that's for sure. With help from the assistant she decides on buying two, the short dark pixie cut and the other a dark shade of red, cut into a shoulder length bob. Wanting to wear one right now, so she can leave her real self somewhere else, she does. Taking the dark pixie wig back out of the large bag, she looks in the massive silver framed mirror on the wall making sure it's on comfortably. She looks across to the assistant, nice good-looking girl with a great smile, and with a nod from her, walking out of the shop she feels like a different person.

Wanting to explore this side of the city she walks and walks until her ankles swell. Groaning to herself she bends down to rub them and looks for somewhere to sit.

Looking around for a vacant bench she sees one on the other side of the road and heads straight for it. God, she thinks, it's hot out here now especially with this wig on my head so she moves to the other end of the seat where there's more shade. Just for a few seconds she closes her eyes then has a feeling of something touching her hand, quickly opening them to see a robin perched on the edge of the arm of the seat. It remains there for a full minute as if it were there especially for her. She comes into contact with this bird a few more times over the course of the next few days.

Having a closer look at her ankles and noticing the swelling has gone down, she gets up to walk further down the street. Passing some people who are speaking English, she stops to ask them if they know where the nearest museum is. They direct her to the Museum of Communications where they tell her they have just been looking around and would definitely recommend it. After thanking them she finds the building not too far away and she is thankful for the cool air that hits her as soon as she walks in the door. Carly spends quite some time in here, sitting down each time her ankles start to ache. Remembering what Matthew said, *'make sure that you drink lots'*, she looks for the cafe as she didn't fancy passing out again. Following the signs she sees the cafe now ahead of her. It's large with lots of dark wood tables and chairs, typical German interior. She walks straight over to a table in the far corner so she can see everything and everyone right in front of her. She sits people watching before ordering and notices that there are mainly couples here that seem to be happy. Or maybe not, how can you tell these days if the people are really happy. You can't, she decides. Observing them realising that she'll never feel happy again, she could hide in here and no one would know. Hide from the world and never come back.

The waitress comes over to ask what she would like; she wants to tell her a large anything alcoholic and a new life please. But a coffee and a large piece of cake pointing to that very one on the menu, will be fine thank you. When she returns with her order, Carly waits until she is well away from her, then bending down to pick up her bag from the floor opens it carefully to take out the small bottle of brandy she has sneakily put in. Looking around first, she quickly pours some of it into her coffee and takes a swig from the bottle before stuffing it back inside, and feeling a lot more confident drinking it with her disguise on her head. The alcohol helps her get through each day without anyone knowing. She relaxes thinking she likes it in here, a lot.

Matthew comforts her at night but he does smell the alcohol on her, he keeps his thoughts to himself. He is certain that is her only way now of staying sane. Each day she spends alone she wants to go back to the same museum where she feels at peace. She likes to change from one wig to the other so no one would recognise her as a regular visitor as she has no desire to make friends. The second time she visits she walks along the balcony and stops to look down.

Since she was little she has always wanted to fly.

"Wouldn't it be exciting if I *could* fly" she shouts too

loudly. She then feels a tap on her shoulder.

"Are you okay, are you with someone?" The security guard asks her in his strong German accent seeming quite concerned.

"Oh, yes, yes I'm okay," she stutters.

Then quickly walks away so he doesn't ask her any more questions. She hides in the toilet for a while thinking about Matthew, now feeling alone, she decides to head home.

She returns home to an empty house. Going into the bedroom she opens her bedside draw to retrieve her journal.

25TH SEPTEMBER 2015 6PM *I have again been to the Communications Museum today. I love it there, it's the only place I want to be now apart from being with Matthew. I am so depressed; nobody could understand the way I am feeling it is so hard to get through each day. I know my Dad is watching me when I'm walking around that building definitely communicating with me. He was there as a robin like he said he would be. Wow, it's amazing thinking that he is there to keep me company. I will go again this week to say hello to him. I can't wait. Matthew will be home soon so I can tell him. I might just show him my wigs too. Write soon x*

That same night whilst lying in bed with Matthew, Carly is eager to make love to him more than usual. Afterwards she is intent on keeping him awake as she wants to talk.

"Matthew, I miss my family especially my Dad."

He opens his eyes to look at her.

Sighing he says, "I know you do…would you like me to…"

Before he can say anymore she tells him.

"I was his little girl and when he died I was so upset. I cried for months. Mam and Ailish looked after me but I was devastated even though I was only eight years old when he passed. I am still devastated about his death and I've been thinking about him a lot."

She hesitates and Matthew pulls her to him. After sobbing and letting him hold her, she suddenly jumps out of bed, opens the cupboard door and takes out a large pink and white striped paper carrier bag. Matthew looks at her and wonders what the hell she is up to. Hiding behind the door putting on the red wig, she then appears before him.

"Tah Dah, what do yer think?" He laughs loudly so Carly is not sure about his reaction. She frowns at him.

"Carly, you look gorgeous, why a wig, of all things to buy yourself?"

As soon as he says it he regrets it. She throws it right back into the bag and runs out of the room.

'Oh shit' he says out loud.

He quickly jumps out of bed to follow her. He finds her sitting sulking with her feet tucked under herself rocking back and forth. Matthew sits next to her.

"Sorry Carly I love the wig. I was being very stupid to ask why you bought it. I know why you did."

She looks at him confused. They laugh together and Matthew makes the most of her good mood. She runs back into the bedroom and brings out the short wig.

Pulling her down on the floor, he makes love to her. But his afterthoughts are bittersweet.

Matthew now asleep, Carly takes out her journal to write again.

25TH SEPTEMBER. 11.40PM *I am on the brink of wanting to leave this world. The drugs are destroying my mind and now I know I can't go on much longer. My feelings about making love tonight have dulled. I don't enjoy the act of actually doing it and I don't care anymore. I can't keep pretending that I am happy. My love for my family will never die. Matthew will find another girl to love who can give him children. Maria has been such a God send and I will never be able to thank her enough for what she has done for me. I have tried so hard to come off the drugs but it has been too difficult. The only thing that helps me now is the brandy.*

I want to cry and cry until my eyes are sore. But that is all I do these days.

I don't want to write in here again because I don't care. I am so sorry to everyone apart from Ross, he has destroyed my love for life and everything in it. Bye. xxx

Carly places her journal on the table and then quietly climbs into bed beside Matthew. Lying awake staring into the darkness realising now that she cannot sleep, so she pulls her bag out from under the bed and digs deep into her bag for her bottle of brandy. Creeping out of the bedroom she gets comfortable in the spare bed and drinks herself into a stupor.

Matthew wakes the next morning looking over at the

pillow beside him expecting Carly to be there. Now thinking she's probably in the bathroom before coming back to bed, he looks but she's not in there. He uses the bathroom to have a pee then sleepily wanders toward the kitchen passing the door to the spare bedroom. He notices the door is closed which it normally isn't, so he pushes it open to see Carly lying naked on top of the bed with an empty bottle of brandy beside her. He bends down to check her breathing, thankfully she is. He doesn't see anywhere in the room where she might have thrown up which worries him as he knows she could choke on her own vomit. So he picks up the phone to let his employers know he won't be coming in. He tries to revive her but she is unconscious. Now picking her up, he takes her to the bathroom, places her in the bath and then turns on the water, turning the tap so it comes out cool not cold, as he has no intention of causing her to go into shock. The water trickles down her face then he gradually turns up the water speed so it splashes all over her body, then he controls the water so it gets colder. As he does she wakes up with a very high-pitched scream.

"Calm down Carly, I'm trying to help you not kill you."

Screaming again, shouting "Stop, stop I want to throw up".

And she does all over him. Then he steps into the bath with her to clean himself up. "You should have left me alone I didn't need your help" she shouts.

He says, "Stop shouting at me, you will wake the neighbours." "I don't give a fuck about waking up the neighbours." She continues screaming so Matthew shakes her shoulders hard thinking that would make her stop.

"Leave me alone you bastard" she screams again while thumping him on the chest.

That didn't work so he slaps her hard across the face to stop her. Carly looks at him shocked and then breaks down in a fit of tears. Matthew feeling as guilty as hell, but what else could he do, places a towel around her shoulders and then leaves her alone, while he puts the kettle on to make her (and himself) some strong tea.

He finds himself shaking as he prepares their drinks and then jumps as the boiling water splashes onto his naked body.

"Christ that hurt" He turns around to see Carly standing in the doorway, she also naked.

"Think we should put clothes on?" he asks her.

Shaking her head she slowly walks to the table to sit and drink the tea.

Their silence lasts a long time. Then, she gets up as in a trance to walk back into the spare bedroom, closes the door and lies on the bed into the foetus position. Matthew feeling like an idiot wonders what to do next. Should he just leave her alone and go out to work or should he stay to keep an eye on her. He gets himself dressed and decides to call Maria. He explains what has happened and asks her what he should do.

She tells him he should go to work as Carly will most likely sleep for hours now. And just leave her a note to let her know where you are. Maria says not to worry as she would pop around later, maybe early evening to make sure she's okay. Matthew decides that she was right and calls work again to let them know he would be there after all quite soon.

He checks Carly just before he leaves and Maria was right she had gone out like a light. He places a blanket over her, kisses her forehead then writes her a note.

Carly, when you wake up and if you feel lonely, please call me at work and I will be there as soon as I can. Maria said that she would come to see you tonight to make sure you're alright. Don't forget that I love you, Matthew. xxx

He props the note up against the lamp on the bed side table next to her, then heading out of the room he turns around to look at her again. He has a strong feeling that things won't ever be the same again, but shrugs it off as he has to leave. Closing the bedroom door behind him he wishes he had decided to stay with her. Five minutes later he leaves the building to head off to work.

CHAPTER 18

The only way to describe the way Carly feels right now is that she has gone to hell and back twice over, with her mouth feeling like she has eaten sand mixed up with vomit. Her head has grown two sizes bigger than normal or so it seems. Needing water *now* she carefully brings her body off the bed, then looking at the clock telling her that it's early afternoon, she tries hard to get herself to the bathroom. Once in there she throws handfuls of water over her face. Oh God I feel like I have to hold my head onto my body as if it's going to roll off of my shoulders.

Now she needs painkillers, but where would she find them? Searching through the bathroom cupboard, eventually finding some, then throws a few down her throat, nearly choking in the process. After coughing and spluttering for the next few minutes, thinking maybe having a bath might make her feel somewhat livelier as she desperately wants to go to the museum today. Throwing in the designer smelly bath oil she used to love, Carly lies there for almost an hour before getting ready to disappear out of this building. She remembers that Dad always loved her dressed in pink, so decides on a pink outfit. She takes a glance in the full-length mirror and tells herself she has made the right choice. But before leaving she knows the right thing to do.

Carly pulls out a piece of paper from the back of her journal, picks up her pen and sits down to write a note to her Mam and Ailish.

Walking toward the Museum she sees what she has been waiting for, her robin, her Dad. Carly watches it as it keeps pace with her footsteps and then flies off as she gets to the building.

Feeling at peace as she slowly wanders through the door, she looks at her watch knowing that the Museum will be closing in just two hours. She meanders around taking her time just to take in the people and the way they look, interested in life unlike herself. Looking at her watch again she knows that she has half an hour left so goes to the toilets and drinks some of her brandy. Not having taken any of her drugs today her body shakes uncontrollably, although it's also down to her having a terrible hangover.

Thinking about this morning and the way she couldn't help being completely fucked up and treating him like shite, she hopes Matthew will forgive her for everything.

She hears a voice shouting from the loud speaker, that the doors will be closing in five minutes. She opens the door to the toilet and peeks out to see that everyone is heading to the main exit. She hides in one of the cubicles and hopes that no one sees her. She sits there hunched up for the next half hour. Hearing the staff leaving and the security guard closing the large doors, she can now relax. Standing up she swigs more brandy then glancing in the mirror she acknowledges her *pink look* then decides to stay in there for another five minutes. Looking at her watch for the last time she peeps out of the toilet door to discover that the place is silent, no one is around. Now it's time.

She leaves her large yellow bag in the toilet, takes off her shoes and looks out the door again before heading toward the balcony knowing exactly where to go. She's not nervous she's on a high, and having good feelings, which is something she's not had for months. Creeping towards her destiny now, knowing exactly what she wants to do, Carly sees the balcony in her sights and heads up towards the steps to the top. Checking again that there is still no one about; she steps up onto the rail which is so highly polished it is slippery. She knows it is hard to keep her balance but wants to fly now. She sees herself as a child playing with Dad. Him shouting, "Come on Carly jump from the tree you're not that far up, you won't hurt yer self." She is in her own world now and as she puts her arms out to fly, she jumps…yes, I'm flying. Her arms spread out like the wings of an Angel. And then she sees her Dad smiling with his arms out at the bottom waiting for her. They now embrace with a feeling of so much joy and happiness like no other.

The security guard shouts, "Halt, Halt", running, trying to catch her, but he is too late. He is now joined by another guard who runs from the security office after he sees her jumping off when checking the cameras. Bending down to check her pulse and then with their heads on her chest to see if there is any breath in her, they realise that she has passed away. When they look her over, they are very concerned that she would not have survived anyway with the injuries that her head has suffered. Blood pouring from it with a gash so large they could see bits of her brain hanging out. But the look on her face is something they will never forget as she looks serene and full of happiness.

After being so shocked after experiencing something he never thought he would, the younger of the two speeds to the nearest toilet to throw up. Fortunately, he runs into the ladies and that is where he discovers Carly's handbag and her shoes laying on the floor.

He places the bag on the floor in front of the other shocked older guard who is wiping tears from his eyes as he looks through it to find out who they belonged to. They call the emergency services and wait at her side until they arrive. Even though the blood was around her head he strokes her face. He thinks of his daughter who is at home safe and sound with her Mother, who is about the same age as this poor girl lying in front of his shaking body. His tears come even harder now.

PART THREE

CHAPTER 19

Why is it, whilst I've been sitting on the toilet, that something happens which needs my *immediate* attention?

There's one time I can think of unhappily, when I was a bridesmaid at my Aunt Riona's wedding. When all of us, six actually, including Carly when she was little, (can't understand why anyone would want that many in the first place, but she would have had the whole street full of kids as bridesmaids if she could have) had been waiting ages for the car to turn up. When it did arrive, I was on the toilet and could not get off due to one of those situations when you just went for a quick wee, but it didn't turn out that way.

The evening of the 27th September 2015 was the night of all nights. It was a Sunday evening. I had just finished washing the dishes and I was telling Mam that I would make us a pot of tea. But before then I shouted I would just go to the bathroom and told her '*won't be a minute*'. I sat on the toilet and thought oh well, it's going to be a bit longer, she'll get her tea when I'm done. And then I heard this banging on the front door but not the usual friendly knock but hard banging. I look at my watch thinking who the hell could that be? It was dark out now and I don't like Mam answering the door to strangers as she's a bit nervy about it anyway. These days you never know do you?

I shout down "Ma, look out of the window and see who it is first."

"Okay love" she says.

I wait, while at the same time try to hurry up my toilet time. Then I hear her shout up the stairs.

"Ailish, It's the Garda and there are two of them. What do yer think *they* want?" she asks.

"I don't know, I'll be down in a second" I said as I was now done and washing my hands as quickly as I could.

Rushing down the stairs feeling a bit nervous I look at my Mother, who is waiting at the closed door impatiently, with a look of intense worry. When I *do* open it there they are, the police, two of them like she said, a male and a female waiting to enter our home. I look at them obviously with a huge frown on my forehead.

"Can I help you?" I feel my Mam's warm breath behind me on the back of my neck and I hear the male say to me.

"Are you Ailish O'Neill?" I tell him I am, and then he says "Can we come in?"

Then I say "What's this all about"?

"We are here to bring you some news about your sister…"

Then he turns to Ma and says "And your daughter Mrs O'Neill. You are Mrs O'Neill, right?"

"Yes, I am" Mam says. Then I let them in.

254

We are told to sit down and then it comes out of his mouth, the full details of how Carly had committed suicide.

The next thing I know I am packing my suitcase to get on a plane to Berlin.

The rest of that Sunday evening is a blur. All I know is that I had to call my Mam's sister Riona to come to stay with her as she collapsed in a heap (after her very loud screams) when we were told the tragic news. I called my boss to let her know that I'm taking emergency leave and then I booked an early flight with a hotel deal thrown in. I should have been in a state like Ma but my anger has taken over for the time being. I am glad I feel strong, I should really say numbed with shock, as I couldn't sort out everything that I have to, including identifying Carly's body. The thought has put chills up my spine but I have to stay strong because if I don't I will end up having a nervous breakdown.

As I board the plane feeling really exhausted having had no sleep the night before, I walk down the aisle looking for my seat. I see the number and when I look at my boarding card and put the number to the seat, there I see a man sitting in it, my chosen window seat! I tell him, "Eh, excuse me but you are sitting in my seat." My attitude wasn't my best and as I was totally shattered (as he could most likely tell by the way I looked, baggy eyed and all) *and* I had just found out that my sister is dead what would you expect. He gets out of the aforementioned seat and apologises profusely. I am in no mood for chit chat so I mumble a quiet thank you and sit down. I had noticed

though that he looked so familiar to me; don't ask me how
or why, he just did.

I buckle up my seat belt and get settled for the journey
ahead. I sit thinking about what the police officer had told
us about Carly and how her life had ended and wondering
what she has written in her suicide note. Then they told
us that she had a friend called Maria, and she was the
person who made sure that we got to know as soon as
possible before anything else. Her apartment will be my
first stop in my long planned stay in Berlin.

Planning in my head everything I need to do, I close
my eyes and fall asleep almost instantly. About half way
into the flight I feel a nudge on my arm. I wake up
suddenly and see that my head has slipped down on my
familiar mans arm. I jump up in shock nearly hitting my
head on the above storage compartment.

I say "Oh God, I am so sorry" as I feel saliva running
down the corner of my mouth and quickly trying to pull a
tissue out of my bag, I hear him say.

"It's okay it's just that you were snoring really loudly, I
didn't want you to feel embarrassed. Can I get someone
to bring you a drink?"

I actually did feel embarrassed. So, when I have
eventually wiped the drool off of myself, I answer him.

"Oh well, if you are asking then yes, yes I will have a
drink thanks."

I suddenly feel very comfortable with this very nice and
attractive brown skinned man who tells me that his name
is Thaddeus. We spend the rest of the flight talking as if
we have known each other for a long time. I tell him this

then he says with a twinkle in his eye, '*we have*'. I'm not sure what he means by that so I just brush it off and don't ask.

I tell him why I am on my way to Berlin in between my sniffling and holding back the shocked tears, he is very sympathetic about it all. I learn that he is on a world trip as he had taken early retirement from a large financial company and has no living family so he is free to go where and when he wants.

During our conversation he is very concerned about me being alone to look for this man called Ross. Thaddeus is the only person I have told so far as to what I plan to do. He wants to spend some time with me so I agree to keep in touch. We find by checking our details that we are coincidently staying at the same hotel, The NH Berlin Alexander Platz. I chose it as it has a central location. And it's opposite a beautiful park. One of the best places to go to sit and think. Carly used to escape to our local park even when the weather was crap just to sit and think about her future. That thought really gets to me, causing a feeling of my stomach twisting with grief.

I can't believe my luck, as luck isn't on my side right now. This man has me in his grasp but in a very good way and I also feel stronger in his presence. No man I have ever met has had that influence on me, it's a first. We arrange to meet each other later this evening in the hotel bar as the first thing I need to do is talk to Maria.

The next thing I know I'm frantically searching through my bag for a mint to suck on, as we are about to land.

After refreshing myself and changing my clothes I ask

at reception if they could call a taxi for me.

I eventually arrive after a fleeting view of the German sights from the car window to arrive at this very beautiful building where Maria lives, according to the text message I received from her last night. I understand now why she hadn't called as I would have just broken down in tears. I realise it is the same building where Carly was living with Ross as I remember it from the picture Carly had sent from her mobile phone.

I walk into the elevator of this expensive place and feel rather nervous about what I am about to hear. I see the number on her penthouse apartment and knock gently on the door, no answer at first so I knock a little harder. The door now opens and I see this most beautiful dark headed woman standing in front of me. I swallow nervously and then I say.

"Hello, are you Maria Sapienti?"

"Yes I am. You are Ailish?" I nod my head.

"Come on in please" she says in her delightful German accent. As I look around her magnificent surroundings, I tell her.

"Wow, you live in a fantastic place Maria, you're really lucky."

"Thank you Ailish, would you like to sit down, here maybe?" she points to a very large white chunky chair and says, "Could I get you something to drink perhaps?" When I sit down this chair is the comfiest thing I've ever sat in. I think, this is how the other half live. She is waiting for me to answer so I say "Yes please I would love a drink". I surprise myself for my normal behaviour under the dreadful circumstances. I put it down to shock.

Going through a list of what she could offer, I decide on a cold homemade lemonade because I was so taken aback when she told me the lemons are sent to her directly from Italy. Apparently, her Father is involved in growing them. After all the small talk, we discuss my sister Carly.

Maria puts me in the picture with all that had gone on. With her trying to get Carly off the drugs and taking her to see the private doctor. I tell Maria that I would pay her back all the money she has paid out for his services. 'Nonsense', is her reply and I can't change her mind.

She lets me know about Matthew, the lovely young man who stole Carly's heart. But most importantly she tells me all about Ross and that includes his involvement with the illegal (eventually global) dealings with groups of people who are killing women, as the drug leads to severe depression as it had done with Carly. She tells me it had all started when it was only used on prostitutes, and then it became thrown around in front of people like Ross who knew he could make more money from it selling it to the real drug dealers.

That brings me back to the night I was watching the news at home when that information had been put out about the hookers dying in Berlin from this new drug that was on the streets. I tell Maria I had been worried since then. We are silent for a minute and then I have to ask her the inevitable question, when would be the best time to take me to identify Carly's body?

"Oh my love" she walks over to sit on the arm of the

huge chair and says "The room where she's at in the hospital is open all hours and they told me you can stay with her as long as you want"

I break down. I didn't want to, not yet, but I can't help it, I have lost my beautiful sister after all. Maria sits with me until I have stopped sobbing my heart out.

The conversation moves to Carly, the day I first met her when she was a baby and at first, how jealous I was of her getting more attention than me. But that soon became love and a great deal of affection. I talk Maria's ear off for the next hour or so, talking about my beautiful little sister.

Maria goes on to talk to me about Ross. She knows now for sure that she wants him to be put away for a very long time and she would be the one responsible. Also knowing she would have to be very careful as not to be found out, as that would mean the end of her reputation and her successful business. He would put a stop to all of it. I listen very carefully to all the information that she tells me. But after almost another hour, when I stand up with glass in hand, (by then I had a rather strong cocktail) I walk around the room glancing out the window now and again and announce my plan. A plan that would firstly get my revenge on him for what he did to Carly. It would also for once and all, end his desire to have this drug sold globally and that would be the end of him and his large architect company.

She studies my face as I sit in that chair again then goes on to tell me to be very careful as this could cause real danger for me.

Maria walks away and disappears into another room off the very large one we are sitting in. When returning I notice a small white folded sheet of paper in her hand. She tells me that Matthew had given it to her as he was too upset to give it to me in person. She holds her hand out with the white note waiting for me to take it from her. Of course, I know what it is and take it from her very apprehensively. She takes me by the other hand to guide me into a bedroom, which I presume was Carly's when she lived here, where I can read her suicide note in private. As she closes the door behind her I am now alone, sitting on the bed where Carly lay. I hold the note with tears of great sorrow flowing silently down each cheek. On the front of the folded paper is written; *To Mam and Ailish.* Then I read the contents.

My dear Mammy and Ailish,

This is very hard to write. I am so sorry but this is the only way I can let you know how I feel. The depression has taken my life. Don't be mad at me. I know you will be sad and cry but I want to be with Dad now, sorry. He will look after me I know it. I saw him in spirit I did, I truly did.

I want you to love each other and to be happy with your life. I have always loved you both very much.

Maria and Matthew have looked after me so well, tell them I am so sorry. I want you to know that the only person to blame (apart from myself for taking the drugs) is Ross. He should be stopped. I will be happy and at peace again now, only think of it that way, please. I will see you later, you should know that anyway. Love you always, Carly XXX XXX

After reading her note several times, I walk out of that bedroom and ask Maria if she had read it. She nods and says she had and then apologises for doing so. I walk toward her, put my arms around her.

"Please Maria don't be sorry, her note was an open note for all of us to look at and read to be truthful, wasn't it?"

She nods again with her hand in front of her mouth holding back her tears. I put my hands on each side of her head and look straight into her eyes, and then we both let out our well-deserved uncontrollable heart rendering expression of grief.

It's amazing, or terrible as in this situation, how life can change from one day to the next. One day I'm driving to work in my old faithful car and the next I'm sitting in a Bentley, driven by a chauffeur and in Berlin at that. I just wish it was in different circumstances though and not heading to a foreign hospital, where my sister lies waiting for me to identify her body. I feel very nervous, with my stomach starting on that usual nauseous, swirling, wanting to throw up scenario.

The sight of seeing my sister in the morgue is something I will never get over for the rest of my days. When I was told to go in I felt so sick but I knew I had to do this. I cautiously put one foot in front of the other and there she is lying so peaceful, she actually *does* look at peace. I stroke her cheek and then her silky soft hair and just stare down at her. I stare and stare and keep on staring.

Being alone with her I speak to her quietly "Why did

you leave us Carly, I told you I would have helped you."
I hesitate for a while, then speak again, "You should have
come home to me and Mam." I kiss her gently on her
forehead. I sit on the hard chair next to the table she is
laid on and stay with her for the next hour or so. I can't
stop looking at her. I can't believe what I am looking at.

Mam would have been in pieces in here, that's why I
came alone. Before I leave Carly lying here, I tell her that
we will be bringing her back home. And then I kiss her
again on the forehead.

"That one's from your Mam" then I think I have to
leave now, I'm getting too upset. So before walking out I
say "Bye Carly I love you and I'll miss you". I quickly rush
out into Maria's arms where I stay for a very long time.

After sorting out all the details of bringing Carly's body
back to Ireland I need a strong drink. Maria asks me if I
want to go back to her apartment but I tell her I have a
date with a nice man back at the hotel. She was quite
taken aback at that news but I explain how I had met him
travelling here and how we are, very nicely thanks, staying
at the same hotel. I also tell her that I want to visit
Matthew but she tells me that he is too devastated to see
anyone right now. I give Maria the address of our home
in Ireland and say that I would expect to see her at the
funeral.

"She was your good friend after all."

She looks at me and says "Ailish, she became like a
daughter to me', pausing before speaking again. Obviously
holding back the tears. "I *will* be there and I will bring
Matthew with me too."

I tell Maria I would let her know when Carly's funeral will be as soon as I got it sorted out, then she could book hers and Matthews's flight. I thank her for being with me all day. She has helped me get through all the horrible stuff that goes along with dealing with a sudden death in the family.

The paperwork I have to get through to get Carly on a plane back home is ridiculous! I have a lot of papers to sign and a lot of cash to pay out. I am so glad Dad left me some money. It's as if he knew what was ahead, so he made sure it would have been taken care of.

Sitting at the bar with my tall cocktail, I am so glad I decided to shower and change as I could smell *that smell* of the morgue still on my clothes when I got back to my room. I had almost kept them on as I wanted to cling on to it and remember her for the last time the way she looked, but I thought differently of it as it was making me feel too miserable.

I am in a world of my own when I notice Thaddeus standing at my side.

"Good evening Ailish" he says in his deep brown voice. "I see you already have a drink, too bad, I wanted to buy you the first one."

"Oh, hello Thaddeus, that's okay, you can get me another one of these when I get done with this one. That won't be too long either" and I smile at him.

He smiles back and asked "How did everything go today?"

I tell him all about it which takes a while and surprisingly, I keep my tears at bay. We enjoy a few more drinks in the comfortable surroundings, just recently renovated I was told. I would have appreciated it more if it was in normal circumstances as it is very tastefully decorated. While discussing the next time we will meet, for which he said he would be travelling around Germany until he returns to this very hotel, I told Thaddeus what I had planned to do to get my revenge on Ross. He told me that he would be sitting here right at this bar when I return. But he also tells me he will be there for me at any time and don't forget it.

When I get back to my room after a comforting evening with my new friend, I call my Aunt Riona's mobile to see how Mam is doing. She tells me that she has at last fallen asleep as she had been walking around like a zombie for the last few hours. I say I will be coming back home on the next flight out in the morning and I tell her the approximate time I should be at the house. When I lay down to try to sleep all I can think of is Carly in the morgue, lying there cold and alone. I stare at the ceiling and then cry until my body can cry no more. I eventually fell asleep as I dream about Thaddeus telling me everything would be fine. He was my hero in my dream so when I wake up with the alarm the next morning I feel as if he was around me, his presence always in the background. It helps a lot.

CHAPTER 20

Back on the plane now heading for home and my Mam, I think of how I will have to comfort her and try to calmly talk to her about Carly and of course eventually show her the suicide note that she left for us. That was the worst part.

I lie my head back on the seat and say to myself, Oh God; give me the strength to get through the next few days. I wriggle my bottom around to get comfy and ask the air steward for a drink to settle myself for the journey in front of me, when I'm sure I can smell that smell of Thaddeus. He has a nice woodsy smell like it's his after shave or a cologne, but then it seems to me it's just his own masculine smell and not some spray-on stuff to make himself attractive. Just a silly guess, I'm sure. Thinking, that this will be my only chance for some peace and quiet and some time alone, I make the most of it and sit back and enjoy the flight, but still dread what's ahead.

I collect my bag from the airport then head for the taxi rank. As soon as I put my bag down and put my jacket on, knowing it would be a bit cooler here, a taxi pulls up. The driver doesn't bother with my bag so that makes me decide right then and there not to tip him. When he pulls away, I sit in the back with my elbow resting on the door sill and my chin in my hand. I worry how my Mam will react when I arrive home, I dread the thought of having to deal with it all, especially with my Aunt Riona being there. She does mean well, she has a heart of gold, but tends to fuss about too much. I know she will have to comfort my Mother but who is going to comfort *me*? I am the only child left to sort out the horrible reality of the funeral of my baby sister.

Life is going to be very hard from now on, dear God how am I going to cope with it all?

Noticing the taxi is going down my street now, I feel that familiar nervous feeling creeping up from my stomach and into my throat. I let the driver know which house it is and he pulls up outside the door. I look out of the car window to see the curtain twitching. Now paying the driver with the exact amount I owe him, I notice the look he gives me but I don't give a shit. I leave the taxi, retrieving my bag from the floor, then slam the door behind me. He pulls away with a loud screech showing me how he feels. Fuck you I mumble to myself.

The front door of the house is open before I even get to it. My Aunt is there to greet me with half a smile on her face. I wish that I could just be alone with my Mam but that's not to be. At least it will give me the chance to deal with the funeral arrangements without having to deal with her too. I give my aunt a half smile in return and walk towards the kitchen to put my bag down and put the kettle on for that long-awaited cup of decent tea.

"Ailish I can do that for yer. You've had a long trip so why don't yer just sit down and relax for a bit love."

I turn around to face her with the kettle already in my hand filling it with fresh water.

I answer her "I'm fine Riona. I've been sitting for the last few hours, I need to move around or else my legs will seize up."

Then I ask her where Mam is. "Laying down" is her solemn reply. This didn't surprise me at all, it's what I expected I suppose. Then as the kettle starts to boil loudly, which dulls my hearing for a minute, telling me, I think, that she had to call the doctor as she wasn't sleeping enough. "You called the doctor for what?" I ask.

I did hear right first time; my Mammy was prescribed sleeping pills.

I sit drinking my tea at the kitchen table listening to my aunt talking and talking. Well I'm not really listening, I hear bits of what she is saying as I am so tired and this house feels strange and empty. And thinking about what has happened to our lives in a matter of a few days, I'm not in the mood to hear her constant whining tones. What I do hear coming from her mouth is, *'it is so sad and your Ma will never be the same and she's been crying a lot'*, blah, blah, blah.

I have had a hell of a time in Berlin looking at my dead sister and tomorrow I have to deal with planning her funeral and…I put my head in my hands and cry. My aunt cradles me in her arms and rocks me like I was a child again. When that crying session is over I tell her, I need to go up to my room to lie down for a while so I can get some well needed sleep. When I awake, I can pluck up the courage to talk to my devastated Mother.

I drag my body up off my chair and pick up my bag then thank her for just being there. I wander slowly and very wearily up the stairs and when I get to the top I hesitate in front of Carly's bedroom. Shit, shit, shit, I whisper as I gently bang my head off the door to her room, why is this happening? I never hated anyone so much as Ross right now as he is the one who did this to my sister. I walk over to my Mam's room and listen at the door, maybe she is awake now but I don't hear anything so I go into my own room. Throwing down my bag on the floor I get changed into my stretch pants and shirt and lay down on my bed. I set the alarm for…I think…, well it's now almost one pm, so three hours should do it. My head should be clearer by then as it feels, right now, like it's full of dark clouds with some smog thrown in just for the hell of it.

Oh, frickin hell what's that noise? Then I realise it's the alarm by my bed already going off! I feel like I have just dropped off to sleep. I must have slept as soon as my head hit the pillow as I remember dreaming something strange about sitting in a large room feeling cold and scared. (That's so weird.) I lay for another five to ten minutes debating what to do first and thinking what an awful list of things to do. But when I start getting that sinking feeling of desperation again I notice that shadow, like the shadow of a man in the corner like I used to before… then I hear a quiet knock on my door, then the shadow suddenly and quickly disappears. I don't think any more about it for the time being, I pull myself up, walk to the door and then slowly open it. My eyes open wide with surprise.

"Mam." I pull her into my arms right away.

She doesn't cry and neither do I. I look at her face and notice the dark grey shadows under her eyes.

She grabs a hold of my hand and quietly says "Let's go downstairs Ailish and you can tell me all about what happened."

Then as we are walking down the stairs she is telling me quite happily how she had seen a couple of white feathers out in the garden. I am so pleased to hear that, as she had always told me that when you see a white feather after a death it is their spirit letting you know that they are still around.

When we get into the kitchen I felt *my* spirit has lifted somewhat so I am ready to tell her what I had found out in Berlin, but I am still dreading giving her Carly's suicide note. I am hoping it won't bring her down in the dumps once again, (but that would be like telling her never to drink tea again, if you know what I mean), but I should be expecting it shouldn't I.

I know better than to interfere when my Mam is in the kitchen but when we shuffle in she just wants to sit down. I look around for my Aunt Riona but she is nowhere to be seen so I leave the kitchen and pop my head around the living room door, not there either. I ask where is she. Mam says she went home as I was here for her now. I make the usual pot of tea; sort through any goodies that are in the cupboard (not much in there apart from some broken biscuit bits in the bottom of the tin) pour her and my tea in our familiar mugs and sit beside her at our table. I begin to talk. She puts her hand on mine and tells me she wants to know everything that happened in Berlin.

She sits and listens to me telling her about how Maria had helped Carly and the beautiful apartment she lives in and how Carly had fallen for Matthew. But when it comes to telling her the day when I had to identify her body, my poor Mother breaks down. She cries into her skirt until it is soaked through. The time has come to show her the note Carly had written but not before insisting on changing into a dry skirt. But I'm sure her crying will start again and her change of clothes will once again be drenched with her tears.

I'd put the note securely in an envelope in the desk in the hallway, Dads' desk. I go to retrieve it and cautiously hand it to her. Then I watch her read it with so much sadness on her face. After reading it she placed it on the table.

"Ailish, how are we going to cope with this, I just want her back here at home with us" and then she says "I want to kill *that man* that did this to her. I realise that he is responsible for her death you know, I'm not *that* stupid."

"I know you're not stupid Ma" then I tell her, I had nothing to lose did I, "I am going to go back to Berlin after Carly's funeral…"

Oh, shit I still haven't called the funeral office, too busy walking about like I'm in a dream, no, in a nightmare.

"And I'm going to sort things out with him but don't

worry as I'm not intending to do anything stupid and…"
she stops me immediately.

"And what have you in mind young lady, you can't go
off just like that without getting the police involved, he
has to be reported as he *is* a criminal."

I tell her that I have talked to Maria who knows him
very well, and we would arrange what to do with him
when I go back and that would eventually be involving
the German police. I quickly get up to use the phone,
calling the funeral company to have them come around
tonight to talk to Mam. Thank God that they aren't busy,
they tell me they will be at the house at seven pm. I look
at the clock in the hall, Christ, that's only half an hour
away! I tell Mam and she looks down at her still wet skirt,
looks at me and says while lifting the skirt from her legs.

"Well, I had better get out of this I suppose" then as
she passes the mirror in the hall I hear her say "not much
I can do with this face though Ailish".

She rushes upstairs to change and *maybe* tidy herself
up. I don't change my clothes I really don't need to; I am
not going to dress to impress am I.

The funeral director approaches the door with his arms
full of folders. He introduces himself as Chris Bennett.
He is a man I would say in his forties, well spoken, a
bit overweight as his dark jacket is tight around his waist.
When Mam takes him into the sitting room he asks if he
could put his catalogues on the coffee table, very polite
too.

Mam decides with my help, to have a white casket
for Carly and flowers of all types but she wants them to

be all different colours of pink. The same company also dealt with the flowers, so less stress to deal with as far as I was concerned. Mam wants a catholic service for her like she had for Dad, so he sorts that out too. He tells us he would also call the priest, all within the almost two and a half hours he was there. He probably would have been at the house half that time but Mam had insisted I make him tea (two large cups) of course, the healer of all things known to man. But there is one thing in those two and half hours that she wants to choose without my help, and that is the headstone. Selecting what she wants as soon as she sees it. It is a large beautiful stone angel with a bird in each hand. Very *spiritual* she tells me.

When Chris Bennett eventually leaves I hear my stomach rumbling.

"Mam, are you hungry? I am."

I realise I haven't eaten anything since we had those bits of broken biscuits earlier today. I ask her again.

"Well I should eat something I suppose, shouldn't I? But I don't want to start cooking now, it's a bit late now."

"No, I know that, I didn't expect you to. I was thinking I could go get us some fish and chips, what do yer say?"

She is walking around the room looking lost, so I wait patiently for her to decide.

"Okay then, I'll have some if you are love"

So, I go to the chippy. I am on my way driving and thinking, until I know I have to pull over. I notice the car park is empty in the local Co-op so I drive into a space, turn off the engine and that's when I break down. I cry so hard and loud it wouldn't surprise me if the staff in the shop had heard me. It has hit me so hard now after the funeral director has been, I realise now it is *really* happening. It somehow hits me more than when I actually saw her. I realise now that Carly is dead.

I eventually bring home the food and Mam asks me if they had been busy, she hadn't expected me to be *that* long. I lie *'yes that's why it had taken me a bit longer'*.

I lay out the warm plates and put the fish and chips out on the table. We both sit down to eat. Then suddenly she calmly puts down her knife and fork, and then looks right at me as if she is looking into my soul. I think I am going to get a telling off as I have forgotten the peas, but no, that's when she leaves the table whilst grabbing a tissue out of her pocket then runs upstairs to do exactly what I did in the Co-op parking lot. I pick up her plate of food and put it in the oven to keep warm. Maybe she will come back down to eat, maybe she won't, and I really don't think she cares right now. I'm not in the mood to eat either but I know I should try. I sit there alone pushing the food around my plate and feeling like shite.

CHAPTER 21

Carly's body was flown home the following day. I've been up most of the night and I know Mam has too, I can hear her coughing and moving around in her bedroom.

I was told everything was taken care of. From her being taken from the morgue in the hospital in Berlin, to the airport and then flown home to us in Dublin. Then the funeral home will take over from there and she will be placed in the chapel of rest in our hometown. I had to pay a fortune for it to be done but had no choice. Maria had even suggested that she would help with the cost but I told her absolutely not. Mam hasn't even thought of asking how much it will cost, it is the last thing on her mind.

The flight was an early one so she is expected to be laid out by three pm. We were told that when she is ready to be viewed we will get a call soon after. This is in our thoughts all day. Pacing the floor trying to keep our minds occupied. Even weeding the garden, which has never been known for me to take up such a monotonous chore, but I did. Aunt Riona turned up trying to keep our minds busy with her chit chat but mostly she got in the way, my reason for going outside to get out of *her* way.

The clock in the hallway chimes three o'clock but no call yet. Mam walks into the kitchen, looks over at me as I am fiddling with a cloth wiping up an already clean table top and shrugs. She is already dressed up to see Carly with her best floral summer dress on as we are having a glorious Indian summer. We are getting really anxious now.

Another hour has passed and I can't take it anymore. I tell Mam I am going to call the chapel of rest but just as I am about to pick up the phone, it rings. That spooks me out a bit; but I pick up immediately.

"Hello, yes, it is, okay we will be on our way as soon as I put the phone down. Thanks, see you then, Okay Bye."

I tell Mam and Aunt Riona it is time to go. I pick up the car keys and my bag and make sure I stuff a bunch of tissues in it.

We are quiet all the way there. Mam is already sniffling beside me in the passenger seat. I check out Riona's face in the rear-view mirror and can see that she has a subdued expression on her pale face. When we arrive 15 minutes later, Mam is first out of the car. She looks around at us impatiently, not wanting to be held back for a moment.

I let her go on ahead with her arm linking her sister's. I watch them as I follow slowly behind and I notice that Mam has a slight stoop now, she looks a lot older than her years. Aunt Riona opens the main door helping her through as if she was a doddery old lady. She holds the door for me where the friendly looking man at the reception is waiting for us. He then shows us where to go. I want to be alone with my sister for a while, so I hold back. I watch Mam open the door to the room where Carly lies in her coffin and then I hear.

"Oh God, Carly, my little love" then the cries are cries of a very distraught and grieving Mother.

The day of the funeral is a day like no other would ever be. Four days before, we had been to see her in the chapel of rest, Carly is now here in this familiar church where she and I had sat ten years ago, not being able to understand why God had taken away our Dad.

The church is quite full with friends of Carly's she had known from school and there are my nieces and nephews who I haven't seen in years and Molly my friend from work. Then I spot Maria. She was insistent like she usually is, not coming to our house before the funeral. She told me that she had sorted out a nice hotel for her and Matthew for the next few days. She is dressed beautifully, as normal, in a fitted black suit which clings to her small waist. Then I notice the very sad young man sitting next to her, obviously Matthew. In normal circumstances he would be very good looking but his eyes are red rimmed and swollen.

The service, including Carly's burial, is the most full on, long lasting and devastating affair you could ever imagine. One thing that *does* go our way is the sun that has been out all day as if it was her shining down on us to try and cheer us all up. It shines onto her magnificent headstone which makes it glow like a golden monument to celebrate her short life with the angel and the two birds in her hands, smiling down on her. But there is something strange about my mother; she has been very quiet the whole time. Being in denial of her daughter's death is an understandable reaction, but I would have thought she would have been chattier with everyone. She isn't much interested in talking to Maria and Matthew, just the quick hello and that is it. Maybe it has just hit her that she has lost Carly.

Back at the house every one of us looks tired. My aunt and I take care of everything, rushing around on auto pilot. Mam takes to her chair in the sitting room, parking herself there for most of the day. She looks devastated. There seem to be more people here than was at the church. I notice the neighbours from each side and also Carly's best friend Eileen, with her parents. There is Mam's friend Brenda who she's known for years. It seems to become chaos with all the guests to see to, so I sit in the garden and take a break and that is when the young man who came with Maria stepped outside to join me. He asks if he could sit next to me and I tell him of course he can. He tells me who he is, Matthew of course, and I apologise for not acknowledging him before now. I put my head in my hands only because I am so worn out but he thinks I am about to cry so he takes my hand and squeezes it gently as if to say *I am here for you, I will comfort you.* I quickly look up at him and see that it is *he* who needs comforting. His tears were to join mine, we both needed to be comforted.

After our tears stop flowing we talk about Carly. Matthew talks about the first day he had met her and then couldn't keep her out of his mind after that. But when he found out what kind of man Ross was and the drugs he was giving Carly he knew that he couldn't bear to be near that man again. That's when he quit wanting to be his chauffeur. He talked about Maria who has become a good friend of his now. But he said that Carly will always be the love of his life, the way she excited him every time she was near him and the times they were together they always laughed even though she knew deep down that getting off those drugs would be an impossibility. But he told me that the last few days when she became more depressed, he never realised that she was that bad and would do what she did. He then breaks down and between the sobbing he apologises to me for not being able to stop her. I want to hide him away from everyone here so he can just let it all out.

I ask him quietly, "Would you like to go somewhere quiet to be alone? It might be better for you just to let it all out and get those tears out of your system."

He pulls another cotton handkerchief out of his pocket and blows his nose while at the same time shaking his head, saying "No, no, I'll be okay in a minute, so sorry Ailish that I'm behaving like this but I really did love her."

"Yeah I know Matthew, so did I, very much so."

The rest of the day is less eventful but I am so frickin tired. I've had enough of playing waitress so I disappear upstairs for a bit. But instead of going into my own bed room I want to go into Carly's room as I am grieving for her. It seemed that downstairs I wasn't noticed as the grieving sister.

I open the door and the first thing I notice is the sun is still out and shining very brightly through the window. The next thing I notice is the peace, it is so peaceful in here. I walk over to the window and look down into the garden where I see a couple of people with glasses in their hands. I honestly wish that they would all go home. I want to be with my Mam, just the two of us, to be in each other's arms sitting on the couch and talking about Carly. I sit on Carly's bed and pick up one of the teddies she had left there. I smell it; I can smell the days of our childhood. That seems very weird to me for that soft toy to still capture that childhood scent, but it does. I know I shouldn't do it but I open up her wardrobe. I touch each dress, each top, and each pair of shoes. I put them up to my nose I want to smell her and I do, then I pick up her handbags. If Mam could see me doing this I'm not sure whether she would approve. But I carry on looking, I so need to do this. I find shopping lists, old bits of tissues and when I stick my hand in a bit deeper it comes out with a hard toffee stuck to it, which makes me giggle. I remove the sticky sweet off my fingers and keep on digging through her once private stash. I don't find much else in this bag so I take a large yellow one out and I don't know what I want to find, but I did find something I wish I hadn't in a way. But I am glad I did. As I pull it out with care, I realise now that it is the bag that she had with her the day she committed suicide. It was delivered specifically to Mam and I didn't know where she had hidden it but now I know she hadn't even gone through it. What I found was a gorgeous black velvet book with a silver oak tree on its front and the top corners have an angel and a dove. It is so beautiful. I could imagine Carly finding this and knowing right away that she wanted to buy it. I open it up and then sit down to look at it more closely. I turn the pages with interest realising that it was her journal, the last written words of her life. It saddens me so much I have to put it down to wipe the tears from my eyes, I don't want to ruin it with my wet tears dripping onto the soft velvet.

I read every word of it. The days she seemed to be happy wanting to explore the city and her words when she found this journal, I was right; I knew she would love the book as soon as she picked it up off the shelf in that book shop she described so well. The day she visited the zoo she was in a good state of mind and then it went on to say how she had been abused by a horrible Frenchman. Fucking bastard, God if I knew where he lived, I'd smack him right in the face. And of course, the day finding out about Ross and who he really was. Ah, my poor sister. Reading the words that she wrote about her pregnancy broke my heart. I just wish she would have contacted me. I also realise now how she adored Matthew. But the worst part being the way she must have been feeling knowing she'd had enough of her life, which completely riles me to the point where I could scream from the rooftops.

The way the drugs took her away from us is just an unbelievable criminal wrongdoing on Ross's behalf. How he could have given them to her in the first place when he knew the consequences, is so unreal. Was he doing it deliberately? Is he really a woman hater? I will eventually find out, I am determined. I finally put the journal back in to the bag wondering when it would be the best time to show Mam. I lay on Carly's bed wanting her to be there with me, to chat about what we had done that day and the times that I would tickle her to give me one of her toys.

I want to drift off to sleep and get away from this reality of not being able to chat with her again when I hear something at the window. I get up off her bed making hand prints on top of her duvet cover. I then walk over to see the creature, a lovely small robin looking right at me. It doesn't move when I get near to it but the tiny thing looks at me as if it is my friend. Ma had always mentioned the way birds can come to you after a death, as one had done with her when Dad had passed. I feel as if it is Carly checking to see what I was up to in her room. It eventually flies away but it has left a peaceful feeling with me, as if it had known I needed that reassurance. I realise after that wonderful encounter that robins are less visible at this time of the year.

I now hear voices at the front door, someone leaving. I check myself in the mirror, then walk over to the bed to smooth out the duvet cover. I wasn't sure what to say as I've never done the '*goodbye thanks for being here at my sisters' funeral and wake*'. I rush down anyhow and see that it's my aunty leaving and taking her (my nieces and nephews) kids with her. I tell her '*thanks*', that's all I said and gave them the usual hugs. Mam wasn't there behind me waving them off as she would have been in the days when we were all together as a family, she was still sitting eyes wide in her own little world of disbelief.

Before Maria and Matthew left, they were the last to leave, we discuss briefly when I will be coming back to Berlin. I tell Maria that I will let her know as soon as I know myself. They also try to talk to Mam but she is nodding off in her chair. I tell them I would see them very soon once I got sorted out taking care of my Mother and who would be there for her whilst I am away. I don't want to leave her on her own, that would be a (another) disaster waiting to happen. We all weep on each other's shoulders at the front door step while we hug each other; there was no reason why we shouldn't have, we all loved Carly very much.

When I put my Mother to bed that night, it is if she has had a few drinks, maybe she has as I haven't been keeping an eye on her, her legs seem to have become made of rubber and her speech is a bit slurry. Never thinking that it would be something serious, I had left her with a cup of tea on her bedside table as she didn't want to eat anything. As always saying she'd be fine, so I kissed her and she kissed me and then I left her to have some peace and quiet. I left her door ajar just in case she might shout down for more tea.

But two hours later, after I have sat down with my thoughts after finishing clearing up, I go upstairs to get ready for bed. As I get to the last stair I can hear the sound of Mam crying. I quietly pop my head around the door and I see that she is sitting up holding her face. I know right away what is wrong; she had had a stroke as one side of her face is drooping very badly. I rush to her side and call an ambulance immediately. I try to calm her down telling her the ambulance will be here soon. Then she pulls my face down to hers and tries to tell me something, at first, I couldn't understand but then I know what she is saying.

"Don't, I don't want to go to hospital, just leave me here" This upsets me more than I can say as I need her to be around.

I say to her "For God's sake Ma, don't you be saying things like that. I love you, I want you to be well" then I cry, can't help it.

I've been through enough already and don't need another death on my hands. Then I hear the siren so I pull myself up off her bed.

They rush up the stairs and take care of her; in the time it takes for me to turn around, they have her on the gurney. I do the usual, grab my bag and my keys and then I am in the ambulance holding her hand with sweat pouring from my face. There had been some rain that night and the only other noise I can hear apart from the beeping sound coming from the heart monitor is the wheels of the ambulance speeding through the wet road and over those dreaded pot holes.

When we arrive at the hospital, she is taken away from me right away. I know I have to try and think straight so I sit down and think *what should I be doing now*? Then I go outside to use my mobile. I ring my Aunt Riona to let her know what is going on. She tells me that she'll be at the hospital as soon as she can. I walk towards the receptionist who suddenly and silently points to the nearest place where I can purchase a hot drink (the drinks machine). I obviously look as if I need one. I thankfully have some coins in my purse, decide on the hot chocolate and then as I find the nearest fairly comfortable seat I sit in silence, wondering what the hell I am going to do if she dies? Finishing off the fairly decent drink and feeling so worn out from all of the day's drastic events, I think of all the days my Mam has to get ill she picks this one.

Half an hour later I hear footsteps coming toward me in the silence of this clinical white corridor. My aunt arrives looking as worn out as I am. She asks me what had happened and how is she doing? I tell her what I had seen with her drooping face and all, but I still didn't know anything yet about her condition.

That news doesn't come for another hour, from a young-looking doctor dressed in a very white coat (obviously new to the position). He tells us that she'll be alright as she was brought here in time to keep the stroke from getting any worse. He goes on to tell us that she's been very lucky that she hadn't been alone. I ask him if we could see her and he tells us just for a few minutes as she needs to rest. He also informs us that she will be kept in hospital for the next few days.

When we walk into the side room where she is laying I honestly think she has died. The blood has drained from her face, helping it to look grey in colour. It scares me to see her like that and as I turn to Riona she says just what I was thinking. "God Ailish, she looks like she's dead." Then we both take her hand and it feels warm. We look at each other and smile with relief.

The doctor comes back in later to advise us to go home

as there is nothing we can do for her. Sorry Mam but I don't hesitate I am knackered. I am out of there in a shot just wanting my bed.

Riona drops me off at home and I say I will see her at the hospital tomorrow. Sitting in the car heading back home the thought just hits me, how could I have been *so* stupid not to have thought that she may not have been feeling well all day, being stuck in her chair while I was practically ignoring her. She is so stubborn that way; she would never tell anyone if she wasn't well, never has.

When I put the key in the door and throw myself in, I go straight upstairs, pull off my clothes and fall into my bed. I lie my head on the pillow and think please God let tomorrow be better. And then I drift into the land of nod and dream I was a kid again.

The next few days are spent driving back and forth to see Mam in the hospital. When she is eventually allowed to come home a list of essentials is placed in my hand.

'And don't forget my makeup' she says, I think well at least she's still interested in what she looks like.

Arriving home with Mam dressed as if she was on a hot date, I ask her what she would like me to cook for dinner tonight. Answering in a boisterous manner, which isn't her at all, (I was told by the doctor that this was normal for a while after someone had a stroke) that she was quite capable of cooking, thank you. So later on, that evening I let her prepare whatever she wants to cook and I leave her in the kitchen to get on with it. Ten minutes later I hear her shout out.

"Ailish can you come here a minute please?" when I

walk in she is sitting down at the kitchen table shaking like a leaf.

"Ma what's wrong?" I ask her.

"I tried to cut the carrots but my hands won't let me, what's wrong with me?"

I sit down beside her, take her arm and say "You were told by the doctor that it will take a few weeks before you can fend for yourself again, that is why I told you that I would cook."

"But you will have to go back to work soon Ailish and then what will I do?"

We sit and discuss all options to this. I eventually tell her that I am going back to Berlin to visit Maria and Matthew and have planned to stay there for a couple of weeks. I also mention to her that Riona said that she could stay with her while I was away.

"Can't I come with you to Berlin? I just want to see where Carly was and where she lived. I need that Ailish."

"I know you do but you're not well enough to do that yet, now are you?"

She looks down at her shaky hands and nods her head realising I am right. Then asks me when I am going back to Germany. I tell her probably next week which is five days away. We discuss what is the best and safest thing to do including what she says, to have her put in a home which is all she's worthy of now, which is when I tell her to stop being stupid, then agreeing to live with her sister until I return.

Until the day I leave for Berlin, we have time at last to sit and talk about Carly. We cry a lot, we look at photos and we just talk and talk, until we are so worn out with everything we fall asleep too many times in front of the television.

I have booked a late afternoon flight, so on the morning of my departure Riona comes over to get Mam and all of her things. She picks up her very full suitcase and when Mam leaves the room I looked across at Riona and see a puzzled look on her face.

She asks whispering, "What the hell has she got in here?" Shrugging my shoulders I whisper back, "Don't ask."

She was making sure she was ready for anything I'm sure. Riona never questioned anything after that but I could tell she was looking forward to having some time with her sister. And as I watch my Mam bustling about as much as she could, I could see that she was too. After the kisses and the hugs and the "be careful what you're doing" I say my goodbyes for now and they leave. I watch the car as it went down our street and then turned the corner until it is out of sight. I pray to God that she will be okay and be well for my return home. The house is quiet as I walk back in, too quiet. I think in fact, eerie, that is it, quite eerie.

The house is locked up, I am on my way to the airport with *my* very full and heavy suitcase. After all, I really don't know how long I am going to be staying there do I.

CHAPTER 22

I have booked in at the same hotel. The young woman (well about my age) remembers me as I check in, and asks how long I think I will be staying this time. I tell her I'm not sure. She tells me that the hotel isn't as busy at this time of the year, so there will be no problem in getting a nice room.

I settle myself into my large room, by collapsing on the large bed (I've been upgraded this time) then pull out my mobile to call Maria to let her know I have arrived. The porter has dealt with my suitcase thank the Lord. We arrange to meet later to have drinks and to talk about what I have in mind for the next few days. When I am busy putting my toiletries in the bathroom I hear my phone ring, thinking it is Maria calling me back. I pick up and notice that it isn't her. I answer it not knowing who the number belongs to.

"Hello?" I ask suspiciously.

"Hello Ailish, its Thaddeus" he says in his polite way.

"Oh Hi Thaddeus, didn't recognise the number, thought it was someone else."

"I hope I haven't interrupted something, if I have, please let me know" he says.

"No, no, you haven't." I tell him. "I'm back in Berlin at the same hotel; I just arrived about fifteen minutes ago. Where are you?"

"I'm in Fulda, a nice town further north. It's really nice, but I rang to let you know I will be back in Berlin in two days, so if we can meet at the bar sometime. Wednesday evening? I would love to see you."

I remember he said he would like to see me again but I wasn't sure whether he would, but he has kept his word.

"Of course, I would I'm looking forward to it."

He says "Eight o'clock be okay?" I agree and then the conversation ends.

Later that day after having forty winks, I shower and change my clothes into something a bit dressier (I know Maria would be dressed immaculately). I don't want to look like a slob dressed in jeans and a T-shirt so I put on a pair of smart navy flared dress pants and a floaty blue and white blouse. Put on a bit of jewellery and sprayed myself with some…then glancing at the bottle, (not sure what I brought with me, I buy for the smell not the name) ah yes, it's…Oh right, now I know. I didn't buy this one, it's the German perfume that Carly had bought for me when she came back from her first time visiting here. I sit on the bed and smell it. It brings back memories of when I'd opened it and when she'd had it wrapped up so beautifully. I remember when I *did* open it; my first thought was oh, its perfume. My thoughts on buying someone else perfume arc not a good one as it could smell so different. But what she chose is gorgeous and it suits me so well and the name of it is so appropriate for me in her eyes (probably the reason why she bought it) as the name translates to *Pure Living*. (Everyone thinks I'm still a virgin.) Ha, they couldn't be more wrong. There's only one person who knows different, is my friend Molly.

I had a quick fling with a man who I met at a party that Molly and I had gone to a couple of years ago when I was almost twenty-two. His name was Mick and he was very sexy so we ended up doing it in the back of his car and quite a few times actually.

'Very romantic', Molly had said.

"Well we are young and have nowhere else to do it," I told her. Our secret relationship lasted six months. I've never had sex since, unfortunately.

I go downstairs to the bar and Maria turns up before I have even ordered my drink. She walks in as predicted, immaculately dressed in an expensive looking burgundy trouser suit with a floppy hat to match, which is perfectly placed over her dark silky hair. I greet her with my smile and we order our drinks which she insists she will pay for. We order cocktails and then sit in a quiet corner of the lounge. She takes off her hat and crosses her legs looking elegant, myself now feeling inadequate, unknown to her of course. Now I know I need a new hairdo when I look at her. I feel so out of date with my auburn brown bob.

The first thing I let her know is how my Mammy is and how she is being looked after. Which is a Godsend as it helps me not to feel guilty about being here in Berlin. Maria says she is so sorry and then takes a long drink and then says she has some news about Ross. The sound of his name makes me cringe but I am on the edge of my seat hoping she is going to tell me that he has been strung up in the middle of the street and is being tortured by all and sundry. I listen with interest.

Apparently Ross had noticed Matthew walking around the shops in the area where he lives and he followed him thinking he would find Carly. Matthew eventually walked home and Ross determined as he is, knocked on his door to ask him face to face if he could come in and just say Hi to her.

When Matthew opened the door Ross drunkenly shouted "I know you live with her, I'm not stupid."

Matthew couldn't help but realise that the man at his door was in a drunken stupor. The next thing he knew Ross pushed open his door and...

"I am so sorry Ailish if this is upsetting you, me talking in this way." "I'm okay honestly" I lie.

"Well; Matthew became very angry, told him to get out. Then Ross became angrier and told him that he wanted to see her *now*. Matthew took a swing at him right in his stomach and that is when Ross fell on the floor in pain."

"Good God Maria then what?"

She continues, "Matthew now shouting at him, told Ross if he wants to see Carly...sorry Ailish..., he would have to go to Ireland, he will find her there...but...you won't be able to speak to her as she is..."

I then put my head in my hands as I know what she is about to say.

"Oh, my love, sorry, he went on to tell Ross the truth

and then Matthew hit him again, very hard apparently."

That is when I laugh. I laugh so hard it almost turns to tears. Maria is so pleased to see me laugh, she tells me so, and we end up laughing together. She goes on to tell me, in between laughing, that Matthew threw him out and said if he didn't get out of the hallway now, he would call the police.

She says, "Matthew told me has never seen anyone move so fast."

I think now, Ross knows what he did to my sister.

I ask Maria when she thought would be the best time to visit Matthew. Texting him then and there the answer comes back as any day this week or next as he's working nights. I can't wait to meet him again as he is lovely. I can *so* understand what Carly saw in him.

I now want to remind Maria briefly of my plan of getting revenge on Ross Carmichael. She sits and listens very carefully at what I have to say.

I know I have to do this alone and I don't want him to know who I am. Maria has let me know where he drinks and where his office is in the city. She tells me she doesn't like what I have planned as it could become a bit risky. He might find out who I am as he is very crafty. I tell her he won't. She doesn't like it. Suddenly she pulls out an item from her handbag. Handing it to me, I'm shocked to be looking at apparently a photo of Ross. When I look at his face it takes my breath away, like it was déjà vu. I hate to say it but he is very attractive. Maria saw my expression and gave me a look.

"What?" I say.

"You know what I am thinking Ailish, I know he is very good looking and he is very charismatic too. Bill Clinton, ex-US president is like him with his charm and charisma. I met Bill years ago. That is what I meant when I said you need to be careful. Do you understand now?"

I am still looking at his photo and say, "Yes I do…but now I see the man that took my sister away from me." I sit staring at the photo as if putting a magic spell on the man. A bad one at that.

The photo now put in *my* bag, we order another drink and then I tell Maria about the man I had met on the plane the first time I came here.

She says "He sounds very interesting, you must introduce me to him soon." I have a feeling this will never happen as Thaddeus is just around when I want him to be, not for anyone else. Anyhow that thought flung to one side, and a few cocktails later, Maria says that she has some business to deal with later this evening so we part to meet another day.

The next morning, I am up with the larks as I have planned to tour the parts of the city that Carly visited. I want to look at the places she looked at and walk the streets she walked. It could or maybe would help me with my grief, even for just that day.

After having one of the hotels delicious breakfasts once again, I ask the lovely girl at the reception if she could call a taxi for me.

My first stop is the shopping area of Kurfurstendamm where Carly bought her journal. Stepping out of the taxi after I have paid the driver I look around and am suddenly taken over by a chill in the air. I pull my thick jacket further up around my neck and feel excited in a strange way of looking around where Carly had been. The shops are really nice here and I stop by a few, but the shop I am looking for I haven't found yet. I know it is off the main street as she had written in her book. I walk further and turn a corner and then I notice that this street seems quirkier.

As I walk even further I notice the book shops now. I remember Carly said that there was a cafe downstairs so I look in a few and then I know right away when I enter this one. I see the small sign that tells me that the cafe is downstairs.

But before I go down the few steps, I look around, then I see on one side where she had bought her journal. Then I notice on the shelves the Peacemaker books. I pull one out and I get goose bumps knowing that she had stood right here on the spot where I'm standing right now. They are all beautiful and made with so much care and thought. I look at all the nice books and decide to buy myself a small notebook that is made by the Peacemakers too. This one is covered in midnight blue velvet, with a silver moon stitched onto the front cover and I notice at the top of one corner is a small owl looking down as if it wants to jump on the moon. At the other top corner is a silver star. It is so pretty.

Then I look for an interesting novel to read to help me relax before sleeping. I find a book called *Beside you Forever*, quite appropriate as that is what I want Carly to be, beside me. As I walk to the checkout to pay for both of the books, I feel upset thinking that Carly *should* be here with me right now, shopping together is how it should have been. The young man who serves me looks at me in a curious way, I feel a tear roll down my cheek, but he doesn't ask. I thank him after I pay and then wander down to the cafe. I sit in a corner table just as she did. I order the same, coffee and a strudel and I try not to cry.

I spend the next few hours just wandering the streets that Carly had walked. Looking in windows and just thinking and wondering how my Mam is going to cope with our huge loss. I text Aunt Riona to ask how they are both doing and then I hear my phone ring.

I answer it immediately, "Hello."

"Hi Ailish hope you don't mind me calling yer."

Then I hear her mumble "Sometimes my fingers can't move very well on these small buttons".

"Yes of course it's OK Riona" I say, "But how's Ma doing"?

"Well she *is* upset, but she gets depressed too. But the doctor said she would, under the circumstances. I was saying to Colin (my uncle) that it's just as well she had a stroke."

What? I look at my phone as if *it* is the problem.

"I know that sounds bad Ailish but if she didn't she would have been on her own while you go to Germany and all that, telling you that she would be okay, when all the time she wouldn't if yer know what I mean love."

I say "Yes I do know what you mean. Can you tell her that I'm okay and I'm enjoying some time with Carly's friends? And give her a kiss from me too".

"Okay love, will do, bye now." Then she hung up.

Still holding my phone to my ear as if she's still there, I want to tell her that I will be home before Christmas as it's only six weeks away. I know I told them that I'd be here for a few weeks, but as Carly won't be around it will be hard for Mam, well for all of us really especially at this time of the year.

I decide after another four hours have passed, (Christ, four hours that time went by quickly) to return to the hotel but don't want to grab another taxi. I look for the tourist information centre where Carly had been. I want to jump on *some* form of public transport. I do eventually find one, maybe it isn't the same one but at least I find out how to get back to the hotel using the underground metro.

Back at the hotel I decide to have food in my room, as all that walking (which I wasn't used to) has tired me out. I change and shower and ordered a soup and salad with a lot of crusty bread and a pot of coffee. When it arrives I realise how famished I am and I eat the lot within a short time. Afterwards I lie on the large bed and pick up my new book, but before reading I think about what I have planned for tomorrow.

Getting out of bed the next morning, I have a feeling that something strange is going to happen today. You know that gut feeling yer get, don't ask me why but it is the atmosphere in the air that I think is a bit too calm for my liking. The calm before the storm. All I have planned for the day is to visit the zoo. Then tonight I am to meet up with Thaddeus again. Cannot wait to see him; he always cheers me up and helps me feel energised no matter what sort of mood I am in.

I want to take the underground again so I study the map of the entire system to make sure I get off at the correct station. When I do arrive at the right place, I have to walk a short distance and as I do, I notice ahead of me what Carly had described when she wrote about the entrance to the zoo. It is just as she had described. The entrance looking very oriental with it's colourful archway. I feel quite sad again but want to see all the animals that she had seen and the cafe of course, she loved the cafes. This entry though is where she met that Frenchman who had crossed her path for a short time and had treated her badly, the rotten bastard. Poor Carly she was a good person she never deserved the hard times she went through.

Once I have spent my time here and had a coffee to relax, I think well, the day hasn't been as bad as I thought it would have been. But the day isn't over with yet, is it.

Heading down to the underground to get back early enough to relax before meeting with my friend, I stand at the station waiting for the train and that is when I see him...I quickly go through my bag to take out the photo and...My heart beating faster now, I look again and it definitely *is* him...Ross Carmichael. What is a very rich man doing here when he is used to having a chauffeured driven car? Maybe he hasn't found another driver to come to his beck and call. I watch him from a distance and I observe other women looking at him too. Well he is very good looking and he knows it too. Arrogant pig!

I move closer to him to get a better look and then even closer, again my heart is beating faster. I am now standing just about five feet away from him. I really want to get closer to him but I am nervous, oh what the hell, I move in even closer still. I am nearly touching him at this point and I can even smell his (gorgeous) cologne. Oh shit. I feel right now I want to spit in his face, grab him by the balls and bang his head against the side of this train. That makes me feel very nervous thinking he can stir that emotion in me. They do say that anyone under stress could commit a murder if they had good reason. And I have a *very* good reason.

The train has now stopped at the platform. As soon as the doors open I notice there are a few seats that are vacant. I sit right next to him. I accidently drop my bag off my lap and we both go to pick it up but he reaches it before I do and then we come face to face with each other. He smiles at me and I nervously thank him for handing me my bag.

"Are you alright…" he asks me "you seem to be a bit flustered".

His voice is throaty and sexy.

I gulp and answer him "Oh Yes, yes" I stutter. "Just a bit hot in here", I say.

I fan myself with my own hands, and mutter "Phew" I can't think of anything else to say.

I find out that he is a fast mover as he asks me then and there if he could take me out for a drink as it may help to cool me down.

I must have had the face of thunder as he then says "I am sorry if I said the wrong thing, you're probably married or at least have a boyfriend".

I'm in a panicked state now. Do I call my whole plan off and get the police on to him, or do I stick to my guns and just go for it? So, I take a long breath in and say, "Well, I can't tonight but..." Oh shite "I could see you for a drink tomorrow if you still want to".

I notice some good-looking women listening to our conversation as if they are thinking, bitch; I would love to spread my legs for *him*.

He answers "Yes I would love to, how about if I pick you up or meet you somewhere if you prefer."

I can't think quickly enough as my brain is in mix up mode, so we exchange mobile numbers and I tell him I will get in touch with him.

Just as he is about to get off the train he turns to me and asks.

"Oh, by the way what is your name."

I again panic, then thinking quickly I say "Eh, Rachel, yes Rachel."

Then he says "Ross, nice to meet you".

He then steps off onto the platform and he is gone. I know where he is going; little does he know I know more about him than he thinks. After he got off I knew I had to tell Maria as soon as I got back to my hotel room. I sit my head back on the seat and realise that I am shaking. I have to concentrate on where I am as I don't want to miss my stop. I check the map on the wall of the train, I have three more stops.

When I enter the hotel, I rush straight up to my room as I need to get my head around what has just happened. When I change into my sweat pants and out of my sweaty underwear, I go to the in-room bar and pour myself a strong drink, shit, I need it *badly*. I sit on the bed holding my glass thinking, what have I done? I have to think straight so I have another drink to calm my nerves. I now know what Maria meant when she said Ross is a dangerous man. I need to plan out my idea with great care if I decide to see him. I have already given him my alias name as Rachel but I have to think of pretending where I'm from and why I am in Berlin in the first place.

Before I text Maria I pour myself another drink, then I think, I don't want to be drunk when I meet Thaddeus, so I pour a small one. I decide on a text as she said she had business to deal with so I don't want to disturb her by calling her. *Maria, seen Ross 2 day on the U. Ground, asked me out. Nervous need your advice, Ailish*. Her reply comes back much quicker than I thought. *What the hell is going on Ailish, how did that happen? Call u later; it be quite late, round midnight, hope that ok. M.x*

I reply. *Yes, midnight is ok, A.*

My mind is in turmoil but I know I have to try and relax as I am looking forward to seeing Thaddeus. I don't want him to see me *this* way. Checking the time, I decide to shower and change my clothes. I don't usually shower twice in one day, but my nerves are causing extra sweaty bits.

I dress casually in smart jeans and a silk emerald shirt, matched my eyes I was told, and spray on some of my special Pure Living perfume. I check myself out in the mirror, fiddle with my hair and then head down stairs to the bar. As I walk slowly past a couple of tables where guests are sitting enjoying their meals, I see him already sitting in the lounge looking through a newspaper. I walk up behind him and put my hands on his shoulders, he turns quickly with a big smile on his face.

"Ailish, you look lovely, and you smell gorgeous too." He stands up and we embrace.

"Thaddeus it's *so* lovely to see you again. You will have to tell me all about your adventures."

He says "I will, but first what can I get you to drink." We both decide on a beer with some bar food, a good extra posh bratwurst with French fries. It is the best I've ever tasted. (But what should I expect when the last one I had was from the local shop in Dublin.) Thaddeus tells me, in between bites of the delicious German sausage, all about his trip around Germany.

Then it is my turn to tell him what I have been up to and how everything went with Carly's funeral and then I tell him how my Mam had had a stroke.

He takes my hand and strokes it while telling me "Ailish you have to be strong, you can get through anything if you have faith."

Then he says "There is something else bothering you what is it?"

I sigh then tell him about my encounter with Ross on the metro and the way I felt that I could have killed him then and there. He says that it is only normal I feel like that as that man is responsible for Carly's death. I also tell him how I feel nervous about seeing him for a drink and was it really the right thing to be doing?

He says, "Ailish I told you I would be right beside you if you need me. You only have to call. I'm going to be in Berlin for a few weeks as I have lots of things to see and do here so I won't be far away."

I feel a bit happier after he tells me that.

He looks at me in his calm way then says "I know you want to get revenge on him but you still have to be careful for your own sake."

I say, "I know that Thaddeus and I know it would be easier to just get in touch with the police but really there isn't enough evidence to prove what he's up to, I need to do it *my* way anyway."

"Well, you've just answered your own question, then haven't you?" he comments. And I know I have.

Our evening is so enjoyable with him telling me more about his journey around the country and reminding me that he's always there for me. Then I notice the time. Christ it's almost midnight. I know Maria will be calling, so I bid him goodnight. Thaddeus says he was heading for his bed too, so we walk up together. Embracing in the hallway my phone starts to ring.

"Sorry, got to go" then I kiss him on the cheek. Oh he smelt so good.

I close the door behind me and still standing with my back against it, answer my mobile.

"Hi Maria."

"Ailish you have to tell me what is going on. What happened, where was he?"

She said, sounding very concerned. "Well?"

I move away from the door and tell her.

"I was coming back to the hotel on the metro standing at the station and I saw him a few feet away from me."

"Oh my God Ailish, what happened?" she says. I tell Maria how I felt when I saw him and how he asked me out.

"I can't believe it, he is such a bastard. He sucks women up like a spider to a fly."

I say "My thoughts exactly. But of all the good-looking women on the train he picks me, don't know why."

Then she says, "He picked on you because you *are* very attractive Ailish."

I answer her in shock, "What me, with my boring brown hair and lanky legs?"

"You with your shiny auburn brown hair and beautiful long legs more like. *That's* why he asked you out."

She continues, "When are you going to call him?"

"I think I will do it now, no time like the present" I say.

I hear her quickly inhale as if she is shocked.

"Just kidding, although…I *could* wake the bastard up right now what do yer think. Sorry, seriously though I thought maybe tomorrow."

"You seem more positive about it than when you left a message earlier this evening" she answers.

"I saw Thaddeus tonight, he gave me the confidence to just get on with it, he said he would be there for me if I needed him." (Funny thing is, he always seems to be around even when he's not.)

Then Maria says "My advice for you as you did ask, is

to keep calm and don't do anything stupid like sleeping with him".

I am shocked as I have no intention of sleeping with that creep.

Then she tells me, "Keep in touch Ailish and let me know what happens okay?" I agree, and then we end the call.

My revenge with Ross is about to begin.

Chapter 23

I wake early after a good night's sleep. My first thought is of Carly, it is every morning since her death. I miss her so much. But this morning I also feel strong and the thought of my plan is in my head. I jump out of bed and head to the bathroom to take a shower, not like me as I usually like breakfast first, but I am full of energy and ready to change my routine. While showering I start to think of Ross. The way he looks and how I despise him and the way I have to act as if I really like him. I think of what I'm going to tell him when he asks why I'm in Berlin, which I know he will and then my thoughts turn to Matthew. I had promised to visit him after I'd met him at Carly's funeral. I feel as if calling him today would be a good idea and I'll ask if I can pop over for a chat.

Maria has given me his address so I decide to take a taxi as the weather has turned from cool to cold and is threatening rain. I am glad I have packed some warm clothes.

Matthew greets me with a warm smile on his lovely face and asks me to come in and sit on one of the comfy looking chairs. The apartment is lovely and I can tell that Maria owns it as her stamp is written all over it. It is beautifully done out with classy furniture and neutral colours everywhere to make the place look so light and spacious. I know Carly would have felt the same even though she had lived here for just a short time. Matthew is pleased I have called, he tells me so. I take off my coat and make myself comfortable which isn't hard as he just makes me feel that way, just like a brother would. If things had been different he possibly could have been my brother-in-law. He makes coffee and he's obviously already prepared the food as he brings it all out on a tray. There are a few assorted sandwiches and some delicious looking pastries. I notice that he looks a lot different from when I last saw him so I tell him this. He answers me by telling me that he doesn't cry so much now, but he misses Carly very much. We talk about Carly for the next thirty minutes then I change the subject and tell him how I saw Ross and that I am going to meet with him. His face shows shock and disbelief. I go on to tell him of my plan to set the man up so I can then eventually hand him over to the police.

He says "But Ailish you are mad, how you are going about doing that, you could get yourself into real danger".

I say "Don't worry I have my ways of covering my identity from him and the plan I have to catch him with those people he deals with well, I'm hoping to get to them too."

"My God, you must be insane. But you know, you pretending to be someone else, you'll have to stay away from me and Maria. If he sees you with either of us, he will know something's not right. But call me if you need me though…For anything Ailish please, do you hear me, *anything*."

"Yes, Matthew I do hear you, I promise I will."

We enjoy the rest of the afternoon together eating and drinking coffee until it is coming out of our ears. I know he has to work tonight so I leave not long after my umpteenth caffeine fix.

He reminds me before I leave, to not forget what he had told me. I hug him then agree and off I go back to my hotel to put my plan into action.

When the taxi pulls up to the hotel I step right out into some nasty rain which hits my face as the wind sprays it in my direction. I am glad to be inside to dry myself off.

The first thing I do after drying off and warming up is to text my aunt Riona to ask how Mam is doing. While waiting for her reply I change my outfit and sit against the pillows that I have propped up against the headboard. Then I hear the ping as the message comes through. Her reply tells me that Mam is doing fine. She had her out in the garden today but she's still a bit weak. She adds "It will take time Ailish", but this I already know. She then tells me that Mam was asking after me so I tell her to tell Mam I will be fine as I have friends here to talk to and they are showing me around the city. She didn't need to know anything else.

I look at my watch and notice it is nearly three in the afternoon, so I wonder what to do to keep myself occupied before I call Ross. I bend down to reach my bag off the floor and pull out my note book. I decide to write myself some ideas of where to tell him I am from and why I'm here. Oh, and a fake last name too just to be on the safe side. Oh God, I have been brought up not to lie and here I am lying like slippery rocks on the seashore ready for my fall. No, I will not slip and fall. I will think positive and be strong, for Carly's sake.

I watch a bit of TV and try to find something of some interest. I find the news channel and listen to what's going on in the world. I flick it to another channel but change my mind when I hear the subject they are now discussing, *Drugs in Berlin and London*. I remove the remote from my grasp and listen with a lot of interest. The news reader is saying that things are getting worse as more young women's lives are being destroyed by the drug known by the name of Higher Love. And I know one of them I thought, my sister. The news stated that the police were still looking for the people responsible and if anyone has any information or idea please come forward and they will be protected. This news makes me more determined to do what I have to do. Checking the time once again I feel like it is now time to call Ross to meet up with him tonight. Hopefully he will be free to see me.

We arrange to meet at eight pm. He says he will pick me up from the hotel where I'm staying. From there he will take me to one of his regular haunts.

It takes me a while to decide what to wear. I pull out a low-cut pale blue dress, no, too seductive for the first date. Then I choose a navy trouser suit, not that either, it's too formal. I take out a blue (am I addicted to blue clothes?) fitted blouse and find a dressy pair of (Oh my God, different shade of blue, but they look good) pants to go with it as the weather is crap tonight. I try them on, yes perfect, third time lucky. I choose a pair of kitten heels to finish off the outfit. I don't want to tower over him. He is tall; my five-inch heels would have me looking down on him, not a good idea. I take another shower and get dressed with not a lot of jewellery. Spray my perfume over my neck and arms for good luck and now I'm ready. I pour myself a large drink from the bar in my room just to calm my nerves a bit. Then toss another down my throat.

Walking out of my room, I lock the door and take a deep breath before I head downstairs to the bar, as that is where I suggested we meet before going elsewhere.

I turn the corner into the lounge and then I see him. Looking tall, good looking and beautifully dressed standing at the bar. FUCK!!! Thank God the alcohol I have in my system did the trick as I feel confident enough to casually walk towards him. But before I get near to his body, he turns around and sees me as if he has sixth sense. I smile at him and stand next to him and notice that he looks less tired than when I first saw him. He smells (gorgeous again, damn it) like he knows how to attract women. He tells me that I look very smart. SMART? Makes me feel like his sister or an aunt. Just as well I guess, it's better than making me feel horny. I thank him and he asks if I would like a drink here or would I prefer to go out. I suggest going out somewhere else as it would be nice for me to go somewhere rather than here again. He finishes off the small amount he has left in his glass and then he pulls out his phone. He presses a button then hangs up.

He puts his hand in the small of my back then says "Ready Rachel?"

Then out we go to the front of the building. He steers me towards a car that has just pulled up to the curb and then the chauffeur opens the door for me and him. I see he is back to his rich way of living with his chauffeured driven car again. So, I say, pretending to be surprised "Ooh this is nice, never been driven around like this before".

Whilst travelling in the back he comments on my perfume and asks what it is as he has never smelt it before. I tell him it was a gift from a friend and I can never remember the name. He asks if it was from a boyfriend, I tell him yes but he's not in my life now. He says that it is unusual to keep things from an ex when normally you would throw them out. I then answer him by saying but why, when it's so lovely like this perfume. He smiles at me, shrugs his shoulders then says, "Whatever you say." Then the conversation *really* starts.

"What are you doing here in Berlin, do you live here?"

I swallow then I tell him "No I don't live here, I'm visiting alone. I work for a travel agent in Northumberland (a county where I've sent a lot of people on holiday, so I know a bit about it). I was chosen as best selling sales person for the year with the company so I came here with a friend as a prize. But at the last minute my friend had to pull out as she had to work, so I decided to come anyway."

I say it with a definite light tone in my voice, quite

happy with that. Oh God, I hate to lie but that's the name of the game isn't it.

He asks me "Your accent doesn't sound as if you're from the north east, sounds as if you have a bit of Irish in you".

Oh God help me.

"No, no, definitely not Irish" I feel the sweat trickle down from my armpits. "I used to live in Wales for a while, it's probably a mixture of both." I look out of the window swallowing hard with nerves and trying not to look at my reflection.

He said "I see, well it's really cute and you're cute too".

He leans into me as if he wants to kiss me already. Holy shit! He must notice my embarrassment so he moves away, but I notice a smile come to his face as if he enjoyed it. Fucker!! The next thing I know, we pull up to a nice-looking classy bar, his kind of place. We walk in and I hear voices greeting him as if he is a regular here.

Someone takes my coat and Ross knows exactly which table we are heading to as if it's his *lady table*. We sit down at a quiet secluded spot and he orders drinks for both of us. Cocky bastard, not my kind of man, he's too sure of himself.

He smiles and says "I know you will love this cocktail Rachel if you don't well, that will be the first".

Christ, the first of how many women have you had? I think it very weird that he was supposedly so in love with my sister and now he is acting as if she never existed. I don't say anything but act in my innocent *lovely* manner.

He looks at me while we wait for our drinks then asks

me "I never asked how long you are here for?"

I tell him "Well, the trip I won from my employer is for two weeks but I also had my holiday booked for the two weeks after that, so I'm here for four weeks."

"Wonderful" he said "We can get to know each other and I can show you around my special places."

Good God, every woman he's been with has most likely been to his *special places*. Our drinks arrive and then he orders the food for me. Very annoying, he makes me feel like a child.

Again, he says "You will love what I've chosen for you, it's the chefs' speciality unless you are a vegetarian, are you?"

I said "No I'm not" I have to be kind "I'm sure I will love it" and I smile. YUK!!

I spend the rest of the evening listening to him telling me about his architecture offices in Berlin and London and also his latest one in Dublin. Then out of the blue he asks if I have any siblings. I hesitate, then I tell him no, never had. I am shocked by his next comment. "I thought you may have done, you remind me of someone."

I feel quite sick after that so I ask for a glass of water. I notice the strange look he gives me. (He couldn't know, as I don't look a bit like Carly.) As our evening comes to an end, well that's what I thought; he asks if I would like to go somewhere else for a drink. What the hell, so I say "why not".

I am taken to a dark, cave like bar with seductive corners and lots of women dressed in sexy clothes. It's like something you would find in Morocco, full of bright colours, reds and yellows with lots of funky lanterns hanging from the ceiling. He steers me where he wants to go and we sit and I tell him this time what *I* want to drink. He approves of the domineering woman I have suddenly become so he decides to place his hand on my leg and then he sits back on our cushioned seat and pulls me back with him. I laugh as we are now almost sprawled out on this low banquette but I don't want him to get the idea that I want sex with him. But...he comes down on my face as if he hadn't had a woman in years. He kisses me with a passion I have never known. I really don't want to kiss him back but I have no choice I have to go along with it. We have a few more drinks which make me feel relaxed and fancy free.

Then he says "Want to come back to my place?"

Oh shite, I don't want to go and I am afraid that Maria might be watching out of her window. But I act with carefree abandonment and say I will. The alcohol is my friend tonight and I could drink more as I'm not to the point of throwing my head down a toilet. He looks pleased with himself when I decide on his way.

He is now in a hurry to leave as his mind is only on getting me into his bed. His car takes us to his posh apartment and of course I have to pretend as if I have never been in the building before.

"Wow Ross, this is such an incredible place." I tell him followed by my sickly smile.

As we enter his home I again throw comments around about his beloved apartment. I look around imagining Carly living here which sends me off into a solemn mood for a minute, but before I know it, he is standing with his back to me pouring our drinks. He walks towards me with a determined look and I notice the glass is quite full of clear liquid.

"Ah water" I say laughing.

He likes my sense of humour and laughs with me.

While handing me the drink he says, "I hope you like gin and tonic".

"Yes, that's fine. I don't mind as long as it's not spiked with anything."

He looks as guilty as sin and says "Why would I do that I am a good boy" Then with a sexy innocent smile he says, "Don't worry it's not, just get it down your neck".

He places his glass on one of the expensive dark wood tables and walks over to the other side of the room, presses a couple of switches on the wall and then there is music. Music I think to get a girl in the mood. He then walks towards me, pulls me to my feet and does what I call, the *sex dance.* He moves his hips next to mine and gets closer and closer as if we are about to have sex. He takes my drink and helps me to drink it, which I thought was a bit strange. After the drink is finished he, to my amazement, pushes me slowly down on to the thick carpet, pulls down my pants and goes down on me. My head is in a different place now which is not unusual, when I *am* frustrated as hell. I haven't had sex in years. He pushes his tongue right into me and I moan and groan with pleasure. My mind is thinking I hate you, I hate you, but my body is doing quite the opposite. This fantastic oral sex lasts a while and I come twice. I thought I would feel ashamed but I hate to say, I don't. After another kissing episode he wants me to go down on him but I pull myself up as I need the toilet.

I look at myself in the bathroom mirror and I am very flushed. *Ailish*, I say out loud *you fool; you really enjoyed that sexual encounter didn't you*. I use the toilet and sit there thinking I want sex with him, I really do. I can't wait to get his dick inside me.

Something has changed and I know it, maybe he has put something in my drink after all. Then I start to think, oh my God, what if he *has* put one of those drugs in it that he gave to Carly, because I want him so bad. I finish up and go back to him. He's now standing in front of me stark naked. I look at him but I don't say a word. He lifts me up in his arms and takes me to his bed. He slowly takes off my clothes and lays me down, caressing my whole body. He touches my breasts with his lips then down onto my thighs then licks my throbbing vagina with his sensual tongue again. But I want him inside me I can't wait, so I pull up his head and see his large erection ready for me. He enters me with a slow and seductive way I have never thought possible. I am so hungry for him. The feeling of such pleasure wraps around my whole body. I wrap my thighs around him and I feel him getting deeper inside. We move together as if one and I get wetter at every move. Then I come not once but again and again. I feel like I'm in heaven. Kissing him, moving with him, feeling him getting harder each time, I want him more and more.

It's four am when our lovemaking ends. The thing is I still want more, but I don't tell him that as he walks out of the room to make us some coffee. I sit up and wonder what I have done, but at this very moment I don't care as I had never thought sex could be *so* good.

I had wanted to be where Carly has been and walk where she walked in this city, but I should have realised that in his bed would have to have been included in my plan. If I don't do this how could I expect to catch him in the act of drug dealing? I also have to seduce him in to doing what I want. Ross comes back into the room with the coffee before we have sex once more.

I awake with the sun shining through the sheer white long billowing curtains in his bedroom. He is not beside me as I look around the large room. I check the time, Christ eleven am already. I stretch my body to try to feel alive but I have a hangover that makes me feel like shit. I get up slowly feeling my head throbbing and walk through this vast apartment to get to the kitchen. I search for coffee and a cup, and then I see a note propped up in front of the coffee maker. (Shit no instant.) I open up the note and read.

Good morning Rachel or maybe afternoon if you've been feeling lazy. I would love you to be at my place when I get home but I'm sure you will need a change of clothes. Can I see you again tonight? I would love to continue where we left off, what do you think? Call me. Ross. X

I feel horny just thinking about what we did. Obviously, I will call him, but sex can't be the only thing in this relationship. I am going to have to ask him what he *did* put in my drink then I can start the ball rolling finding out more about it and asking him where he does get this drug from, but feeling guilty about the whole thing as I do.

I get back to the hotel around one in the afternoon feeling slightly better than when I woke up earlier.

I walk in feeing slightly guilty as the staff can see that I've been out all night just by the way I look. The same clothes as when I left last night. I enter my room and strip my clothes off and get in the shower. I feel the luxurious warm water run down my face and body. I pour the body gel on my hand and touch my body as if it was Ross. I can feel myself becoming very aroused thinking about what we did and how we did it. I suddenly feel strange wondering if this is how it all started with Carly. Then I come to my senses and think about my plans tonight with Ross.

Dressed up to the nines, with a low-cut black (not blue this time) dress with my *cum fuck me* shoes on my feet; I wait for Ross to pick me up. He said he was taking me somewhere special for dinner tonight, so why not.

His car is such a treat I love being in it, makes me feel like I'm a celebrity. He tells me that the journey will take a bit longer this time so I sit back and relax and enjoy the ride.

The car turns down a quiet road, along a gravelled driveway until we get to a spooky looking stone building which is lit up with fairy lights. I see other couples arriving, one woman dressed up in a sparkly number with a slit just about up to her crack! Thank God I had a decent dress to wear. I get out of the car pulling down my dress slightly as it has moved up to show off the tops of my thighs. Now I do feel sexy and special.

We enter the building and are seated in a large room with dark curtains and candelabras on every table. Ross tells me that it is an old crematorium (a shiver runs down my spine when he tells me that) pop up restaurant which has been run by two chefs only for special events. The event tonight, being the birthday party of a celebrity who he knows well. I ask who, but he says he will introduce me to him later. I pick up the menu and notices it's a set menu. There are some things on it which I'm not sure what they are but I'll take my chance as I'm starving.

Before the food is brought out, he excuses himself from our table, then he walks over to a couple of men standing near the door. Looks a bit like a secret rendezvous to me, the way they stand looking suspicious but that's probably my mind working overtime. (Or maybe not.) Eventually he walks back to the table with a grin on his face as if he *has* done a deal.

I really do enjoy the fantastic food that is served and the atmosphere is magic. Ross now stands up taking a cigar out of a case (Yuk) and off he goes outside to meet with other men I presume. He leaves me at the table twiddling my thumbs which I am not very happy about.

Boredom now sets in. I want to move and nose around outside. Pushing my chair back I pull my dress back down again and grab my handbag from underneath the table. I decide first of all to go to the ladies to redo my lipstick. I open the door but it's quite busy so I am in and out in a minute. I want to get some fresh air so I wander to the doorway and open the large wooden door and see lots of nooks and crannies in the grounds where you could hide yourself away from everyone. I quietly wander then I notice the lights coming from lit cigarettes. I hide behind a tree and see that it is Ross with his two male friends again. I listen carefully to their conversation, it sounds like they are talking about setting up something. I take out my phone and set it to record. I'm scared but this is my chance. I hear them talking about a deal that will be going down in London very soon. Good God, I'm shaking now really bad, just imagine what they would do to me if they found me listening in. Then I hear them talking about it being sent to other people. I know this is what I have been waiting for, at last some evidence which I need badly. When I think I have enough information I decide to quietly go back inside to sit back at the table before I'm found out. I look around to see if there is anyone I recognise while waiting for my *drug dealer* boy friend. I don't notice any one of interest so I ask the waiter for another drink and then I see Ross walk back into the room. I take in a deep breath before he sits next to me. He looks so innocent as he sits back down.

Then he puts his hand on my leg and says "I forgot to tell you, you look so sexy and gorgeous" then he says "Back to my place?"

I nod and then his hand wanders further up my thigh, heading straight for my cunt. I want him now. Coming back into the car, I ask him why he didn't introduce me to the celebrity as he promised that he would. He said 'Oh, I didn't think you would be interested.' I ask who it was. He says some name I haven't even heard of, so I shrug it off. He sees my reaction then tells me which film he's a star in and the part he plays. That is when the penny drops.

I say "Oh my God I love the new Star Trek, he is *so* good." Selfish bastard, I could have met him.

The rest of the evening becomes a repeat of last night but something is not right as I feel different. More confident, sexier and everything I have ever wanted to feel. He leaves the room and I hear my phone beep as a message comes through. Oh God it's from Maria. I just hope she hasn't seen me from her window as we got out of the car. I read it.

Hi Ailish hope everything well with you. I worry about you, just keep me informed ok Maria X.

I send a message back to tell her that I am fine and I will keep in touch. My legs ache a bit so with my phone still in my hand I walk through to see what he is doing. With his back to me again pouring drinks, I can still see that he has a small bottle in his hands so I quietly hide behind the door to watch him. Well, I was right, he is putting a pill in my drink. I set my phone to camera and take a picture of him in the act. I tip toe my way back to the bedroom, lay on the bed as if I haven't moved and think, shall I drink it or not.

I have to be honest with myself, I want to experience what Carly did to an extent. I remember her telling me that she was taking two each day but that's not what I will be doing, so I might as well go through with it. If these drugs make me feel the way I did last night well, I will take more. I am sure I will be okay; I'm not as naive as my sister was. God rest her soul.

CHAPTER 24

Taking off my coat, the most important thing, is listening to the conversation I recorded last night. I sit on the bed in my hotel room and reach for my bag and pull my phone out. Getting comfortable with the pillows behind my shoulders, I press the button and listen. It's quiet, so I turn it up to the highest level.

(Ross speaks) That warehouse near the airport in Feltham the building we used a couple of months ago they are bringing it in a van with ALJ LOGISTICS written on the side. Pete and Danny will be there this time. The drugs are in several red and green boxes with Christmas decorations on the top to cover them. The bottles will have Harvey pharmaceuticals on the labels, and then after they are checked the boys will deliver them. (Unknown man's voice) Okay, we will check them out but you will be there to make sure that the money is right? (Ross speaks) Yes, I will I don't trust anyone. They should be there at 8 o'clock on Monday evening so I will see you then.

Oh my God I feel very excited but nervous. This is great

evidence but I still need more. I recall the conversation I had with Ross before we fell asleep. He told me he was going to London for a meeting with his architects but he should be back in a couple of days. I told him I would love to go with him because I don't want to be without him in his bed. But he said no, quite a firm no too, but I wasn't going to leave it at that, I couldn't.

I eventually weave my web by the power of my woman hood. (Sitting on his face, sucking him off...I could go on.)

Going to London is my big chance of getting the evidence I need, I hope. I just need the guts to do it. I have to let Thaddeus know where I am going as he asked me to, especially if I'm leaving the country.

I also let Maria and Matthew know where I am heading. Both are worried and still think I could be in danger. I tell them I already have some evidence but not enough to get him convicted. Maria tells me to call it off as she is scared for me.

But I say "Maria I have got him under my thumb, I know what I'm doing."

She knows right away what I mean by that and says "Ailish?"

I say "No, it's Rachel".

"What? Oh, right your alias. You have slept with him, haven't you?"

"I had to" I say. I can't believe the new found force in my voice. "There has been no getting away from that, I had to get close to him."

I hope she doesn't think I am being mean by shouting.

She says, "Just be careful my love and do not take anything he offers you, Okay?"

I answer, "Yes Maria, I won't do anything I shouldn't. But I *do* need to be with him and get what I want."

We are both silent for a moment then I say, "I have to do this, he cannot get away with what he is doing to women, Maria you know that".

She agrees and we end the conversation. But not without another 'be careful watch your back' etc.

The meeting in London is tomorrow. I have to pack my bag as Ross is picking me up this evening to stay at his place, before getting the 10 am flight in the morning from Heathrow.

Last night Ross told me right out what he has been putting in my drink.

I was quite shocked at first, but stayed calm and smiling and said "I thought you may have been giving me something like cannabis or similar as the sex is *so* wild. Why didn't you just give me something to smoke?"

He said "Well, it is a bit stronger than cannabis and it only comes in tablet form. I wanted to surprise you to let you see what it does, you may have refused."

"I might have done but I'm glad you gave it to me, it works wonders."

I smile at him while thinking, *you fucking bastard I could kill you, you're nothing but scum.* Even though I still love the sex I really have changed into someone else, I *am* becoming Rachel the Spy.

Sitting on the plane to London, I go through my bag for an antiseptic wipe and then I find rolling around in the bottom, guess what, a bottle of tablets just for me to throw down my throat. I sarcastically think, how kind of him to think about me. I pull them out and nudge him as he is reading a newspaper. I just look at him with the bottle in my hand waiting for an answer.

He says "You can take one each night if you still want some wild sex, as you like it so much"

"Right, okay I will" I tell him with my *put-on* sexy smile.

I love this. Getting great sex with the help of an enhancer which is not harming me (surely, I would be getting moody by now), I will make the most of it while I can. I place them back in my bag, sit back and flick through my newly bought magazine trying to concentrate on something other than revenge, for now.

We arrive at the Savoy which apparently isn't far from his London office; I lower myself out of the taxi and have to pinch myself as I am at my dream hotel. We enter into the foyer and my eyes are all over the place looking at the beautiful decor.

We are taken to our suite by a lovely polite porter who asks if we want anything else. Ross turns to him and says he would like some Dom Perignon on ice brought to the room. The porter leaves the room but not before getting a huge tip from Ross.

I say "Champagne, are we celebrating something I don't know about?"

He says "Well actually it's my birthday today so I thought I would start with a decent drink."

"Well if you had mentioned it I would have bought you

a gift." On saying that I think, I'll buy you a gift alright, the first fucking ticket to fucking Mars.

I have become so sickly sweet being so polite and hiding my real personality I make *myself* sick sometimes. But I only intend for this to go on just as soon as I get those pictures sent out when I find him at the warehouse doing the drug deal with his friends in tow.

He says to me "Oh, what would you have bought me?"

I think for a bit and then I say "I probably would have bought something for us to share".

He looks at me with a quizzical expression.

So, I say "You know a sex toy, something to pleasure us both".

He says "So you like that sort of thing, do you?"

I have never had anything like that in my entire life but I don't let him know the boring sex life I've had in the past.

He then says, as I watch him watching me teasing him, as I begin to undress "I could take care of that, I will put my order in when we get back".

A knock on the door, then our champagne arrives. The porter opens the bottle, pours out two glasses and leaves again with another huge tip. We take two sips then begin our two hours of wild sex.

"Would you like more coffee madam?" asks the very smart waiter.

Sitting in the dining room of this magnificent hotel we have just finished our amazing evening meal. I accept the coffee and ask Ross when his important meeting is. He sips his drink and as he places it slowly back onto its saucer he looks at me and says. "I am going out later this evening to check some papers at my office which is only a walk away. But tomorrow evening I will have to leave you on your own because I have an important meeting at eight o'clock."

He then calls the waiter over and asks for a bottle of champagne.

I said "What, more?"

"Why not it's still my birthday."

The sex and the Dom Perignon we had earlier today was the best time I've had in a long time.

I think about Carly, she most likely tasted the same thing when she was with him. I feel rather solemn thinking about her but then I have more champagne that will cheer me up again.

After drinking a few glasses, I still feel a bit down. I know sometimes alcohol can get you that way so I just brush it off. Ross asks if I am ready, as we could walk down to his office and he can show me around. He helps me with my coat before we venture out into the chilly night air. It's nice outside as the atmosphere is becoming quite Christmassy. He tells me with a glint in his eye that we'll be alone in the building apart from the security men at the door as if to say, more sex? I don't mind at all. It doesn't take long to walk to his offices and when we do get there, the security doorman greets him and lets us both in.

The foyer is vast with a large high atrium, bright neutral colours and large stainless-steel light fixtures hanging from the ceiling. We enter the elevator and press the button for his personal office on the top floor. He opens the door to an enormous ultra modern, sexy but tasteful room. I walk in and see it has an en suite bathroom, so I pop my head around to have a nose and can't help but notice the huge jacuzzi. *Oh, Bejaysus.* So glad I did not say that out loud or I would have given myself away.

I say to Ross "Would be lovely to have a go in that thing".

He says "That's good I was thinking just that, we could get in there after I get the papers I need. In fact, why don't you put the water in and I'll meet you in there."

I was very excited as I had never been in a jacuzzi before, never mind had sex in one. I do as he says and strip off my clothes and wait. I relax in the warm water wondering what he is up to. I start getting impatient and the water is getting cooler so I step out and dry myself off with one of the large fluffy white towels and quietly open the door. I listen for his voice as I expect him to be on the phone, what else would he be doing? I don't hear a thing so I get brave and walk into the room. He isn't here, what the hell is going on? I go back into the bathroom and pull a bathrobe around myself then I go to investigate.

The door to his office is closed which I think is a bit strange, because if we are alone why did he close the door and where the hell has he got to anyhow? I slowly walk towards the door to open it but when I try, it is locked. Christ, I suddenly feel scared, why would he lock me in? I stop to think and then I hear my phone ringing from inside my handbag. I look around before answering it then grab it quickly.

"Hello?"

"Rachel are you standing there naked ready for me to seduce you?"

Oh, for fucks sake, this is weird. "Ross, why have you locked me in here?" I try to keep it light.

"Have I been naughty?" I say.

He says "Well, you tell me".

"I'm not sure what you mean" I say.

"I saw you Rachel when I was outside the restaurant in Berlin talking to my friends, you were hiding behind the tree and I also noticed that you had your phone in your hand."

Oh, shit what am I going to do now, think Ailish, think. After my hesitant reply which involved feeling completely nauseous I say, "I was lonely and I needed some fresh air and then I saw you so I took a picture as a reminder of the lovely surroundings outside." I hope he will go for this.

"Okay I will be with you in a minute and then you can show me the picture that you took, Bye." Then he hangs up.

I know what to do, I immediately send my recording and the picture I took of him and his two friends to Maria, Matthew and Thaddeus then I hit delete. Thank God I *did* take some pictures of the fairy lights around the trees or else I would have been in dire straits. I then run to the bathroom and throw up. I need to watch myself now very carefully. I wash my mouth out with the alcohol I poured earlier, then put more hot water in the jacuzzi and get back in.

With a huge sigh I lay back and wait for him, trying to be calm. I didn't wait long. He was next to me within the next few minutes with my phone in his hand checking out my pictures, thankfully he was satisfied. We did have great sex, a bit more aggressive as if I *had* done wrong, but after telling me that he doesn't like his photo taken at any time, never has.

I will be very glad when I have got back to being Ailish and being in my bedroom at home with all this behind me. I lay here with this Ross person next to me in this king size bed in this fantasy hotel of mine thinking I don't feel too good.

I want to tell Maria that I have been taking this drug he has given me and that I'm now scared that it has taken over my body like it had with Carly. But I have to get tonight over with and get the evidence I need to get this man put away for a very long time. I want to be alone today. Maybe I will be if I tell him I still want to buy him a belated birthday gift then I will disappear into the crowds of Christmas shoppers for a while.

Ross goes with my excuse of wanting to be alone. Even though I will have to buy him something.

I dress like myself today in jeans and a T-shirt with my scarf and gloves at the ready. Ross has already left for *his* day whatever that is going to be. When I do get to the foyer of the hotel to leave for the peaceful day on my own, I am surprised by the most beautifully decorated Christmas tree standing there in all its glory. I have to stop before going out of the door to inspect it and to see all the glittering gold baubles and the pink bows and crackers tied onto the branches. It brings a tear to my eyes thinking of memories from the past when I was a child with Carly by my side, opening presents on that special day.

I notice the receptionist looking and smiling in my direction. She is blonde and about the same age as Carly was when she…I stop and think now, Oh shit, I didn't turn my phone back on after I sent the recording and those pictures to my friends. I wander and find a seat in a beautiful room and sit near the open fire which is crackling with the sound of the logs burning and search threw my bag to find it hiding in the bottom. As soon as I turn it on, the messages are coming through from each of them. I read them and each one is saying *Ailish you have to call me and let me know what is going on now. I am worried.* I call Maria and Matthew and tell them what had happened and that I am on to him. I still want to tell Maria about the way I am feeling but I don't, not yet. Then I call Thaddeus. I tell him where I am and what I am about to do tonight and at what time. He tells me to be very careful and he will be there with me (in thought obviously). I leave the warmth of that fantastic room with hesitation.

I wander around London feeling glad to be alone. I wonder if this is where Carly walked and shopped when she was here with Ross. Walking for an hour or so, I feel hungry so I stop at the nearest nice-looking cafe. Feeling the warmth as soon as I enter, I put myself down at a table near to the window. I order coffee and a sandwich and settle myself for the next half hour or so. As I wait for my food I pull out my notebook and pen and write down how I feel today. As I start to write I get a sudden flash back of when I found Carly's book in the shed when she started taking the drugs, and then the notebook of her feelings of depression. I am scared now as I think it is starting to happen to me. I think of Mam and decide to call my Aunts house. It's a while before someone picks up.

Then "Hello".

"Mam is that you, it's Ailish." She talks with a bit of a slur so I have to listen carefully.

"Ailish where are you love? I miss you."

"I miss you too. I'm in London right now doing some Christmas shopping." I couldn't tell her that I'm really your lying daughter, getting revenge on the nasty bastard named Ross.

She says "I thought you were in Germany".

"Well I was, I am only here for a few days. How are you anyway?"

"A bit better I suppose", answering in her slurry voice. She lies too.

"Riona is looking after me very well. I should be a lot better when you come home, when will that be?" I really do not know what to tell her as I do not know myself.

So, I tell her. "I should be home just before Christmas then we can go to Christmas Eve mass together. What do yer think?" It is back to reality when I can talk in my normal Irish accent instead of putting on my fake *Rachel voice.*

"That will be nice love, hope to see yer soon" then she says, "I'm going to have a lie down so I'll go now".

I reply "Okay Mammy take care, I love yer".

"Love yer too Ailish bye." She hangs up. I sit looking

at my phone until I am interrupted by the waitress bringing me my food. I'm very sad not hungry but I don't want to starve myself either.

I find a shop on Bond Street that sells men's scarves as Ross had forgotten his when he packed his case. I pick one up that (is long enough to strangle him with?) is warm and just his style but then I think, hell no I'm not paying that price for him. I'm not that generous. Then I look for a nice shop where I can buy my Mother the perfect Christmas gift, so I head for Harrods, she would love a gift from there. I find a cheaper scarf for Ross too, it hurts me to get out my wallet to buy him something but I have to carry on with the pretence.

Feeling tired after my shopping day I lay on the bed in the hotel and drift off to sleep. I dream about my Dad and this time Thaddeus is sitting talking to him. I try to listen to what they are talking about but then I am woken by the sound of Ross coming into the room. I am annoyed as I was tired and enjoying my good dream.

I say shouting "Why did you wake me, I was fast asleep?"

He looks at me as if he had never been shouted at before and says, "Don't you dare shout at me like that ever again or I will…"

I get up off the bed very quickly feeling really pissed off and say to him "And you will do what Ross, come on tell me…I am waiting"

I am getting brave but I have had enough of him, I don't care anymore. He doesn't say any more just leaves the room and gets himself some alcohol. I follow him into the room and we sit parted for the next half hour.

And then he says "I am sorry Rachel; can I pour you a drink?"

I sigh and think, may as well get pissed out of my brains as I need a lot of courage for what I'm about to do tonight. He pours that drink and sits looking at me with his spoilt schoolboy look. He asks me to sit next to him so I do. Then after a few gin and tonics I give him his gift. Then as he wraps the scarf around my naked body, we have sex again. Those frickin' drugs, now that I know I *am* addicted to them I am becoming very worried.

Trying very hard now to hide my erratic moods we eat dinner together in the Riverside restaurant in the hotel (great place to eat) even though I would have rather called for room service. He keeps checking his watch most of the time during the meal. I'm sure he's expecting a call very soon. I now check my watch (six thirty, one and a half hours before his meeting) and he has the nerve to ask me why I'm doing it.

I say, "What is the problem, I still feel tired and was only wondering whether I should take a nap or not."

He says "You may as well; you know I told you that I have a meeting tonight. We could do something when I come back if you like".

I tell Ross that I think I will take that nap. I leave the restaurant and head back to the suite.

I google 'AA route planner' on my phone to check how far the warehouse is from the hotel so I will know when I need a taxi. It tells me 35 minutes. I decide that it would be better for me to be there in plenty of time, hopefully finding a good hideout, so I can watch him walking into the building. So, I ask reception to get a taxi to pick me up at 6.45 pm which will give me plenty of time.

I put back on my jeans and a warm sweater and stuff my large bag with scarf, hat and gloves and a bottle of water and of course my phone to get the evidence I need to get him and his cronies arrested. I'm not really sure how long I will be there. All I know is that I need to be back at the hotel before he is. I'm ready to jump into bed fully clothed if he comes back to the room. Thankfully he doesn't.

CHAPTER 25

I am now on my way, sitting looking out of the window into the darkness of this city. After some slow traffic, which caused me to panic trying to calm my nerves down a bit, I notice a road sign that says Feltham/ Bedfont. It seems it can't be far now so I ask the driver and he tells me about another five to ten minutes. I am sure he is wondering why I want to go to a warehouse at this time of the night.

I know which one it is when we are in the area as the lights are on and there is a truck outside that says ALJ LOGISTICS. It looks ancient. A building that in the past has been blackened by the smoke fires that were common in its day. With its main windows low and arched it looks Victorian. Seems to be one of the oldest and spookiest buildings on the site.

Even though I've had a few drinks I still feel nervous. I tell the driver that this is the one but I ask him to drop me off at the back of the building. He gives me a strange look so I feel I should make an excuse (don't want him to get suspicious), I tell him the building has been hired for a large party and it has been arranged for me to go in the back door. I am getting good at lying now.

I pull my warm woolly hat on and thank God that it's not raining before paying the driver, then I get my phone out ready to get some evidence. Stepping out of the car, hearing the gravel beneath my feet, I feel the cold air on my face and watch my breath like a small cloud in front of me. I know the first thing I have to do is to get a picture of the license plate on the truck and there is also a car here which obviously belongs to the two dealers.

I feel my heart beating faster now. I have to try to control my breathing as I don't want anyone to hear me panting when I get inside. I watch where I walk trying to find the grassy areas as not to make a sound with my boots. If I need to, I will take them off, but it is not necessary as yet. Sneaking around the building I check my watch then I hear a car pull up. I slowly walk around towards the front of the building, then quietly hunch down feeling the sweat build up between my cleavage and trickle down my back. Then I see Ross getting out of his car. It is too dark to get a picture outside as I can't use the flash. But I'll wait until he's inside then I can quickly put the flash on to get the plate numbers of both the truck and the car. With that done I have to figure out how I am going to get inside. I wait for him to close the door to the warehouse, then I wander around looking for a window to climb through or have I been watching too many films when there always is a window open. I feel more confident so I keep looking and hoping.

Believe it or not I *do* find a small window open at the

side of the building which is most likely a toilet. I'm not a large woman so I might be able to get in. I pull myself up and my feet are dragging on the brick wall so this is now the time to take off my boots. I unzip them and stuff them in my bag. I can now get some grip with my thick socks even though it takes me at least five minutes to get my whole body in.

When I do eventually get in the room it *is* a toilet and a small room at that. Phew, it stinks in here it has to be the Gents.

My nerves are getting the better of me which makes me want a wee, so I do. Best place to enter the building then wasn't it. After I relieve myself, I open the door of the room and I am thankful it didn't make some kind of noise. I listen carefully and stop, then I hear talking. I move slowly toward their voices until I am right outside the door of what seems the main room in this building.

I see a small window so I move toward it but it is too high for me to reach. I look for a box or something to stand on which isn't difficult as I see a lot of pallets thrown here and there. I pick a couple of them up with my shaky hands. I gradually lift my head up to cautiously look through the window and there I see Ross with his two dealers and another man who must be the driver who brought the drugs here. I see boxes of drugs in front of them, piled high full of the bottles and Christmas decorations that had been thrown on the floor. I get my phone ready and take a few pictures, then I send them straight to my friends. I know better this time.

I say a prayer for help to calm my breathing amongst

other things, so I can listen to their conversation. I hear with shock that the drug has almost been doubled in strength for the last few weeks, so no wonder my reactions happened quickly. They do not care who they are harming, they deserve to be jailed for a very long time. They go on about where the drugs will be delivered to and who will be responsible for them, names and all. Then I hear a remark from Ross that makes me shiver. He is telling his friends that so far that his new experiment (meaning *me* I'm his experiment? What the hell) hasn't had any side effects as yet? Then the real shocker, now I hear him say that the last one killed herself. Oh my God, he *is* a real criminal I can't believe what I am hearing. I really thought he cared for Carly, obviously not. I then start thinking I am getting into something very dangerous, more dangerous than what I had thought. Maria was right; he is a man not to get involved with. My stomach is doing somersaults now. I feel like throwing up but I can't. Concentrate Ailish, think about your safety, anything but throwing up. I have got what I came here for, all this information on my phone that is what matters and I've sent it all to my three friends.

And then something happens, after I send the last recording my phone starts to make a beeping noise. I try so hard to shut it off but it won't, then as I know it has been sent, I throw it down to shut it up and it breaks into several pieces. Oh fuck, I'm in trouble now as I hear nothing but silence, then footsteps heading towards me. Then I see the door opening and there he is standing in front of me. I look at him terrified.

"What the fuck are you doing here Rachel, if that is your name?"

He then picks me off the floor and says "Are you a cop, if not, what are you playing at?" I am shaking so hard that I think I will throw up all over him. That wouldn't be a bad idea. He sits me down on a very hard chair. He turns to his men, signs and checks some other paper work and then tells them to leave.

When they walk out of the door, I hear the truck leave and then I know that I am now alone with this killer. I am very scared and terrified that I'll never get out of here.

He pulls up a chair and sits opposite me but not before giving me a glass of water telling me to drink it, NOW. I gulp it down in one and then I know why I had to drink it, he has probably put in a load of drugs trying to harm me even more. Then we talk.

"Well, little miss, what is going on, whatever your name is. Is it Rachel or not?"

I don't say anything. He grabs my arm hard and I squirm with pain.

"You *will* tell me you know, as I will leave you here if you don't, in the dark, with no food or water. Do you want that?" I shake my head and start to cry.

He then sighs. "Okay if that's what you want I will leave now."

He starts to leave and then I say "No, I will tell you."

Then I tell him everything, apart from the recording and pictures that will eventually get to the police. But they won't be sent until they know that I am safe.

After spitting out the truth he says "Ailish I care about

you and I cared about Carly, the drugs are just a bit of fun not to harm anyone. Why should you think any different? I know you think it was my fault that your sister died but it wasn't, it was a mistake, she wanted to take them. I didn't force them on to her."

That is when I take my fist and punch him, SMACK, right in his eye. My knuckles hurt so much, but it is worth it just to see his reaction. He gets so angry he slaps me across the face very hard.

And then he says "That's it; you are staying here until I think of what I am going to do with you."

I am very, very frightened now. I do not want to be left in this dark building on my own.

"No please don't leave me here. I want to go back to the hotel with you, I am sorry I was so stupid."

I thought he would take me with him but I see his face change as if he knows something is just not right here. He walks toward the door and looks back at me sitting on this hard seat, terrified. He turns out the lights and I scream as loud as I can, then I hear him locking the door. I suddenly fall to the floor and just break down.

After crying for what seems a very long time I look at my watch, as it thankfully has a glow dial on the face and I see that it is now nine thirty. What am I going to do.? I have no phone, nothing. I have to do something though. Right think Ailish, I know, back out of the window I came in.

I can hardly see much at all. I walk carefully towards the door that I came from, when I was found out. I eventually get to it but fuck, it has been locked and I can't reach the window to try to break it. I can't see to find anything to stand onto anyway. I scream again out of frustration but it's pointless knowing that no one will hear me. The time is passing and I start to get cold and I am very hungry and very thirsty, wishing I had eaten more earlier. I remember the water I put in my bag so I search for that. Then I remember that it's locked in the next room, I think I am going to die in here, and then I lie on the floor and cry even harder.

I must have spent another hour just lying on the floor when I hear a car outside. I hear the footsteps and then the door opens and to my relief I see Ross standing there. He has brought food for me. Sandwiches and a bottle of water. I get up off the floor and sit back on the hard chair.

He hands me the food and water and says "I really think something else is going on Ailish and you are going to tell me, aren't you."

I have already got the food in my mouth so I shake my head and make a noise telling him no, no nothing. He opens the water for me and throws a couple of the drugs into the bottle and forces it down my throat. I nearly choke and start coughing it up but he makes sure I get all of the liquid into my body. He sits and watches me eat the other sandwich and then he forces more water with another two tablets into my body. Now I know I am in *big* trouble. He sits with me asking again and again what else I have done and still wondering if I am an investigator. I begin to feel really strange as if my body is coming away from my head and when he looks into my eyes I now know then, he realises its time.

He walks away, turns on a switch to an electric heater and brings a large blanket that was stored in the corner of the room. He walks back and throws the blanket on the floor and pulls me down. He kisses me with a force that is so uncomfortable, it hurts like hell. Then he strips off my pants, then his and then he forces himself on to me. I want the sex, as he has given me enough of those drugs that I would have had sex all night long. But in my mind, I know I am being savagely raped. I don't cry as I am so out of my head, so I just let him.

After he has finished with me he turns off the heat and just leaves me again in the freezing cold. I want to pull myself up off the floor, but when I try to get up I can't, as the drugs have left my legs unstable. It takes me what seems like hours to put my pants back on. I feel kind of numb all over but I can't get to the light switch to get out of this unbearable darkness.

This is when I pray from the bottom of my heart and soul. I speak to my Dad and Carly and ask if they are listening to me. I cry and tell them I need help. I don't know how long I have been laying there, but a strange thing happens that I will never forget. I am becoming even colder when I hear a noise like an animal walking toward me. Before I know it this fluffy thing lays next to me, snuggles up beside my legs and puts its head on my lap. Am I hallucinating? I don't feel scared as I am so cold it's a blessing. I find its head to pet and wonder if this was heaven sent. It must have been, as I never noticed any kind of dog lying around when the lights were on. It takes some time for me to pull myself up in a sitting position but when I do, I look and see a golden glow all around the animal's body which puts some light into the room. Trying to focus, which has become a struggle, he looks up at me with the face of an angel, looking at me it seems, to help me feel reassured, and he *so* does. I begin to think is this my guardian angel? Has he come to save me from my death? I don't know as I can't think very clearly, as I feel that the drugs are slowly destroying my body. My head spins now and I'm feeling very dizzy. The more I try to lift my head up the more I become scared. I lay my head on the warmth of this furry guardian lying beside me and I think about my home and wonder if I will ever see it again. I think about my past and the way things used to be. The lovely happy times I spent with Carly and my Mam. Wondering how she will feel finding out her other daughter has died. I really don't want to die like this. I'm beginning to feel colder now and I can't feel any sensation in my feet and the feeling is travelling up my legs. I wish I could just pass out so I won't suffer. Maybe I will eventually, then I can pass away not knowing what happened. I'm now feeling much weaker and I begin to think this is my time.

I try to snuggle more into the warmth of the dog and feel my head going under as if I'm starting to become unconscious. I think I'm about to pass out when I start to see a light coming from underneath the large warehouse doors. I think it's the sun coming up but I am so drugged I don't have the strength to lift my head anymore. This beloved dog is still by my side protecting me and when I try to move my head to kiss him goodbye, he moves *his* head up to try to tell me something. I then hear a noise outside and that's when he leaves my side to move toward the doors. I squint to try to get my eyes to focus. I can see him as the light from the dawn breaking through the cracks in the doors shines on his golden fur, and then suddenly a brighter light forms in the room as if someone is standing with a torch shining onto my whole body. I see a man appear before me, just a blur but I know the smell, I remember it, it's my friend, Thaddeus. I hear him speak to me.

"Ailish let me get you out of here." I don't speak as I am in shock but I know my prayers have been answered. He picks me up in his arms and with a whistle the dog follows him. I am put in the back of a car with a blanket thrown over my cold body. I then hear the closing of the doors, and he pulls away from this horrible, desolate place.

The next thing I know, Thaddeus is helping me out of the car after a journey which I thought would be my last. I could feel every tiny bump in the road which was fortunate as it kept me conscious. As he carries me from the car I try to focus on my surroundings, but with my head in a spin it's very difficult.

He takes me into a room and lays me down very carefully onto a soft bed. I lay there feeling warm and thankfully still alive. I listen to his voice in the distance talking to whomever and then he walks in and sits with me.

I hear him say "Nobody can harm you now".

I try to acknowledge him but not with much success. He realises I need to get water into my system so he helps me to sit up. After that struggle to get the liquid down my throat, he holds me safely in his arms. I want to talk and ask questions but my mouth won't let me.

And that's it. I don't remember much after that.

I *do* remember getting on a plane with a kind woman who was a stranger to me who kept telling me "You'll be home soon."

Home, where's that? I'm so confused I don't even know my own name.

I'm in a room now where I'm being told over and over "Yer home now, yer home now" then new words "We are going to help you" that continued for a while too.

But there is one thing that I'm not confused about when my head hits the pillow every night, the thought of that lovely man I was with. I think he helped me. He comes into my dreams and talks to me and tells me that he's my spirit guide who'll always be there for me. When I wake, my thoughts are still of him, mostly wondering if he *is* what he tells me. Other times I sit with a nice lady who tells me she is a doctor and that her name is Rachel. That name always tends to lift my eyebrows, I don't know why. But she tells me that I'll remember everything in time.

I don't have any belongings with me apart from the essentials. But there is one thing that I treasure, which someone (who, I don't remember as yet) gave to me as a gift. I have it by my bed.

I stretch over very carefully, to pick up the white picture frame topped with angel wings. I stroke the white wings whilst gazing at the picture of an angelic-like figure and read the words underneath that look like they have been hand written with care, they say…'When a spirit guide stands by your side, you know you have been blessed.' Is that what happened to me or was it just mind games? I'm not really sure yet.

To be continued…

Coming soon the sequel to HIGHER LOVE,
"IN MEMORY OF…"

ACKNOWLEDGEMENTS

I want to thank all involved in helping to get this book together.

Thomas McFall at Tom Tom Designs for the amazing artwork for the cover.

Bob Randall for typesetting and for helping me with editing. I could not have completed this book without you Bob.

Lazy Grace for design.

Martins the Printers.

You are all so talented. I cannot thank you enough.

I must also thank author Margaret-Ann Maxwell for putting her ad in the local newspaper for her childrens book. This gave me a push to get my book eventually in print.

I so want to thank my husband Tim. He is my soul mate who is understanding and patient with anything I want to do.

Last but not least I want to thank my two dogs Lily and Rose who put up with me ignoring their pleas for treats while I had my head stuck in the computer writing this novel. Trust me, they didn't starve.

Lily now passed away. 2001-2016. But I know she is still around.